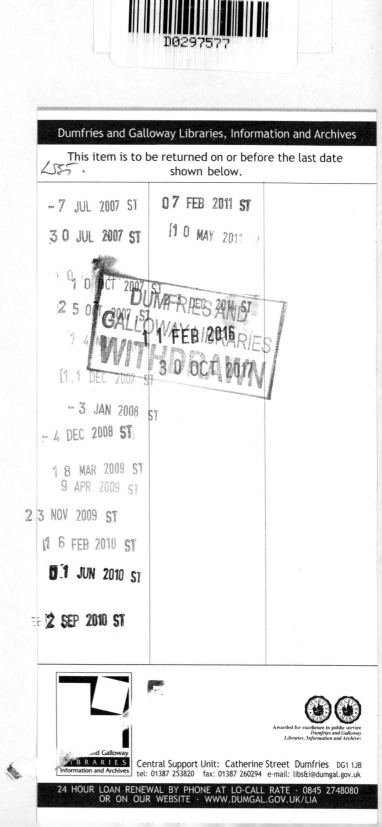

# A Kind of Legacy

# A Kind of Legacy

Mary de Laszlo

ROBERT HALE · LONDON

ISBN 978-0-7090-8292-7


Robert Hale Limited
Clerkenwell House
Clerkenwell Green
London EC1R 0HT

2 4 6 8 10 9 7 5 3 1


*With Much Love to Sam and Damon*

Typeset in 10/13pt Sabon
by Derek Doyle & Associates, Shaw Heath
Printed and bound in Great Britain
by Biddles Limited, King's Lynn

# CHAPTER ONE

ROLAND'S conception was Max's last act on his eightieth birthday. 'With a mother like hers, Cinni was bound to cause trouble', Ruth, Max's sister expostulated. 'Fancy coming to a lunch party with her front all popping out like that.'

'Trust the old devil to go with a bang.' Philip sounded envious.

'He could have waited until after we had eaten that expensive lunch. Fillet of beef is far too rich for every day and that huge cake,' Ruth grumbled. 'It's far too colourful for a funeral.'

'Nothing like a sudden death to cut the appetite,' Stella, one of his ex-wives, piped up. 'Max always had to draw attention to himself.'

Before they had found him Cinni had escaped down the back staircase and through the alleyway to the street behind the house, unaware that she carried the heir to what was left of Max's fortune and this white elephant of a house, home to assorted relatives and hangers-on. When she'd said she'd give him anything he wanted for his birthday, she hadn't meant that.

'Anything?' he'd said, his old eyes glistening. 'Come here then.' He'd opened the door to his study and pulled her in. She hadn't expected the strength of his embrace and once he'd started she'd thought, Why not? Poor old boy, why not give him a treat?

When he'd finished he'd suddenly fallen back on the carpet. He was just exhausted after all that effort, surely he was? But he seemed so still, his face stuck in a strange expression of surprise and pleasure. She panicked, pulled on her clothes and ran away.

Later on the bus she wondered how she had left him, she'd pulled his trousers up but would they guess what his last act had been? He was

5

dead, she knew it. She'd seen dead people before and they were, well, dead, inanimate. Ruth might not guess his cause of death – she seemed stuck in some previous, sexless age, but on the other hand she was always professing her outrage at the amount of sex that seemed to be blossoming from every corner, except for hers.

Some of the other lunch guests were younger, much younger than Max and Ruth. Max Cavanagh had quite a following. He was an artist specializing in moody, mysterious women who sprawled in various stages of undress in gardens, in sand dunes or on forest floors, where the models always complained at the strange prickly things that stuck to their bare flesh.

When Max first started painting as a very young man, the women were swathed in clothes. He became obsessed with cloth, the way it folded and creased, drapery as seen on Roman statues, women in burkas, wrapped in scarves. The older he got the more naked the women became.

'Disgusting, I call it, just an excuse to leer at female genitalia,' Ruth grumbled one day when she was there.

'Just because yours have shrivelled up,' Max retorted maliciously.

'And yours haven't? You're five years older than me,' Ruth threw back.

Despite her anxiety about leaving him like that, Cinni smiled, remembering that day. What would Ruth say if she knew Max was still in fine working order?

Cinni's mother, Fiona, had been one of Max's most famous models but in the days when he was obsessed with drapery. Cinni had a photograph of her favourite picture of her, Fiona swathed in a wafer-thin cashmere shawl from India. The soft folds promised a beautiful body enclosed within, only her face showed – calm, inscrutable, a woman who held secrets.

Fiona had a long love affair with Philip Gardener, a distant cousin of Ruth and Max's who, after a series of misfortunes, had ended up living with them in the large house in Kensington. Stella, Max's second ex-wife – he'd had three – had also fallen on hard times and lived in the basement.

Over the years Cinni often visited the house with her mother and they had been kind to her, fascinated in this childless house with a child as though she was some toy to be marvelled at. Ruth fed her biscuits with hard pink icing, and Max tried to draw her, but she hid her face in her hands saying she didn't 'want to be captured'. After Fiona had died –

nursed so lovingly by Philip – Cinni had kept in touch and, now back in London after various jobs abroad and a long relationship in Scotland, she had returned in time for Max's eightieth birthday party. She'd have gone to the party anyway, even if she and Julian were still together, but she would not have let Max make love to her.

She tried not to think of Julian, the wound of their parting was still too raw. A deep, ragged hole inside her that made her ache with loneliness. She had loved him for years, lived with him for seven and now it was over. The seven year itch, people said and maybe they were right. They should have married after a year or so of meeting, settled down to making a home with children. But people didn't do that today. People lived together, not seeing anyone else, well, not in the romantic sense, so that when these long relationships finished they were left with nothing. No home, no children, no single friends to fall in love with. They had to start all over again.

She was thirty-eight and had expected marriage and children with Julian. Then about a year ago he started getting restless, and she, wanting more than anything to have his child, became frantic. She even threw away the pill in the hope of having 'an accident'. If she became pregnant he would marry her, he'd always said he would. But as if he'd guessed at her action, his lovemaking dwindled then stopped altogether, and then it was over. He couldn't say why. He'd sat there on the arm of the sofa, long legs anchoring him to the ground, his head in his hands.

'I'm so sorry, Cinni, I feel trapped, unable to breathe, I can't love you any more.'

Even thinking of that moment made the tears rise in her. If you fell into love you were just as likely to fall out of it, but she hadn't. It clung to her like the echo of a song, a habit that came with agonizing withdrawal pains. She begged to stay in his life, she'd move out, live further away, give him space. She'd asked if he'd found someone else but he'd said no, he hadn't. Later, friends had said they thought he was having some sort of breakdown.

'I can't leave him then,' she'd said. 'I'll help him through it.' Hope had flared for a moment that all would be well between them again, but he became so agitated when she suggested riding through it with him that she knew she could not stay. He did not want her and yet he felt guilty and possibly afraid because of it. She had packed up and come to London, moved in with Sue Harwood, a friend from school who, by lucky chance, was looking for someone to share the rent in her new flat.

Sue was the same age as Cinni. She worked for Christie's for not very much money and had a married lover who was going to leave his wife when his last child finished university in three or four years' time.

'Women do have babies in their forties these days,' Sue had remarked the other night, 'so I could just get one in with Gerry, or even twins.'

'But what if he doesn't leave his wife, Sue? After all you've been with him over ten years now.' Cinni did not trust men – or time – now. 'If you want a baby, make one or adopt one,' she said. 'It's so unfair that so many women who would make marvellous mothers miss out just because they can't find the right man or if they do he doesn't want children. How many people of our mother's generation were really happily married? They had to marry almost the first boy they kissed and before the age of twenty-five or they were deemed past it, but at least they had plenty of time to have babies.'

'I can't saddle him with another child just now, it wouldn't be fair,' Sue said, her face anguished.

'It's not fair him keeping you hanging about like this. He might never leave his wife, or he'll wait until he is so ancient that she gets sick of him and you'll be left with an incontinent old fool.' She'd spoken more sharply than she meant to, but that is how she felt about Julian letting her down, forcing her back to the dating world to find another man to love, who'd love her back and give her the child she longed for.

Sue had been upset at her warning though Cinni recognized that it was more because she could not bear to face the truth. She'd been the same with Julian that last sad year, but once faced it had to be dealt with and that was always painful.

Cinni could not stop thinking about Max. She had to ring the house. She'd speak to Philip, he was as near as she got to having a father. He'd cope with it. She dialled their number, it rang twice and a woman picked it up giggling. 'Yes, who's speaking?'

She meant to ask for Philip but she blurted, 'Is Max there, is he all right?'

'I think so,' the woman giggled again, 'I don't know if I can find him – oh Jake, leave off—' More giggles. 'We're at his party, can I leave a message or will you rang back?'

Relief swept through her, he must be all right. Max was too vital to be dead. 'Yes, I'll ring later thanks.'

She got off the bus at her stop and bought some supper, smoked salmon, a delicious, expensive salad and a bar of rich, dark chocolate. Chocolate with seventy per cent cocoa was good for you, she told herself as if someone had scolded her for buying it. She'd missed a good lunch after all and she would share this with Sue to show sympathy and solidarity. . . . Two nice, kind women who'd make wonderful wives and mothers to some lucky but unknown men, hurtling towards the menopause and infertility.

It was still early and Sue was not yet back from work. Cinni took off her party dress and showered, washing away all outward traces of Max. He had always been kind to her, told her how beautiful she was: 'Unusual, like your mother, those large grey eyes and that high forehead, reminds me of a fawn with an air of mystery. I shall paint you.' But he never had. Perhaps since her childish refusals of not wanting to be captured, he had dismissed her as too difficult to deal with. Besides, he always had one woman at a time who was his muse and she had never been there when he needed a new one.

Whenever Max saw her he flirted with her. He loved women and saw beauty in them all. She had never thought he would make love to her; she'd never been alone with him, well not long enough for that to happen, and besides he was so old. Today he had taken her by surprise and she had fallen in with it and then it was too late, but it hadn't been unpleasant, she'd enjoyed it until he'd fallen over like that.

She felt cold thinking of it now. That silly, giggling woman had not said she had seen him, that he was standing there in the room. She'd wanted to believe that he was alive so she had accepted what that woman had said as confirmation that Max was all right. At the time she'd been sure he was dead, but no, he couldn't have been. It was just her guilt at letting him make love to her before his party while the guests were still arriving. It had exhausted him, well he was quite a lover, and he had fallen into a deep sleep, hadn't he? She must telephone, again, insist she speak to Philip. They might wonder where she was. She would say she had a headache, a sudden tummy bug, make some reference to Max. She checked the time, 2.40, the lunch party would still be going and it would be a nuisance to ring now and disturb people. That same giggling woman might answer; she must have been standing right over the phone to have picked it up so quickly. But if she didn't ring she was assuming that Max was all right. Cinni had a sudden picture of him, a big man who carried his weight well, face creased with laughter, his booming voice ridiculing her panic. 'Dead? Me? It was only a joke and you fell for it.' He couldn't be dead, not Max. She'd ring them tomorrow before she caught her flight.

She pulled on a pair of jeans and a T-shirt and began to pack. Tomorrow she was going to the South of France for two months to work in the office of Magical Villas, a holiday villa rental company. She'd worked in a travel company in Edinburgh when she lived with Julian and had got this job dealing with luxury villas when she'd come down to London a month before. Someone had had an accident in the Nice office and as she spoke good French they'd asked her to go there until September. She'd jumped at the chance. London was too close to Julian, Nice would be completely different. She had even managed to get the firm to pay her two months' rent to Sue.

Sue had been upset. 'The summer is the worst when Gerry is on holiday with his family,' she said. 'He won't even tell me where he is going. But,' she'd forced herself to sound cheerful, 'that's great for you, Cinni, take no notice of crabby old me.'

'Why don't you come out? I'm staying in some small flat apparently; there'll been room for you I'm sure.' She felt sorry for her and herself too. There they were, two women with no man to go on holiday with.

'We'll see. Get there first and let me know what it's like,' Sue said and they had agreed on that.

So the next morning, Friday – a cheaper flight than on a Saturday – Cinni had left for the airport. They'd stayed up enjoying the supper with a good bottle of wine and Cinni had overslept, leaving in an unglorified muddle. Not until she was checked in and relaxing in the departure lounge did she remember that she had not rung Philip. She had a mobile, but somehow sitting there with all the other passengers waiting to board she felt she couldn't ring now. What if Max had died and she would have to deal with it in front of everyone? By now Philip would be in his office and she didn't have his number and she'd have to speak to Ruth or Stella. Might they not guess what had happened and blame her entirely? Could they even sue her? This thought, intensified by the panic of flying and going cold to a new place with new responsibilities all on her own, took hold like a rabid terrier and would not leave go. Could you sue a woman of thirty-eight who let a man of eighty make love to her? Would they accuse her of seducing him and killing him? There were no witnesses. They had all seen her arrive, she had been early, the bus had charged along as though being chased. She had greeted them all, offered to help.

But Ruth and Stella had refused; they had caterers in though they were 'too young and slovenly-looking so goodness knows how hygienic it all is', Ruth had wailed, rushing in and out of the kitchen hoping to catch them licking their fingers, or picking their noses over the food. Ruth had a horror of 'what went on' behind the scenes in restaurants and the exorbitant prices they charged so had insisted on giving this party at home.

Philip had been useless as always, eagerly getting in the way like an over-grown puppy, until he had been sent into the dining-room to open the wine. There were a few other guests who hung about or went into the garden but Max had had time to whisk her into his study, a small room on the bend of the stairs, though no one had seen her leave, she was sure of that. Perhaps no one had seen her go into his study either so why should she be blamed for any of it? Maybe they would think he had gone into his study and fallen over with a heart attack. She felt sick with guilt. She should have called someone when he collapsed, not run off like that. At the time she'd been sure he was dead but maybe he was not and prompt medical attention would have saved his life? Since Julian had left her she'd become so anxious, so irrational, the sort of helpless little woman she so despised. What a fool she was to think that it was important not to spoil the party by alerting someone and risking everyone knowing the sordid details. She'd spoilt everything for ever by causing his death. But then again perhaps she had not and he was alive and well and laughing about it.

But if he wasn't she would have to confess for surely she would be found out. She remembered a crime series she'd recently seen on television. The forensic doctor always seemed to find out the most extraordinary things, what kind of carpet bought years ago on special offer, what kind of scents or creams someone had used. Finding out Max had just had sex before he died would be easy and her DNA would be there and. . . .

The flight was called, she jumped up and ran to the desk thrusting her passport and boarding pass at the girl, frantic to escape as if, even now, a stream of police cars, sirens wailing were drawing up at the airport to arrest her.

The plane rose in the sky tucking its wheels under its belly with a clunk. She settled back in her seat with relief. She had escaped, she was overreacting as usual, her mind wired up into overdrive. Max would not die so easily. All would be well.

# CHAPTER TWO

$I$T was Philip who found him. Guests were arriving and Max was nowhere to be seen. Ruth, frantic at the caterers and frantic because they did not give many parties on this scale, ran at him like a hysterical chicken.

'Where is Max? This is his party and he should be here coping with the guests. I can't do everything, go and look in his studio, I'll kill him if he's with some woman there.'

'Don't worry, everything will be fine,' Philip said hiding his exasperation. Ruth was getting more and more anxious in her old age like a bee trapped in a bottle. There were waiters holding trays of drinks and most of the people knew each other so the party was going well. He couldn't see Max but he was there somewhere.

He toiled upstairs to the studio at the top of the house, pausing after each flight of stairs to catch his breath. He found it rather embarrassing going in if there was a nude woman being painted. He hardly ever had to go into the studio while Max was painting – only really when Ruth got agitated over something and if he refused to go she'd start on the shaming scenario about 'how lucky he was to be living in such a grand house at such a peppercorn rent'. As he neared the top he began to sing rather off-key, '*Questa notte nessun dorma in Pekino. Nessun dorma! Nessun dorma!*'

All those stairs and his singing left him fighting for breath, his heart hammering in his chest. The numerous attics, little rooms running into each other, had been knocked into one large space with huge windows letting in the northern light. He sang a little louder. Usually Max heard him and cried out, 'Oh do stop that hideous noise, have you never seen a naked woman before?' or some other such insult, sometimes said in a jokey way, other times more viciously. He knew Max despised him,

12

had done so since they were children. He was so much younger than Max, in his prime really, yet since Fiona's death he hadn't had another girlfriend – no other woman could ever take her place – and he was plodding away in a rather dull, dead-end job in a government office and Max accused him of 'wasting his life'.

But this time Max did not call out and when he went into the studio, saying loudly. 'Anyone there?' in case Max was up to – well, he felt quite hot and bothered thinking of what he might be up to – there was no one there. An easel stood in the middle of the room with a half-painted picture of his latest muse. She was sleek and black, lying on a tiger skin, an old, moth-eaten thing Max had found in some dusty antique shop. It was probably against the law to own such a thing now, Philip thought, imagining it glossy and alive, rippling over the muscles of the beast in the jungle.

He went downstairs again and paused at the first floor as he got to Max's study door. He probably wasn't in there but sometimes he went to read, to get away from his sister or his work and he hated anyone coming in. Philip felt rather foolish but he knocked softly, tensely waiting for Max to thunder, 'Who's there and what do you want?' When there was no sound Philip was about to continue downstairs, sure that Max would be there by now holding court when something, he could not explain it later, made him turn the door handle and go into the room.

Below him he could hear the laughter and chatter from the party, the clink of glasses, the sound of the doorbell and people coming in, greeting each other in over-loud, excited voices. The minute he saw Max on the floor he knew he was dead. He closed the door behind him and immediately felt trapped. He took a deep breath and went over to the body.

Max lay on his back, eyes open, with a strange smile on his face as if he was greeting someone he was pleased to see. Then Philip saw his trousers, the old-fashioned fly buttons done up in the wrong button holes, the shirt pulled out and stained, and he knew at once what he had been up to. He'd heard of men dying like this. One story told of a man still attached to his unfortunate woman friend, dead and stiff on top of her. Both had had to be taken out on a stretcher to be released in hospital. He didn't know if it was a true story, but Max had obviously died after making love; there was a faint, sweet smell of some flowery scent. He had not been in there alone.

Panic and nausea gripped him. What was he to do? Go now to Ruth and tell her? He could not tell her what he suspected, what if it wasn't true, what if . . . but he would have to say that Max was dead. Max, the life and soul of the party, would have no other excuse to miss his own birthday party. He'd get Stella to help him; she was good in a crisis.

Philip let himself out of the study, shutting the door behind him and slowly made his way into the sea of people. He was like a robot, programmed only to find Stella, staring with glassy eyes at the people who greeted him. He was aware of their looks, them nudging each other wondering what was wrong with him.

Stella was flirting with a man with lustrous white hair, who had one eye on her while the other roved the room as if looking for someone more alluring. Philip took her arm: 'Stella, please come.'

'Oh, darling, not now,' she drawled in irritation. She was on a constant search for a man to love her, to take her away from here, but it had to be somewhere smart and beautiful. Then she saw his face.

'What is it?'

'Just come,' he said, tugging at her arm and pulling her with him.

'Back in a jif, crises in the kitchen.' She threw a smile at the man with whiter than white hair who did not seem to notice her departure. Philip pulled her out of the drawing-room and to the stairs.

'Whatever is it?' she said. 'Let go of my arm, you'll leave a mark.'

He loosened his hold and hissed, 'Come to Max's study.'

She laughed. 'If I didn't know you better I'd swear you were bent on seduction.'

He blushed, remembering an embarrassing winter's afternoon when both of them, feeling depressed and not a little drunk after a late lunch, had thought that going to bed together might be uplifting. It was not uplifting in any sense of the word and had left him cringing with misery for months afterwards.

'It's Max, he's dead,' he said, not meaning to have said it so brutally but feeling hurt by her jibe about seduction.

'What?' She turned, horror and disbelief on her face.

The sound of the party rose up to them like a wave; people were too busy drinking and gossiping to notice them. He opened the door and pulled her into the study. 'Ruth told me to go to find him and he's here, on the floor.' He shut the door behind them, cutting off the noise, the comfort of laughter.

'Oh my God!' Stella clamped both hands over her mouth as if she would vomit. She crept forward, eyes staring with fear, with horror.

Philip said, 'I think he had sex with someone and that killed him. What can we tell Ruth?'

Stella took some deep breaths as if to calm herself, shutting her eyes a moment. Then, calmer, she said, 'Poor old sod, but it's the way he'd want to go. Who was it he was with?' She sat down on the floor beside him with a little difficulty; she was not that young and agile any more. She laid her hand on his cheek and a few tears splashed on to his face. 'He was a monster really,' she said, 'but I loved him. However badly he treated us all I think all of us still loved him.'

'But what are we going to do? The party's in full swing and here he is dead. We must cover up how he died.'

'We'll dress him properly,' Stella said and went about pulling his clothes together. She did it mechanically as though she was stuffing a cushion, not looking at his face in case it made her break down. 'Now who was the woman? Did you see anyone? Is she still here perhaps, not knowing what's happened?'

'I didn't see anyone, it could be any one of most of the women downstairs.'

'Except for me,' Stella said with a strangled laugh, then she pulled herself together. 'I think he's died of a heart attack. I'll go and tell Ruth and creep round and tell the others, so they will leave. You ring an ambulance; don't say he's dead, I don't think they come if someone is dead, say he's had a heart attack or stroke or something, then they will know what to do. Or maybe his doctor,' she said suddenly. 'Has he been invited?'

'He may have been, I don't know,' Philip said. 'I'll go and see.'

'No, I will,' she said, thrusting her hand at him to help her up. 'I can't stand it in here, poor, foolish old man,' she choked and ran from the room.

Philip went over to the window and looked out at the garden below. Various guests had gone out on to the terrace. It was a cloudy day in late June, which promised rain, but some more intrepid souls had decided it was summer anyway and to go out while they could.

A few moments later to his great relief Eric Naylor, a man ten years younger than Max but still seeing a few patients, came in. He nodded to Philip. 'What a sorry business, but not unexpected,' he said, going over to Max and looking down on him a moment in quiet reflection.

'Pity he had to go before the party but it must have been quick. He had a bad heart. I did warn him to slow down but he argued what was the point of life if you couldn't do anything you wanted?'

'Just like Max,' Philip said. 'But you see, well, we don't want Ruth to
... or the press to ... well, make a story of it and upset Ruth,' he
finished.

'I'll see to it. He died of a heart attack; he had a weak heart and it gave
out. No need to say why. Who was the woman?'

'I've no idea. I didn't see anyone come in here with him.'

'She must be told. I'm sure she'll keep quiet.'

The door opened and Ruth rushed in with Penny, a friend, close
behind her. Eric went to her and held her.

'What was he doing?' Ruth raged, tears pouring down her face. 'I'll bet
there was a woman in it, you read of it, don't you? Old men pegging out
while having sex.'

Philip escaped, leaving her to Penny and Eric. He went slowly down-
stairs in need of a drink. There was a deadly hush intermingled with sobs.
People were leaving, shocked and pale, all party spirit quashed. Mrs
Tadger, who had cleaned for them for years, was stunned.

'It was them bare girls that did it,' she sniffed into a colourful hanky.
'I told him many a time, 'Ain't decent spreading yerself about like that,
too much excitement for an old man. I warned him,' she added, furiously
mopping her streaming eyes before leaving the house 'all of a bother' as
she put it.

Stella was seeing the guests out in a dignified way, almost mechanically
as if she had not really grasped what had happened. She had quietly told
a few of them that Max had had a heart attack and please to leave and
keep it to themselves for a while. Philip went over to the drinks cupboard
and poured himself a double whisky. The woman in charge of the cater-
ing told him she had covered the food and some of it could be frozen. He
thanked her and then she was gone with her young helpers, all shocked,
disbelieving, not knowing how to behave.

He sat there on the chair too drained to do anything. He could see the
people leaving, passing the door on their way to the hall, some smiling
sadly at him, others too upset to notice him. About fifty people had been
invited and he knew most of them and then it suddenly came to him.
Cinni must have been the last woman to make love to Max. Max had
always liked Cinni; she was the daughter of one of his favourite muses,
and incidentally, the one muse he had never slept with. This was one of
the things that annoyed Max about him, for he, dreary old Philip, had
made love to Fiona many times. Fiona was the only woman he had ever

loved, and how lucky he'd been to have her.

Cinni had greeted him with affection – as she always did – she had offered to help with the party and then he had not seen her again. If she had been here she'd have been very upset. She would have stayed, wanting to be here with them, gleaning comfort while she came to terms with it. She must have been the woman; no one else had come forward and she had already left without saying goodbye, which was quite out of character. Had she been having an affair with Max? He thought probably not, unless they had met away from this house. She'd only been back in London a short while and this was the first time he'd seen her for over a year. Maybe she had offered herself as a present? Max was a dreadful flirt, no woman was safe from him. He might have joked about it and she might have obliged.

He had tried to keep it from Ruth thinking it would upset her even more if she knew how he had died, but she had guessed. Straight out she knew. Eric would confirm it and they would all try to keep it a secret.

Eric came downstairs with Ruth and Penny, and Stella appeared and hugged Ruth. Eric said, 'Don't any of you worry, I'll deal with it. There'll be no scandal.'

'Unless those bloody tabloids get hold of it,' Stella said.

'Only we know what happened so unless one of us talks, we're safe,' Philip said, certain that if it was Cinni she would keep quiet.

'*Cherchez la femme*,' Ruth said darkly. 'For all we know at this moment she is closeted with some smarmy publicity agent demanding millions to sell her story.'

'I'm sure not,' Philip said. Then, to his relief before the two women could peck him to pieces with their questions, Eric intervened saying Max's heart could have given out at any time. If he had to he would say that to the press and confirm that sex would have been impossible in his condition.

'He'd hate you to say that, the great lover,' Ruth said with a trace of glee.

Cups of sweet tea and whisky were passed round and after a while everyone began to feel better. The room was littered with glasses and half-eaten canapés, a few bright helium balloons bearing the number 80, floated, tethered to various chairs. A pile of presents, mostly bottle-shaped, stood on a table. Philip felt the house had a *Marie Celeste* feel to it, a party abandoned almost before it began.

'So, who was the woman responsible for this?' Ruth asked, scrutinizing all of them, her eyes perhaps homing in on Stella, who, she always felt, waited like a predator in this house to capture Max once again.

Philip shrank into himself. For Fiona's sake he would protect Cinni. He was the nearest she had for a father, he thought now. Her real father, Theo, was a charming chap who had never grown up himself. It was hardly her fault; he wasn't going to say anything. Max was renowned for seducing women and had probably initiated it, and anyway until he had asked Cinni he had no right to suspect her.

Stella said, 'The only person not here when he was found was Cinni. Why would she leave suddenly without saying goodbye? It's not like her at all.'

Penny said she thought she'd seen her on the stairs just as the party was starting.

Ruth became convinced it was her. 'Fancy coming out to a lunch party with her front all popping out like that. . . .'

Philip, on his third whisky, remembered her dress; it was a bit like a Roman tunic, her breasts barely covered and she certainly wasn't wearing a bra. He felt a wave of lust. 'Trust the old devil to go out with a bang,' he said.

'Max always drew attention to himself,' Stella knocked back the rest of her whisky.

'Such a pity it happened before the party, all that lovely food,' Penny said.

Ruth remarked about the cake being too colourful for a funeral, then after a moment said, 'I'll get Mrs Tadger to re-ice it, something more sombre, and we'll freeze the rest of the food. It should keep until the funeral.'

# CHAPTER THREE

CINNI did not feel at all well, which was hardly surprising, as the job was so fraught. The minute she'd arrived she'd been met by Pascal, her new boss, and whisked off to a small, cramped room, romantically called a 'studio', where she was to stay. Pascal drove fast, firing facts about her job at her in a torrent of French, taking his hands off the steering wheel to punctuate his words, causing her to wonder if she'd survive long enough to take up the position or be mangled on the road in an accident.

He'd given her ten minutes to 'settle in' to her minute flat. All the time he was pacing up and down the room until she was dizzy, before tearing back into the town to show her the office and introduce her to her work colleagues. Colette was about her age, tanned and skinny in impeccable dark trousers and a pale pink shirt. Emma was out, apparently 'millionaire hunting'. Pascal showed her the car to use while she worked for Magical Villas and whirled out again, reminding her that she must be at the office by nine o'clock in the morning, earlier tomorrow as there were guests to put on a flight. She must also be on call for the other hours of the night.

'Don't worry,' said Colette, who had not moved from her desk but just held out her hand to shake Cinni's. She shrugged. ' 'E is always like this when there is someone new. 'E likes to make you think the job is very difficult.'

'It does seem it, but I suppose I'll get the hang of it.' Cinni had sunk down at the desk she'd been given, exhausted already.

She had promised herself she would ring Philip – because he had loved her mother she felt close to him and knew she could depend upon him – and find out about Max, but the days passed and she did nothing about it. Removed from London she felt distanced from it and as the days went on – overflowing with work – it slipped further from her mind. Max was quite famous, and if he had really died in such a way she expected it would be gossiped about in the tabloids. She scanned a few papers and did not find even an obituary. Perhaps he had not died after all. But the job took over and she only had time to glance through the copies of the French newspapers in the office, bought each day for any waiting clients to read.

She could not believe the destruction some people left behind them in the villas they had rented. The tenants were rich – they had to be to be able to afford their villas. Not content with leaving dirty crockery in peculiar places, the leftover food quickly turning rancid in the heat, grubby underwear and used condoms were left behind the furniture, they stained and ripped curtains and furnishings, even pulled light fixtures from the walls – and there was a daily maid to clean up after them! At the end of each tenancy everything often had to be redone for the next guests to trash again.

It was lonely too. Colette, who was nice enough in the office, was married with children and, not surprisingly, spent every moment when she was not working with them. Emma, a young English girl, was on her gap year, supposedly learning French and helping out with office work, but she spent much of her time hanging round the port hoping to meet a millionaire who would whisk her away somewhere exotic in his yacht.

Cinni went back alone to her studio room at the end of the day, trailing along the coast road crammed with cars full of families and motorbikes carrying lovers. Everyone but her seemed to have someone to be with.

Being in her room was like being shut up in a box so she often sat outside on the wall, breathing in the warm, evening air. A few people passed her and when they did they just nodded to her then scurried away to their lives, leaving her feeling even more isolated. There was one room to sleep and live in with a sofa bed. The walls were white, the furnishings beige, a black tube of a vase held some dried grasses as the only ornament. It had a slip of a kitchen, a shower that leaked and a lavatory that smelt sour, whatever scented concoction she poured down it. Although she had bought masses of books with her and had the car to tour around in, it was lonely with no one to share it with. She missed Julian even more than she had in London. Even bad-tempered, distant and no longer loving her he would be a better companion than no one, but she would not allow herself to succumb to the temptation – though it was terribly hard sometimes – to telephone him. Their love had run its course and she would not humiliate herself by begging him to come to her just because she knew no one here. Anyway, she reasoned with herself, even if he did still love her he could hardly throw up his job and come and live here for two months. Nor did she contact any of their friends in Scotland because she was afraid to hear that Julian was blissfully happy with someone else, so it was Sue she relied on.

'Please come out for a holiday, it is pretty and hot and you can stay with me though it's no bigger than a shoebox,' she emailed.

Sue was reluctant to leave London, 'Just in case Gerry could leave his wife and children on some beach' and come to her.

'Don't always be available and anyway think how much more glamorous you'll be with a tan,' she posted back and eventually managed to persuade her to come out the last week in August, two weeks before the end of her job there. Colette said she would lend her a foldup bed.

A month slipped by, the hours were so long, especially hers as she had no family or millionaires to occupy her time. She often volunteered for things just to keep herself busy. Anything was better than sitting worrying about Max and yearning for Julian alone in her shoebox. Weekends were the busiest as Saturday was changeover day. Somehow – and every time it was a challenge – the tenants had to be taken to the airport for an early flight, the whole place cleaned and mended and the new tenants picked up in the evening. On Sunday they always rang her asking – although she had already told them and the information was in a clearly written book in the villa – about shops and markets, secluded beaches and anything else they felt they should get for the money they had paid out. The rest of the week was spent coping with petty grumbles or sometimes major dramas when things caught fire, flooded, blew up and once, Colette told her gleefully, someone had died, locked in the bathroom.

Sometimes Cinni was tortured with the picture of Max falling back like that on the floor, but surely she was overreacting, she told herself without much conviction. He had not died but passed out and was now probably fine, painting away and enjoying life. But other times – usually at dead of night – she was suffused with guilt. What if she had killed him, surely she should at least find out?

One morning after a particularly restless night she was determined to ring him, but she could not find their number in her mobile phone or in her diary. She had written it on a piece of paper and pushed it in there, she remembered, but somehow it had vanished. She had another book with more numbers, which she must have left at Sue's flat though she couldn't think where. It could still be with Julian but she was not going to contact him. In the end, though Max was often in her thoughts, she never got round to finding the number to ring him. The worry and guilt about it added to her feelings of nausea and general malaise.

It was Colette, who suffered from various ailments which she discussed avidly, all to do with being '*fatigué*' or *mal de* somewhere in her stomach, who suggested that Cinni might be pregnant. Cinni laughed. 'Of course I'm not, haven't made love for months.' She wouldn't count Max, he was eighty years old, surely past siring babies. It was the unaccustomed heat, the stress of work, it was anxiety, it was feeling sad and lost without Julian.

'You look like me when I am expecting,' Colette went on. 'Baggy round the eyes, big chest.' She shrugged. 'I just know.'

She could not be. But she had missed her period, or maybe it was just late as she had 'travelled'. Her mother, terribly vague about the reproductive workings of the body after a convent school education, used to be convinced that flying across the world upset one's body's rhythm. But France was next door, hardly across the world. However, before she could give it much thought, Gerry Mitchell, Sue's married lover, strode into her office.

Most people booked the villas from their home country and just appeared at the given time at the airport where Cinni, Colette or Pascal met them and went with them to the villa to settle them in. Gerry Mitchell made straight for her desk, not that she knew it was him at that moment.

'*Bonjour, je veux* . . .' he began imperiously in a very English accent.

'I'm English,' she smiled. He was nearing fifty, a tall, square-shouldered, powerful-looking man, impeccably groomed. He had thick dark hair dusted quite liberally with white, he looked straight into her eyes and smiled.

'That's a relief, my French is pretty rusty. I'm just passing through and I wondered if you had a villa free for the month of August. I know I'm probably far too late but the one we were taking in Spain has fallen through.'

There was only one that was free for the whole month. Though it was shabbier than the others, Cinni rather preferred it to some of the over done-up ones, feeling it had more character. There was an option on it but the client had not called back. She explained this as she showed him pictures of it and offered to drive him there to see it for himself, but he did not have the time.

'I'll take it,' he said. 'I'll sign up now, pay the month's rent.'

'I'll contact you later when I have talked to the client who has an option on it for two weeks,' she said, knowing that the deadline for that was almost up but that it belonged to them until they refused it or the time ran out.

He smiled with a touch of annoyance, a steely glint in his eyes. 'Look, I am here offering to take it for the whole month, with my credit card in my hand, why wait for a client who might not want it or might only want it for a fortnight?'

If only Colette were here to advise her, but what he said was true. If she lost this deal it would be worse, the owners of the villa would be furious and complain, she might even lose her job. The name of the client was down here but not a contact number – no doubt due to yet another of Emma's inefficiencies – and it would take time to find it.

He signed the paperwork and paid, all charm now that he had got his own way, telling her he'd made a detour here from a business meeting he'd had in Marbella and that she must come and have dinner with them at the villa. She smiled and said that would be kind, in a non-committal way. She was so busy concentrating on getting everything filled in right, checking his credit card and the dates of his tenancy that she did not take much notice of his name until he had gone and Colette was back and she was explaining the transaction to her.

'Gerry Mitchell? God, I know someone who is in love with a Gerry Mitchell,' Cinni said in horror. She looked back to the paperwork; he'd said he wanted it for his family, a wife and three children. Sue's Gerry only had two children but perhaps one was bringing a friend. He was coming out here in August and so was Sue. It must be a coincidence, it couldn't possibly be the same man but she had an awful feeling that it was. She had begged Sue to come and stay, pushed aside her reluctance at leaving home in case Gerry escaped to her from his holiday, but now Gerry would be here at the same time with his wife.

She really did feel sick now. What if they met, strolling along in the Place Masséna, in the flower market, in a bar, on the seafront? His villa was in the hills above Nice and her studio about a mile in the opposite direction, but fate being what it was they were bound to meet somewhere along the way.

She explained all this to Colette and to Emma who had deigned to give up some of her precious millionaire-hunting time to help man the phones.

'I'll have to cancel Gerry, say the other client had a prior claim,' she said, not wanting to lie to Sue with complicated stories of why she could not come. It was the only date she could come anyway so she couldn't change it.

'*Mais non*, you cannot do that, it 'appens all the time in France.' Colette threw her a pitying look as if the cold British could not possibly understand such a situation. 'The other client does not want it, 'e 'as not called back in time and every year we 'ave such difficulty with that villa, it is only still on the books because the owner is a friend of Pascal's.'

'What a toad this man is,' Emma said. 'Wonder what his wife is like.'

'Very cold and demanding, apparently.' Cinni remembered Sue telling her how unhappy poor Gerry was with this impossible woman who was bleeding him dry with financial demands but as cold as a dead fish in the bed department. In fact they had not shared a bed since the birth of their second child who was just about to leave school. She'd have to tell Sue he was coming. It would not be fair to ask her to come here knowing her lover was nearby with his family.

Damn him, she was so looking forward to Sue's visit. To be able to gossip and laugh and just chill out with a good friend. She was starved of affection and companionship, but it would not be fair to expect her to come now. Gerry would be here in two weeks though maybe he wouldn't stay here all the time, just install his wife and family and then go off. But if he were here Sue would want to see him and go through endless scenarios to come upon him by accident. The whole thing would be a nightmare.

She rang the flat, but got the answerphone. She rang Christie's but was told Sue was away valuing some country estate. Then Pascal asked her to see to the redecorating of the villa that had caught fire during some drunken party. The smell of fire and the water damage was everywhere and he wanted everything done in the shortest possible time. They used the same shop in Cap Ferrat so all she had to do was coordinate it all, but it was very tiring. She found it hard juggling all the things she had to do and in a foreign language so she forgot to try to contact Sue again, remembering only when she fell exhausted into bed.

Sue did not really want to go and stay with Cinni – as much as she liked her – but she had to make herself. Sue gave herself a pep talk as she opened her carton of soup for supper on Saturday evening. She did hang about too much for Gerry and had lost many friends because of it. Even the most laid back person got sick of her chucking an invitation at the last moment because Gerry had turned up unexpectedly; or when she couldn't make up her mind over some date in case he might be free to see her at that time. But then if she wasn't free when he was she might not see him at all. It was painful to admit that he held all the cards and could control her. She loved him, body and soul, he was the only man she had ever loved and so she waited for him and she thought it was worth it.

He was always so busy with his job and going to things at the children's school, he didn't have as much time as he wanted to be with her. Though they had managed to snatch a few holidays together – little breaks, long weekends here and there. But how precious was that time they spent together? Better than any dinner party or date with a girl-friend. She smiled, her body warm remembering their lovemaking.

He'd dropped in last week; he'd said he'd have to leave after ten to get home. He was meant to be at some do in the city but he got out of it to be with her. She hated talking about his family – of course, he loved his children and she was glad of that, she couldn't love a man who did not like children.

'I wish I could have your child,' she'd said, snuggling up to him, imag-ining having him with her always and their child growing up between them. He didn't like her saying that and she knew she shouldn't have mentioned it, it made him angry. He wanted everything to be above board, his son to finish university, get his divorce and marry her, and then they would have a child, not before. It wasn't right, he'd said. This modern arrangement of single parents was bad for the bedrock of soci-ety, you could see how those sink estates churning out uneducated yobs was bringing the country down.

'But we're not like that,' she'd said. 'We would love and bring up our child properly.' His face had gone hard, implacable and she knew he would say no more on the subject. He'd said he would marry her and give her a child and she must accept the wait.

She sighed, at least she had him still and they loved each other. Poor Cinni, how she had loved Julian. She'd only met him a few times but she'd thought that they were perfect for each other. But he'd changed, suddenly got panicky and opted out, perhaps suffering from some mid-life crises. That is what frightened her, the longer she and Gerry were together in this precarious relationship the more likely it was to break up.

Cinni should have married Julian ages ago and had children, then there would be more to hold him to her. But then again he might not have stayed. There were too many choices today, too many people searching for dreams that did not exist and they were easily enticed away to new pastures, ditching their lives and the people they once loved.

The telephone rang. She took the pan of soup off the stove and went to answer it.

'Please may I speak to Cinni Langley?'

'She's not here, she's in France, can I take a message?'

There was a pause. 'Yes please. It's Ruth Morgan here. I'm afraid I have sad news, Max Cavanagh, my brother, has died of a heart attack.'

'I . . . I'm so sorry.' The news stunned her for a moment. Ruth went on talking and Sue tried to make sense of it. She was about to ask if she would like Cinni's telephone number when Ruth thanked her for handing on the message and said goodbye.

Sue drank her soup and ate some cheese and thought about it. Had she said he'd died at his birthday party? But Cinni was there; it must have been after his party, too much excitement, or drink, poor old boy. She put her dishes in the sink and went to find Cinni's number. She rang her mobile, surely she wouldn't be in the office at the weekend, though the job sounded like a nightmare, but then those sort of hospitality things always were.

'I've had a rather odd call from someone called Ruth, saying she's sorry to tell you but Max has died.'

'Oh, God.' Cinni sounded shocked, near tears.

'I'm sorry, love, I should have broken it better, I didn't realize you were so close to him and—'

Cinni broke in, her voice frightened, 'What did she say?'

'Just wondered if you knew, it was in the papers, death column, he had an obituary and all. I don't know why I didn't see it, but I haven't done more than skim the papers these last weeks, I've been so busy and I'm reading a rather good book. But I got the impression she expected to hear from you. Anyway, they've had the funeral.'

'I should have rung them; I know I should, but it's so hectic here and I hardly ever see the English papers. Did she leave a number?'

'No, I think she assumed that you had it. She said she'd taken ages to find this one, had written it down somewhere and lost it and Philip had had it but he had been away or something. She did sound rather vague but I suppose it's a horrid time for her.'

'I haven't got hers with me. If you have a moment could you look through my things in my room and see if you can find my old address book? I should have it under Philip Gardener.'

'Will do. Max was that old artist friend of your mother's, wasn't he? Died of a heart attack during his birthday party, or after it. Didn't you go to that?'

There was a strangled noise, then a sob, 'I . . . it must . . . I'll ring you later.' She rang off and Sue wished she were with her to comfort her. She'd go out to France that week, of course she'd go. It would do her good to get away, have a holiday in the sun. Cinni was one of her few friends left – probably because she had lived in Edinburgh she had not involved her much with her life with Gerry. Sue did go on holidays alone, or with her sister and mother, but only when she knew Gerry was away. But he was away this month, in Spain with his family. A sliver of panic gripped her; sometimes he made some excuse to his wife and slipped away to her. What if he did so when she was away? No, she must go to France; they might even be able to meet on the continent – that would be exciting.

Cinni had not told Sue about Max's last bout of passion when she'd come home from the party that day. She was too ashamed about it. Another reason she'd said nothing was because then it would make his death all the more likely in her mind. Sue would have made her ring to find out and somehow the whole thing would have been too much and anyway the next morning she had left to come to France.

It wasn't until she had rung off, too overcome with tears at what she had done, did she realize she had not told Sue about Gerry.

She did not want to meet the Mitchell family and settle them in their villa but when Saturday arrived two weeks later one of Colette's children was ill, Pascal was with two other sets of clients who had driven here and Emma was not up to doing it. So she had to be professional and go through with it. Gaston, the driver of the minibus took her to the airport and she waited for them in the small arrivals area, holding up the board saying Magical Villas.

She saw Gerry first, striding through the airport as though he owned the place and everyone in this country should be grateful he had come. Beside him was a young girl, no doubt his daughter, and a gangly youth, no doubt his son, whose passage through university poor Sue waited for impatiently.

A good-looking woman with straight brown hair and a cheerful, enquiring face came behind him, one arm around the shoulders of a young boy. She was chatting to him and they laughed together, her face lighting up.

'Ah, there you are,' Gerry greeted Cinni as if he did not need to be met but as she was here he might as well make the most of her. 'This is my daughter Sara, my son Piers, my wife Helen and my youngest son Ben.'

'How kind of you to meet us.' Helen smiled taking her hand. 'I do hope we haven't mucked up your weekend?'

'N-no, not at all.' Cinni was stunned. Where was the cold demanding wife and what about them not sharing a bed for years? Ben looked like both his parents and could not be more than ten years old. Poor Sue had a very long wait for Gerry to marry her, until she was over fifty, surely – unless she used donor eggs and was incredibly lucky – long past having the child she longed for.

# CHAPTER FOUR

GERRY rang Sue from the airport. 'Can't talk for long, darling, meant to ring you last night but I didn't get the chance.'

Sue was just about to go to the hairdresser's for a cut and to book a wax so she'd look good on the beach. She took enormous care of her body to please him. Well, she'd be a little late, but it didn't matter.

She could hear the bustle of the airport behind him and squashed down the feeling of loss and envy. His wife – the woman who did not love him, did not deserve him, was no doubt making some problem, grumbling about the queues, snapping at him and the children. She should be there by his side, calm and cheerful.

'Might we have a chance to meet up, while you're on holiday?'

'I'll have to let you know,' he sighed. 'There are some friends going to be there, it might be a bit difficult, but I'll do my best, let you know when I see how the land lies.'

'Fine, you can get me on my mobile.' Her heart contracted, a month without him, how could she survive it? But she was used to it. Christmas and holidays were family time, she must be patient until they were a family and she would have him with her for always.

'You know I want to be with you,' his voice curled down the phone into her. 'It's just difficult, Piers has just left school and really it's proba-bly the last holiday we'll have as family.'

His remark lifted her spirits. The children were growing up and they would soon be gone and then they would be together.

'I can't wait for us to be together,' she said, 'going on holiday as a family, our family, not making it a secret any more.' She was about to tell him that she was going to be in Nice with Cinni for a week when he spoke quickly as though he was about to be found out.

'It will be lovely, darling, take care, will ring soon. Love you.' He hung up and she stayed holding the receiver in her hand a few minutes as if she could not bear to break the link between them.

Gaston collected the luggage and loaded it into the minibus; Cinni followed behind. She must stay calm though inside she seethed with anger. Gerry was betraying one of her best friends, pretending he had an empty, cold marriage, implying that he would come to her when his last child finished university. Only he'd forgotten to tell her that he had a third child not even at secondary school and by the time he left the nest Sue would never get the baby she longed for. She would have to tell her now and her heart stung thinking of her pain. What made it worse was that she had a dreadful feeling that she was pregnant after all. But she would not allow herself to panic until she had bought a pregnancy test kit and confirmed it.

Helen was shining. She took in a deep breath of the hot air, looked about her, her eyes drinking in the colours, the light now softer near the end of the day. 'I love the South of France, I keep forgetting how much I love it,' she said walking beside her. 'It must be fun working here, is it?'

'Not bad,' Cinni said feeling too sore to say more.

The minibus started off. Helen sat next to Gerry; she linked her arm through his and leant against him the perfect picture of a happy, loving wife. Cinni sitting in front with Gaston felt wretched. She seemed a nice woman, someone she would in normal circumstances like as a friend and Gerry was cheating on her too, he was cheating on his whole family.

The villa was set in a short drive overlooking the sea; well, you could see a glittering strip of it if you looked out of the top window. A small, rather dank hall opened up to a kitchen with a dining-room on one side and a large living-room on the other. Cinni quickly led them away from the hall and through the living-room to the terrace and the garden. There was a barbecue and a table and chairs under a red striped awning. The villa was shabby but if she showed them the outside – which was after all what they had come for, lying round the pool, eating on the terrace – they might not be put off by it. Anyway there was no other option, so if they did dislike it either Magical Villas would have to poach one from another rental company or the Mitchells would have to go to a hotel or find another villa themselves.

The children ran straight to the pool, Ben even stripping off to his underpants and jumping in, splashing his brother and sister who cursed him good-naturedly, perhaps a little envious of his childish pleasure. Sara went in search of her suitcase to change.

'Which room is mine?' she called as she went inside.

'Don't take the one I want,' Piers said, running in after her.

Ben lay back in the water happy to have the pool as his bedroom.

'It's lovely,' Helen smiled at her. 'I adore eating out, you must come to supper one night. Will you be free?'

'Thank you . . . it depends. . . .' How could she accept such an invitation knowing about Gerry? But perhaps there were two Gerry Mitchells, she thought desperately, and it was just a ghastly coincidence.

'Do try, we've some friends over at St Tropez and when we've fixed something up I'll ask you.' She smiled warmly and Cinni, bereft of friends out there, felt a pang of longing to be this woman's friend. To laugh and joke together, someone to confide in about her problem.

Gerry went in and out of the rooms, giving each one a cursory glance, a frown on his face. 'It is a bit basic, and needs more than a coat of paint. I'd say it needs the complete works.'

'I did explain about that and you did want something at such short notice, all our more glamorous villas were booked up months ago.' She kept the smile on her face. If they refused to stay here it would be very awkward for Pascal who'd blame it on her, but such a relief if they moved off her patch.

Helen said soothingly, 'It's fine, darling. We're going to be outside most of the time anyway and I always feel those really smart villas a bit too much for a holiday. You're on tenter hooks in case the children break something or spill their drinks over white carpets,' she laughed. 'This will suit us fine. Now get into that pool and unwind.' She pushed him playfully towards the garden, smiling at Cinni.

'He works so hard that it takes a while for him to change into holiday mode, but don't worry, in a day or two he won't notice what needs painting and what doesn't.'

Gaston appeared on the terrace. 'The cases are in the entrée,' he said slowly, eyeing her. She knew his ways now; he hated hanging about and wanted her to hurry up settling the family in so they could leave. It had been a busy day ferrying people to and from the villas.

'Thank you, Gaston, I'm coming,' she said. 'I'm just showing them the kitchen, how the hot water works and all, I won't be long.'

'Oh, you do that with her, darling, I never understand boilers and things. I'll start to unpack.' Helen said, calling to the children to take the suitcases upstairs.

'Right, you show me,' Gerry said. 'I suppose the pool is all right, does-n't need anything special done to it?'

'No, ring us if it does.' Cinni showed him how the cover worked. 'Some people like to put it on when they are not using it to stop the birds falling in and drowning,' she said darkly as if such an end would be too good for him.

Ben was splashing about in the pool so she could not say anything to him about Sue, but as she took him through the house the urge to say to him, 'Sue Harwood is my best friend,' became almost irresistible. But each room she came to a child or Helen appeared, and she could not. At last, Helen's plea that she come to supper with them in a few days ring-ing like a death knell in her head, she left with Gaston, who sucked on his cigarette with ill-concealed impatience.

Cinni managed to catch the pharmacy just before it closed and bought a pregnancy testing kit. She was convinced that the whole shop was look-ing at her and wondering, but they probably weren't the slightest bit interested. It was just her guilt making her feel she was under a spotlight. She could not be pregnant from that one time with Max who was eighty years old for goodness' sake. It was only because their lovemaking had killed him that she was overreacting. She still had not contacted Ruth and the shame of it squeezed at her insides. Panic gripped her, there were so many unpleasant things pressing down on her that she had to deal with by herself. Test herself for pregnancy, telephone Ruth, no she'd write, that was easier as Sue still had not got back to her with the telephone number – she didn't know the postcode but a letter would get to her eventually. Finally, she had to tell Sue about Gerry.

She arrived back at her studio, the low building shining white like a wedding cake in the dying sun. There were two small flats one on top of the other and she hauled herself up the narrow outside staircase to the front door, unlocked it and went in. She had closed the shutters against the heat of the day and it was cool inside. She slipped off her shoes getting pleasure from the cold tiles against the soles of her feet. She'd better get this over with, it would only torture her all evening.

She went into the bathroom and opened the pregnancy kit and read the instructions. When the line appeared she stared and stared at it as if she was imagining it. Perhaps the kit was past its sell-by date, or was faulty in some way; she should have bought two to make sure, but she knew in her heart this was not true. She was pregnant with Max's child and he was dead and she had killed him, well, not intentionally but he was dead, no longer here to look after her and the child.

She sat on the floor hugging her knees. She had always wanted a baby, more than one, a family with a loving husband. She had thought Julian would be that but he had left her. At thirty-eight, time was slipping away to find someone new and settle with them, but here she was, against all odds, pregnant. It would be easy to get a termination, it was still early days and Colette was sure to know where to go. She could have it and be back at work in no time, no one need know, there would be no embarrassment with Max's household and that would be the end of it.

She was hit with an overwhelming longing for her mother. This had happened to her – Fiona had fallen in love with a charming but useless second son of a baronet and being rather naïve about sex she had found herself pregnant with Cinni. Her Catholic education had equipped her for most things in life except for the most important, how not to get pregnant.

'It's a grievous sin to have sex before marriage and thereafter it's only acceptable if you want to conceive a child, so it is hardly surprising that contraception is banned. It was also quite difficult to get hold of before you were married,' Fiona had told her. 'And unlike today when babies are shown how to use condoms, we were all frightfully innocent. The man, never the woman like today, had to creep into the chemist and ask for them and it was all so embarrassing as they gave you such looks as if you were some sort of depraved monster, so sometimes you just chanced it, and that's how you arrived.' She'd always hug her then and announce that she was the best mistake she had ever made.

But the difference was that Fiona had married her father though the marriage had not lasted. Theo was still alive, a good-natured but an utterly useless father.

'I could never get rid of you,' her mother had said once when they had discussed it. 'We loved each other and we loved you, though I knew Theo was a free spirit and couldn't settle with anyone.'

She thought of Sue, waiting so patiently for Gerry to leave Helen and marry her and give her the child she craved. It would not happen. How often they and other women her age had talked of finding the 'right man' to settle down with and father their children. One single woman she knew, longing for a child, had adopted one from China. She didn't want to wait any longer for this demigod to materialize, or go through agonies of trying to conceive, of harvesting eggs and squirting them with donor sperm. Other women had got pregnant with men they didn't want to share their lives with but their longing for a child before it was too late was too strong to ignore. Now here she was carrying Max's child.

She'd seen him often throughout her life, visiting with her mother before she had died. He'd always been kind to her, a vital, rumbustious man who took life by the horns and rode it. What would he say if he knew? He had died giving this child life, she could not destroy that and be responsible for both their deaths. She would keep it, she put her hand over her stomach as if to reassure it. In five weeks' time she would be back in London. She would go round to the house and tell Ruth, and perhaps the thought of Max's child would comfort them.

Now she had to ring Sue. She was almost sick with the thought of it. She could do it tomorrow, but no, it would hang over her, better to get all the unpleasant things out of the way at once.

'Sue, love, there's something very difficult I have to tell you. I wish I was with you, but I can't be and you must know at once.'

'Whatever do you mean?' Sue sounded anxious. 'You're not coming back to the flat is that it? You've decided to stay there?'

'No, I'll be back as planned but . . . it's Gerry. He's in one of our villas with his wife and family.' She threw out the words before she could lose her nerve and not tell her.

'Gerry? But he said he was going to Spain.'

'It fell through. He came into the office a couple of weeks ago to see if we had a vacancy for a month and we did, a rather dreary villa but they've just arrived there.'

'Oh . . . I see, and you didn't tell me before?'

She could feel her pain, her sense of betrayal with her friend for keeping it from her. 'I didn't know what to do. You were – still are, I hope – coming out and I hoped that you would not see each other; there's no reason to and it would have been all right.'

'So why isn't it now? I can see if you'd told me before I might not have come. I expect I'll find it very difficult not to try to see him, but I won't, I promise you. It would spoil everything for him.'

'I just feel you ought to know the set up.' Then she wondered if she had said too much. Would it not have been better to leave telling her the rest until she had come here?

'What set up?' Sue's voice cracked with panic.

She had gone in too deep, she had to tell her everything now. 'This is very, very hard to tell you and will be for you to hear but he has three children, the youngest is under ten and his wife, well, she is not a cold demanding woman, quite the opposite in fact.'

There was a silence as Sue absorbed this. 'You must be mistaken, it must be someone else, he has two children, the youngest has just left school, going to university this autumn.'

'I wish I were mistaken but don't you think two Gerry Mitchells a bit of a coincidence?'

'What does he look like?'

'Quite large, yet looks good, lots of brown hair going grey, grey eyes and a little scar sort of puckering up the skin by one eye.' Listening to Sue's sobs confirmed that it was the same Gerry. Cinni tried to offer words of comfort though there were none that worked, as she'd found out when Julian had left her. It was as if half of you and your life had been torn away, throwing you off balance into a terrifying void of uncertainty and loneliness.

'I'll ring you back in a few moments,' Cinni said to give her time to come to terms with it.

It was Sue who rang her back, her voice strained but resolute. 'I know you wouldn't lie to me,' she said. 'Now thinking of it there were a few things I thought were strange but I didn't pursue them, didn't want to believe things were not as I hoped. I want to come out as planned, I want to see for myself.'

'Look, love, you can't do that. Come out do, have a holiday but don't try to see him.' If only she hadn't told her; now there might be a row, not that she'd blame her, but Pascal would be furious with her for disclosing the privacy of clients. She could invisage endless complications ahead.

'I want to see for myself,' Sue said firmly. 'I've given ten years of my life to him, I want everything out in the open now, know exactly where I stand.'

# CHAPTER FIVE

Without Max the house became dull and quiet as if it had lost its heart. He had been such a presence in all their lives, a noisy, demanding, lovable man and without him they all felt diminished.

Philip kept expecting him to turn up suddenly, saying, 'Joke, got you all then didn't I?' and ridicule him for being upset. He was surprised at how upset he was. He was a distant cousin and as a child he used to go and stay at their estate in Yorkshire. He was younger than Max and Ruth, and their mother – Cousin Amy – used to call him 'poor Philip' and tell them to be nice to him because his mother was not well and often had to go to a 'quiet place' to rest. How he'd hated those times, even now it upset his insides to dwell on it, but almost every summer holiday until he was old enough to make his own plans he had gone there, though Max and Ruth were often not there.

Max and Ruth had fought since childhood. Max had been the first born, the son, born to a delicate mother and a wild, half Irish father into a vast crumbling estate in Yorkshire. Various miscarriages had followed in this turbulent marriage then, when Max was five, Ruth was born, pretty and fragile-looking like her mother but as tough as anything. Max resented the fuss made of her, the way the staff and friends coming to the house made much of her when it used to be him who was lavished with all their attention.

Ruth resented the way that Max, as a mere boy, was given so much, sent away to school to be with other boys his age, taught to shoot and fish and roam the moors as long as he wanted to. As they grew up she saw how the gillies, the estate manager and the men on the farm paid homage to him as if he were a future king, while she was only the pretty daughter who would no doubt marry someone suitable and move away from her beloved home.

But Max's heart was in his art and he turned his back on the estate to study at the Slade. There were terrible rows at home. Their father was convinced that he had spawned a 'nancy boy'. At that time Max was in his drapery phase, swaddling women in yards of fine wool or silk. This proved to his father that he found female bodies offensive and what normal, hot-blooded man felt that?

It was Ruth who took an interest in the estate. Their father was furious she was not a boy, was convinced that somehow the genes had got mixed up and she should have been the painter and Max the heir. But he let her help run the estate until he drove his car into a tree late one night during a snow storm. It was then discovered that there was no money and everything had to be sold. Their mother took what money was left and bought this huge house in London off Ladbroke Grove and ended her days happily playing bridge with a handful of quiet, dependable friends. Ruth made an unfortunate marriage to a man called Ralph Morgan who thought women and animals needed beating to show them who was master. It was fortunate that he died on the hunting field before Max could kill him. Max took her in as he ricocheted from one affair to another, which ended whichever marriage he was in at the time, making his name in the gossip columns as well as on the art scene.

Ruth ran the house for him. Even when he was married she kept the upper hand but he married rather useless women – except for Stella – who were more like toys than grown-up, intelligent women. Stella was the exception, she was gutsy. A woman of the world who chose men like one might an outfit, discarding them when the fashion changed. She loved Max and married him but she tried to take control and and it didn't work. But ten years on, when her life was in a mess, he had given her a room here.

Philip too had ended up here, drawn in and through apathy had allowed himself to be. He had loved Fiona, Max's one-time muse. He had cared for her during her cancer, kept the truth of the seriousness of the disease from her, from them all, knowing that was how she wanted it. Caring only for the beautiful things of life, ignoring the ugly, Max admired him for that and when he'd been down on his luck he'd suggested he come and stay here while he sorted himself out, and he had never left. He'd always felt that Max despised him for not having women in his bed most nights – well, any night – except for that one shameful moment with Stella. He only wanted Fiona, he still missed her, the way she wrinkled her nose when she laughed, her delight with life. Anyway, if he had brought someone back it would probably have rendered him impotent thinking of Max charging round the house, perhaps listening outside the door ready to ridicule whatever performance he managed to put on.

But now Max was dead what would happen to the house? Had he left it to Ruth? Would she want to continue this arrangement or might she rather sell it and buy something more manageable, with heating that worked and a roof that didn't leak? She complained enough about the draughts, the gurgling water pipes, the many stairs. Neither Stella nor Philip dared ask her her intentions. With the housing market today neither of them could afford to buy a property in a decent part of London. Both wondered, but neither asked the other if they could afford a house or flat somewhere together. This house was large enough for everyone to live apart, only Max roaring out for attention, slamming doors, clattering about the place with whichever woman was the muse of the moment, had disturbed the peace. Did either of them really want to live together in a far smaller place? But if they did not where would they go? Both worried about this but both felt it indelicate to discuss it so soon.

He knew that Ruth was worried too. He'd overheard her on the telephone. What if, like their father's estate, there was not enough money to keep it on? What if Max had left the house to one of his women, or mortgaged it up to the hilt? He'd made a lot of money with his pictures – ironically had his success come in time he might have been able to save the estate – but he spent a lot too, buying old cars that were meant to be an investment until the price of petrol put paid to that. He dashed off to exotic places to paint, flying first class, staying in expensive hotels. They could all be out on the street and it frightened her. She didn't want to go into an old people's home and even if she did her small income would soon be swallowed up.

They held the funeral two weeks after his death – Mrs Tadger re-iced the birthday cake a rather mournful beige, having added coffee to the white icing sugar. The birthday food was taken out from the freezer and unwrapped but there was not enough for the many mourners that turned up. Mrs Tadger made masses of thick doorstep sandwiches remarking, 'There's nothink like a funeral to increase the appetite.'

The will was read the next day. A Mr Savage, a round rather pink man who had recently taken over Max's affairs, appeared at the house.

'We must all three be there,' Ruth said, not quite looking at them but all three knowing without saying anything that this was something they were all dreading.

They sat together in the drawing-room each on their own chair, no one on the sofa, as if they wanted to show their independence from each other. Stella endeavoured to look positive and cheerful as if somehow Max could see her and would change his will to her benefit. Philip felt he was shrinking away hearing Max's derisive laughter as he packed up his things and searched for somewhere else to live. Ruth was very still but there was an energy about her as if she would jump up and scold Max as she used to when he was alive and did something to upset her.

Mr Savage took a long time putting on his glasses. He opened the case warily as if they might jump out and escape, he polished them with the little cloth in the case, then he put them on, squinted through them, took them off again, polished them again until finally he was satisfied. Then he began to read, slowly, languorously as if he might miss out some vital word.

All three of them tensed, Philip's knuckles were white, a small tic throbbed by Stella's mouth. 'Do get on with it,' they all silently screamed.

'This is the last will and testament of Mr Maximilian Joseph Cavanagh,' he read out as if they had no idea at all why he had summoned them here. 'Unless I have a child either legitimate or illegitimate I leave the house at Landsdowne Crescent to my sister Ruth and ask her to let Stella Norris and Philip Gardener stay there as long as they wish to or they die.'

There was an audible sigh of relief from the three of them. Philip felt tears rise in him and he bowed his head, the ghastly visions of flat hunting and basement flats and lonely, dank rooms receded. Max had no children, they'd have turned up by now if he had, attracted by his glittering success. These last ten years or so his fame had faded, they were safe, they could go on living here as before.

Mr Savage went on reading through the complications if one of the tenants died, how Max did not want Ruth to sell the house but leave it to the nation on her death as a monument to him, turning it into a gallery or an art school.

'Boastful old buggar,' Stella said with affection. 'You'd think he was Picasso the way he thinks of himself.'

There were various bequests to some of his muses, a thousand pounds to Mrs Tadger – which made her 'come over all funny' when she was later informed about it.

'So that's all very straightforward. We needn't change our way of life,' Ruth said with relief. They had got used to each other and their living habits. Philip looked after the garden, Stella cooked the meals they ate together on Sundays and special occasions. Each paid their own way and there was a kitty for communal things like whisky and wine, which they drank, together in the drawing-room or on the terrace in the rambling garden in the summer. They all contributed to Mrs Tadger who cleaned or, as Max used to say, 'swirled the dust round a bit' for everyone.

'Well,' Mr Savage said slowly, folding up the will and putting it down as if it was made of spun glass and would shatter at the slightest clumsiness. 'We have to be sure there are no children, legitimate or illegitimate. I understand . . .' he went pinker, coughed, wriggled on his chair, 'that Mr Cavanagh had quite a colourful life.

'He did,' said Stella firmly, 'but there are no children. I was married to him and though I wanted children he was not the person to have them with. Most women knew they would have been left to bring them up alone.'

'But he leaves specific instructions to leave his house to any child he might have had, so I think that tells us that he may have a child somewhere,' Mr Savage said anxiously as if afraid of igniting their anger.

'It is rather an odd thing to put,' Ruth agreed, 'but he didn't have any children. I'm his sister and I would have known. I'm afraid one or two women did get into trouble but . . . well they didn't go through with it. As Stella says, women knew he would not stay with them five minutes and would certainly not share childcare like men are supposed to do today.'

'He liked children, though,' Stella said. 'He enjoyed playing with my nephews and they loved him.'

'Yes, he liked children but did not have the patience to have any of his own. He was too selfish, and I think afraid they might turn out to be better painters than he was, take the limelight from him. No, Mr Savage, you can rest assured there are no children,' Ruth said.

'All the same I think it would be prudent to make inquires,' Mr Savage went on.

'As you wish,' Ruth said scathingly as if he were wasting his time, but then lawyers were like that. He would sit on things and ruffle some more papers and no doubt charge them a fortune for it. 'But I hope it will be settled soon so we can get on with our lives.'

When Mr Savage had left Ruth opened a bottle of warm champagne. 'Here's to Max,' she said, 'for at the end behaving quite out of character and leaving everything shipshape.'

# CHAPTER SIX

FOR once the office was quiet. Pascal was away for the day so Colette and Cinni relaxed over their desks. Emma was off millionaire-hunting again so they were alone. Cinni told her she'd been right, she was pregnant.

'*Mon Dieu*! I knew it. What will you do? Will you marry the father?'

'He's dead.'

'Dead?' Colette's eyes were round with horror. 'Dead like in dead?'

'Yes, he was eighty and—'

'Eighty! What were you doing with a man of eighty?' Colette cried out in disbelief as if Cinni really must be desperate to have to sleep with such an old man. 'But it cannot be 'is, it must be someone younger. *Non?*'

Cinni, shocked that she had divulged so much, hastily skimmed over the details, implying that he had died some time later, and she had somewhat exaggerated his age. But as she talked about it the enormity of her position struck her like a punch to the heart. Being pregnant was the least of it, what would she do when it was born? With Max dead she could not ask for help in supporting it. She had a minute bit of money from her mother. Her father – if she could find him – never had any. Theo pretended that modern finance was too complicated for him. Her mother might have found this trait endearing, but Cinni soon sussed him out. He was not too stupid to understand such things as bank accounts, tax returns, credit cards and indeed mobile phones and computers, he was simply too lazy. Why should he engage his brain with such mind-numbing trivia? So, she'd get no help there, in fact he'd probably find the prospect of becoming a grandfather far too grown-up to cope with.

She earned a reasonable wage, could earn more if she went back to being manager of a travel company as she'd been in Edinburgh – if anyone would take her on now, but she'd have to pay for childcare and schooling and God knows what and. . . .

As if she could mind-read, Colette began a litany of all the pitfalls of parenthood. Being happily and securely married gave her a slight air of smugness which added to Cinni's panic, each of Colette's words like a stab wound making her wilt under the enormity of it. How could she cope? Perhaps a termination would be more sensible, it would be far easier, the end of nightmares, but it might throw up another kind of pain. Spending her life mourning a child she could only speculate about. She might never be pregnant again, though if she had this child she certainly would never get another chance, for which man would want to take her and a child on? But somehow the extraordinary way it had happened made her feel she must go through with it. She'd been fond of Max, he'd made her laugh and her mother had loved him. She could not pull the plug on his child; he would surely come back and haunt her.

'So 'e 'as no family, this old man?' Colette went on incredulously. The British were supposed to have a reputation for being so cold and repressed sexually, she had never heard of such a thing.

'He might,' Cinni hedged. Apart from Ruth she did not know what other family Max had, perhaps he had other grown-up children dotted about the world. She was not going to tell Colette his name. She might never have heard of him and he might not be as famous as he used to be but she was not going to turn this into a media circus, employing publicity agents and goodness knows what else to make money from it. She wondered why she had told Colette so much and wished she hadn't. No doubt it was because she was so shocked and afraid and yearned for someone to confide in. When she returned to London she would go round to the house and tell Ruth. She had a right to know of her brother's child and the child should know its family, but there was no need to reveal Max's identity to anyone else. In fact she began to re-invent him, saying that he lived in Scotland, alone in a large house.

'Is 'e rich?' Colette had to find some reason for Cinni's strange passion.

'No, he's . . . there won't be any money, he was . . .' her mind struggled to find a profession she could give him as far away from painting as possible. 'A doctor, a sort of professor,' she said lamely, wishing she hadn't started down this road at all. She should not have given his age. A surprise pregnancy was hardly news but if the father was eighty it instantly became more exciting. Colette might gossip and someone – though goodness knows who – might hear and put two and two together and get the right answer. She started to say that she was hopeless with numbers in French and she had really meant sixty not eighty when the telephone rang.

It was a client asking for someone to come and remove a dead bird and disinfect their swimming pool; at least it distracted Colette's attention. Cinni skimmed through the local newspaper. She told herself it was better for her French not to read the English papers but she also admitted to herself that now the news of Max's death was out she was afraid she would come across some sordid sensational story of the 'Who was the mystery sex siren?' variety plastered over the tabloids. But surely Sue, with her job in the art world, would have heard about it even if she didn't have time to read the newspapers.

Thinking of Sue made her feel anxious again. She'd insisted on coming out for that week as they had planned. What if she confronted Gerry? Snipped holes in the front of his bathing trunks, put snakes in his shoes? Pascal would sack her and the office in London would not want her back, and she probably wouldn't get another job worth having. It didn't bear thinking about – sacked and pregnant with a dead man's child.

To cap it all, Helen Mitchell came into the office after lunch. She wore a bright blue loose linen shirt and sparkling white shorts, her skin was beginning to tan. She was smiling. Cinni wished she didn't want her for a friend; it made everything so much more difficult. If only she had been the cold demanding woman Gerry had described to Sue, then she could have understood why he looked for love elsewhere, but to cheat on such a nice woman labelled him a bastard of the worst kind.

'We've just come in to shop and have lunch. I, we, hope you can come to supper tomorrow. I know it's short notice but the Johnsons – our friends – are only here until the weekend.' She looked so eager for her to come that Cinni felt her spirits lift before they sunk like a rock. 'I do hope you are free,' Helen went on.

Of course she was free, she was free every night and was sick of it, but she could hardly go 'dining with the enemy' when Gerry had behaved so badly and destroyed her best friend's life.

'About 7.30 if that's OK,' Helen continued. 'Ben loves to stay up and the Johnsons have young children too and they get so scratchy if they don't get enough sleep.'

'I'd . . . I'd love to, thanks,' she heard herself saying. How she longed for an outing, an evening spent with other people and not alone in her shoebox reading or watching television, her fears haunting her like ghosts. Sue would understand, she need not talk to Gerry, or, on second thoughts, perhaps she'd better find a chance to tell him that Sue was coming out and that she thought his behaviour despicable.

'I'm so glad. See you then, oh, it's casual by the way. Gerry's doing a barbecue. It's the only cooking he ever does.' She laughed, gave her a small wave and was gone.

'That was a nice invitation.' Colette had just put down the phone from persuading Gaston to go and remove the dead bird and now felt she ought to go to the villa and see if they really had to drain the pool.

'Yes, but I don't want to go. I told you her husband is having an affair with my best friend.'

'Oh, that is who they are. Well, you can see how it is, spy on him for your friend.' Colette didn't think there was much of a drama, so many people she knew were in each other's beds all the time. She picked up her bag and car keys and went to the door. 'I don't know 'ow long I'll be. If they 'ad put on the cover the bird would not have fallen in. Some people are so *difficile et sans doubt* they leave the place disgusting with their own dirt when they go.'

The following evening Cinni drove up to Villa Rose. Sue had rung her that morning, but she had not told her about the invitation. Sue had sounded even more resolute, she would confront Gerry and ask him to explain himself. She would not make any decisions about their life together until she had heard his side of the story.

'I shouldn't have told you, I'll probably lose my job,' Cinni said desperately. If she wasn't pregnant it would be worth the sacrifice but she hadn't told Sue about the baby yet, knowing how much she wanted Gerry's child. 'There's client confidentiality and all that. We often get well-known people renting the villas and obviously they expect privacy and if they don't want it they are the ones to ring the papers.'

'Don't worry, I'll find a way that won't involve you,' Sue said darkly and rang off.

Cinni put on some long billowing trousers in a soft, bright pink. She'd bought them in the market and they had a pattern of zigzag lines and elephants traced in black and white on them. She wore a plain black T-shirt.

Their daughter, Sara, opened the door for her and led her through to the terrace. She could smell the meat cooking and hear the babble of voices. For a second she felt a flutter of nerves and wished she had not come. Gerry was hunched over his barbecue, Helen and another woman were arranging the table. Helen looked up,

'Cinni, lovely to see you, come over and let me introduce you. Piers, pour her a drink, Kir OK? Or there's wine if you'd rather.'

Usually she loved both but since her pregnancy alcohol tasted metallic in her mouth. Piers had half-poured a glass and she had not the nerve to ask for something soft, not that there seemed to be anything else on offer but Coke. 'Kir would be lovely, thank you,' she said taking it from him.

'Now, you know Gerry and our children. This is Maggie Johnson, her husband Keith, their son Tom and daughter Katie.'

Cinni shook hands. The children were Ben's age and ran off chasing one another emitting loud screams as they went. Maggie homed in on her as if determined to do her social bit, saying how lucky she was to spend the whole summer out there. Cinni noticed two more men; one was young, early twenties and the other her age. He looked rather out of it, supercilious as if he was used to better company. She wondered if they were 'together'.

Maggie went on to explain that they had a villa out there, near St Tropez. It had belonged to Keith's grandparents and really it would make sense to rent it out for part of the year, only you didn't know with people nowadays how they would treat it. Cinni sipped her drink, wondering if she could put it down somewhere and ask for water. She tried to look interested. Gerry waved to her, the children smiled at her before going off somewhere in the garden, and now the young man joined them.

This is Harry Ellis, my nephew, who is staying with us for a few days before he goes back to the vineyard where he is working,' said Maggie.

Helen called Sara and went into the kitchen with her. Keith and Gerry were talking about the City over the cooking. The younger children were racing around in the garden, the older son lolling about. Sara, who kept coming out to the terrace with a plate of something, eyed up Harry who seemed not to notice her. Cinni was stuck with Maggie who was now describing her villa in minute detail, glancing at Harry for him to verify it. Cinni had never felt so trapped in her life. The other man stayed out of it all, sitting in his chair, long legs crossed, a drink in his hand staring disdainfully out into nothing.

'Darcy.' The name came to her and may even have slipped out, for Maggie looked at her sharply.

'What? What? What did you say?' she asked.

'Sorry,' Cinnie smiled at her, fixed her expression into one of interest over these tedious descriptions.

'. . . and there is another bathroom downstairs but there is a plank over the bath and we use it for flower arranging.'

Darcy, Cinni said again, this time to herself. He is like Darcy – too smart to join these people or maybe, she thought as Keith bellowed with laughter over some schoolboy joke, he feels as completely out of it as I do.

Food was cooked and passed round. Helen had made some wonderful salads, a cold ratatouille, mixed lettuce with herbs, baked potatoes encrusted in sea salt. There was no formal seating, they all just sat down where they wanted, the younger children taking their plates to a rug as if at a picnic. There was a lot of activity, in-jokes and laughter. Cinni felt utterly alone, standing there beside them all with a smile pinned on her face. It was families, she thought. There they were providing food for their children, laughing at their antics. Sometimes one of them remembered something funny some mutual friend had done and they recounted the story, laughing uproariously all the while. Helen even turned to her and said, 'This is this mad friend we have who cooked all these poussins he'd bought in the market and they all had their insides still in.'

Cinni laughed, wanting to join in yet not knowing how to. Would she be joining this family thing, binding herself with other families with stories about her own child? Or would she be an outcast as she felt now, on the edge of the crowd of people enjoying themselves, and from which, through no fault of theirs, she was excluded? She watched Gerry spearing steaks and putting them on plates, joshing around, a thoroughly 'good mate'. She wondered if Keith knew about Sue. Did he have someone too? Did they boast together about their sexual adventures? There was no way she could get Gerry aside and ask him about Sue now. Surreptitiously she glanced at her watch, just past nine, when could she go home?

Keith bought her a plate of meat. 'Here, you look hungry,' he said thrusting it at her then going away. She stood there holding it, the smell of it made her feel slightly sick.

Helen said, 'Do sit anywhere and help yourself to salad and these baked potatoes.' She pulled out a chair for her, smiling, seeing she had everything, before moving away to lavish attention on someone else, leaving her isolated again. Maggie, having finished her description of her villa, had long left her to hang around her husband and tell jokes about him or their children in a shrill, excitable voice.

The other man was standing on the other side of the group, the glow from the barbecue throwing shadows over his face, making it seem longer and thinner. Someone thrust a plate at him and he came towards the table, walking slowly as if he was hating every minute of this evening. But it was the only way he would be able to eat his dinner and he was hungry. Helen had settled Cinni at the table, urging her to start before the meat got cold. Maggie had a plate of food and had put it down a few places away from her but was bobbing around still talking. Sara managed to get Harry to sit next to her. Keith, a loaded plate in his hand, hovered and she would almost have welcomed him to sit next to her and not make her seem such an outcast, but he continued standing.

The man sat down opposite her and stared at his plate as if he was not used to such simple food. The chatter and laughter rose and fell around them. It was just her and him sitting down at the end of this long table. Which one of them would speak first?

After a minute she realized it was not going to be him. He drank his wine, picked at a piece of bread and contemplated his food as if it held some complicated puzzle. Perhaps he did not speak English, he was quite dark and could be French? She leant over and said, 'Bon soir, je m'appelle Cinni.'

He looked at her as if annoyed to be addressed. 'You needn't speak French, unless you want to. I'm English.'

'So am I,' she said rather feebly, not knowing what else to say.

'I know,' he said. 'It stands out a mile.'

By now she had got her bearings and she said, 'Does it? Some people out here think I'm French.'

'Only foreigners, not French people.' His arrogance was maddening and she had an urge to prick it as if it was an over-inflated balloon.

'So, are you French?'

'I said I was English.' His voice was tinged with boredom as if she wasn't going to listen to what he said and it was far too exhausting to talk to her.

The others sat down around them but they were all participating in a story about Gerry being stopped by some foreign police for speeding while on holiday. The Johnsons had been there too for everyone threw in a snippet about this hilarious event, turning their back on the arrogant man and Cinni.

Seeing this Helen did try and include them in the story, which now included a faulty breathalyser, but soon gave up when she saw that it was hopeless.

'With all this noise I didn't catch your name,' Cinni tried once more.

'I didn't give it,' he said putting a piece of steak in his mouth as if he was plugging up his mouth against any more conversation.

Keith, well away on Kir or something stronger, suddenly began to whoop, waving a towel in the air as if it was a whip. He described how on one business trip they'd been on together, Gerry had gone into a sex club by mistake.

Cinni wanted to get up and leave; what was the point of wasting an evening where she was completely excluded, had nothing in common with any of these people, and the man opposite was an arrogant prig? Her book, lying on her bed – a saga set in the war – suddenly seemed exciting and she wanted to find out what was going to happen in it. If only her phone would ring she could pretend there was a drama in one of the other villas and escape. She ate her dinner because she felt quite hungry; she'd barely eaten all day and she didn't want to faint or anything. The noise was so bad she would have had to shout at the man if she wanted a conversation. He probably wouldn't hear her anyway and she'd get a sore throat and it was not worth it.

At last, unable to bear it any longer she went inside to the loo and rang Colette. 'Just ring me and say there is an emergency, a flood or something in one of the villas. Please?'

'What is 'appening? Is the lover after you?'

'Tell you tomorrow.' She went back to her place at the table and a moment later her phone rang. The man opposite eyed her as if he knew exactly what she was up to. Cinni ignored him, got up and walked into the garden to answer it. She went back to the table and bent over Helen.

'I'm so sorry. There's been a fire at one of the villas. I must go at once and sort it out.'

'Oh, must you go, can't someone else do it? You haven't had your pudding yet.' She looked crestfallen as if she genuinely did not want her to leave. Perhaps she had thought by just asking her here and letting her get on with it she would enjoy it.

'No, I really must go. Don't let me disturb your evening any further. Thank you so much,' Cinni smiled, laid her hand on Helen's arm before slipping away in relief into the darkness.

# CHAPTER SEVEN

CINNI couldn't sleep, so she got up early and went to the flower market. She was usually tired during the day, especially in the afternoon when she was hit by a creeping languor. Occasionally she managed half an hour's sleep on the sunbed in the small back terrace at the office, but she went to bed early, quite exhausted. She would wake up around five and became restless with all the anxieties that fought with one another in her head.

It was almost a week since her dinner with the Mitchells. She had sent Helen a thank you card and been relieved when she had heard no more from them. Though she had felt left out – unable to compete with friends who had experienced so many adventures together – they were nice people. Well, Helen was, Gerry was a king-sized shit. Being here without her friends, getting used to the great hole inside herself without Julian had taken its toll. She should not have gone, being in a group of happy people had made her feel even more lonely, more isolated. She longed for Sue to come and yet she dreaded it. What would she do to punish Gerry? And would she also hurt Helen and the children? It was all bound to come out; the family and Sue would be destroyed and it was all Gerry's fault.

The flower market was just open. She wandered under the patchwork of awnings among the brilliant colours and scents of flowers mingled with the soft fruits glistening in their punnets. Further on there were slabs of pâtés decorated with orange slices, cherries and herbs under a shiny cover of aspic. Sacks bulged with spices and herbs and there was bread and cheese. She wondered what to buy, there was so much to choose from. The smell of the cheese and pâtés made her feel nauseous so she moved back among the flowers. She'd buy a hot pink bougainvillea to liven up her stark little room and she was just deciding which one to choose when she saw the man she had nicknamed Darcy. But now the nickname no longer suited him for instead of that arrogance, that superior look, he was smiling, no, actually laughing.

There were quite a few people about, milling round the stalls, choosing things, taking photographs and it was difficult to see who he was with. His face was quite different when animated and she would not have believed he was the same person. She watched him but pretended not to. He was talking, smiling, his hands like swooping birds as he emphasized his words. No doubt there was a woman there, a beautiful sexy one, and to her surprise and chagrin she felt a pang of envy.

That is stupid, she scolded herself, why would you want anything to do with a man like that who thinks he is too grand even to tell you his name? Anyway, in a month or so you'll be too fat with a dead man's child and any man with any sense will run a mile. She turned away and walked in the opposite direction. She'd buy some of those cherries, round as deep red marbles. She paid for them and then for some melon, she didn't feel like cheese – it made her feel sick and pâtés were too greasy although she usually loved them.

She suddenly had an overwhelming urge for olives. She looked around until she found a stall, china bowls filled with every different kind, some with garlic, peppers, black, green, tiny ones and larger ones, some spliced with almonds or pimentos. She bought two large plastic containers of them. She could not resist eating one there and then, it was bright green, a kind she had not seen before. She bit around the stone, then not liking to throw it on the ground, curled it into her hand. She ate six, had six stones in her hand and went in search of somewhere to throw them, and bumped straight into 'Darcy'.

He had his supercilious look on now; no doubt it was very vulgar to stuff oneself full of olives in public before breakfast, worse still to have a handful of chewed stones behind one's back. She felt mortified but she was not going to reveal that to him.

'So, we meet again,' she said. 'I'm sorry, I don't know your name, mine is Cinni, Cinni Langley.' She almost said but stopped herself just in time, 'I think the name Darcy suits you.'

'Lucian Fielding.' He said his name as though it was so precious she must be honoured to know it, and yet she remembered seeing him laughing a few moments ago. She glanced round; no doubt any moment some woman would appear and whisk him off. She was welcome to him, she had given up men and love, and was saving it all for the child she carried.

She could not think what to say: 'Great party the other night,' or 'How long have you known the Mitchells?' All quite pointless remarks. He seemed lost for words, his expression becoming more arrogant as if she was lucky to be breathing in the same air as he was.

'So, you like olives?' he said and she thought there was a spark in his eyes but it must have been her overworked imagination.

'Yes. I'm pregnant and I got a sudden craving so I made a pig of myself. I've got a handful of stones and I'm just going to find somewhere to dump them.'

Shock crossed his face although he tried not to show it, but she had seen it. His eyes darted to her fingers, he said, 'I didn't know you were married.'

'I'm not,' she said, 'and the father of this child is dead.' The pain and fear of her predicament rose in her like a snake. 'It was his last act before he died,' she went on, wanting to shock him, wanting him to leave her, to go and find his beautiful girlfriend.

He frowned. 'I'm sorry, sounds as if you're in quite a mess.'

'I am,' she said, 'but there it is. I got myself into it and I'll have to get on with it.' She glared at him as if daring him to reprimand her, waiting for him to turn on his heel and leave her. If the Mitchells and the Johnsons were not good enough for him she must be complete dirt. But she stood taller, looked into his face defiantly and said, 'I must go now. Goodbye.' And she turned away, dropping the olive stones into a bag of rubbish as she passed. Then she remembered that she had not bought her pink bougainvillea and she was damned if she was leaving without that, she had quite set her heart on it to brighten her room.

She walked on to the stall under the striped awning, which had a profusion of pink and purple plants in pots. He came up behind her.

'I haven't had breakfast yet, I wondered if you wanted a coffee,' he said.

She turned quickly, expecting him to be directing this question to the woman she imagined he was with.

'Me?' she said, perhaps too sharply.

'I'm not asking anyone else, but if you can't I'll leave you. I'm dying for a cup.'

She felt suddenly tired, her head swimming. The cool of the early morning was being blasted away by the sun, and the olives had made her thirsty. She longed for a drink. 'Thank you,' she said. 'I just want to buy one of these, then I'll come.'

Lucian, who had a few discreet bags hanging from his arm, carried the plant for her. As they made their way to a café Cinni half expected this glowing girlfriend of her imagination to materialize and claim him but no one came. They sat down at a table and she ordered tea, coffee made her feel ill, and then at his insistence a golden, flaky croissant.

'That party was awful,' he said at once. 'I hate parties like that, the Brits can be poisonous, drinking and bragging about their stupid exploits as if they were still at school.'

'I agree, but why were you there?'

'I'm Keith's cousin, our grandmother left us the villa. I never go there. Maggie rather took it over when they had children – I don't blame her, taking children to hotels is murder, for the other guests anyway. But . . . well, I needed a break so came here. They've gone now, so all is quiet.' He smiled.

'I thought it was Maggie's villa, she asked me how to rent it out. I work for a villa company out here. The Mitchell's villa is one of ours.'

'We always talk about renting it out but I think we'd have to do too much to it before we could. There are too many rules concerning such things today.' They talked about the complication of bureaucratic life and how everything one used to be able to do was now tightly tangled in red tape. Then suddenly she realized the time.

'I must rush, Pascal will kill me.' She got up, began to pick up her parcels. 'Thank you so much for breakfast, just what I needed.'

He got up too and offered to help her to her car. 'If you're free we could have dinner,' he said casually as though he was not bothered one way or the other.

She wondered about this. He wasn't as bad as she'd first thought. She guessed there was something he was hiding deep inside himself. Perhaps like Gerry he had a wife somewhere and was hoping for a quick affair, though why would he want an affair with her? A pregnant woman with a craving for olives?

'My office is in Nice, Magical Villas,' she said. 'Call in if you are passing.' She smiled at him and opened the car door. 'Thank you again, goodbye.' She got in and drove away. Perhaps he just wanted someone to play with and would dump her as soon as he returned home. But tea and a croissant hardly signalled a commitment. Was she now going to size up every man as a possible saviour for her predicament? She did hope not. No, she was still missing Julian, feeling unbalanced without him by her side. What would he think if he could see her now, or rather knew of her pregnancy? Of the way she got pregnant? He'd be horrified, he liked to plan his life, have the days unfolding like a frieze of calm, until he had been inexplicably hit by some cruising idea that insisted he must change everything.

She was late for work and Pascal was steaming up and down. '*Mais alors, quelle heure est il?*' He tapped his watch as if she did not know what the time was.

'I'm sorry,' she said. 'I got held up. Where is Colette?'

'The *bébé* is ill.' He tore at his hair. Any moment he would start about how this would affect his liver. He had opened the office, she was only fifteen minutes late and no one seemed to have come in. They didn't usually until the evening, although sometimes there were telephone calls.

'I am here now,' she said, wanting him to go so she could bring in her bougainvillea and stand it in the shade outside and put what was left of the olives and her fruit in the fridge, but if he knew she had been to the market he would be angry.

She settled down at her desk while he prowled round breathing heavily.

She rather wished he would sack her then she could go home before Sue came out. The phone rang with a complaint about one of the cleaners, and on the day went. Emma dashed in, her face glowing, completely ignoring Pascal's temper. She had found a man who had chartered a yacht and might have a space for her, then she would slip away into the sunset with him.

'Oh, please do not find a millionaire before the end of the season,' Colette had warned her before. 'You will give Pascal a 'eart attack and the business will close.'

Cinni thought it would make little difference if Emma were here or not. It was far easier to do things herself than wait for her to do them.

Pascal fortunately had a villa to see and left them. He always had a villa to see around lunchtime and was not seen again until about five. Colette had told her he had a girlfriend near the port, who because he was married he could only see during the day. This made Cinni dislike him even more. Her anger with Gerry hurting Sue, not to mention his wife, boiled over on to any man she heard of who was cheating on his wife.

When he had gone, Emma began painting her toenails, she was chewing gum and had the air of someone thoroughly bored.

'When you've done that,' Cinni said sharply, 'you can put those new brochures into envelopes and get them ready to post. There's a list of people to send them to in that filing cabinet.'

'Oh, all right, when my toes are dry.'

'It may be very boring, I'm bored working but I have to to pay my bills,' Cinni said. 'I would be grateful if you could at least pretend to be interested like the rest of us.'

'Sorry,' Emma sat up regarding her shiny blue toenails. 'I'll be out of here next week anyway. This man is going to take me away and he's not an old lecher.'

'I thought those were the only kind looking for young girls,' Cinni said.

'There are others,' Emma said disdainfully. 'Some of my friends have boats, or go with anyone as long as they are rich, but I have to like them as well.'

Cinni laughed, it was none of her business. This spoilt young girl seemed to be able to look after herself. She had come out here as had so many others for a good time. A summer cruising around the sea and then in the winter she and countless others like her would head for the mountains and get taken in there, helping in chalets or shops just to get months of skiing.

'So, who is this millionaire, anyone we know?' she teased her.

'His name is Lucian Fielding,' she said. 'I suppose he's rich; those boats certainly aren't cheap.'

# CHAPTER EIGHT

'I'M wondering if we should have another lodger,' Ruth said as the three of them sat in the drawing-room with a drink before dinner. Since Max's death they had taken to having more meals together. No one had suggested it, it had just happened. Philip assumed it was because Max's passing had left such a void in their lives making each one of them feel more alone.

'Do you need more rent from us?' he said, knowing it had to be faced but dreading it. He had expected their expenses to increase now that Max was not here to pay his share.

'Oh dear, I don't know if I can . . .' Stella became flustered, her fingers fluttering near her mouth as if to conceal her panic. Philip was sorry for her. The then adequate money she'd been left in her divorce settlement from Max did not cover as much as it used to, besides she often 'helped out' young creative men she met at her literary gatherings. 'If he could just finish his poems/novel/play it would be a masterpiece,' she'd say with enthusiasm. She'd got quite cross with Philip when he had suggested that the man in question might find hard work more successful than handouts she could ill afford.

'I don't want any of us to pay more, I know how we stand but I've met this man. . . .'

Philip's heart sank. Ruth was always 'meeting men'. Max used to say unkindly, 'Well, I suppose they know they'll be safe with you and they won't need to invest in Viagra.'

'Oh, not one of those sad ones who needs a nanny?' Stella sighed with exasperation.

Ruth pursed her mouth. 'He's had a sad time, yes, but he can't help that. He has nowhere to live at the moment and – Max's rooms are empty and—'

'But we can't put anyone in there yet? Max is barely dead,' Stella broke in as if Ruth was talking about consecrated ground.

The lines by Ruth's mouth tightened. 'But Stella, dear, he is dead and we must get on. We're not that young and any moment we too might die. But whatever happens I don't want to live out my last years in poverty. We can't sell the house, even if I wanted to, as Max wants us to turn it into a shrine to him. I don't see why we can't use his rooms to generate more money before it comes to that.'

'But who is this man, is it anyone we know?' Philip asked her. They had quite a few friends between them. If it was someone he knew it might work, even up the balance a bit. He was fond of Stella and Ruth but really they could get so hysterical over such small things. Hissy fits sparking up like flash fires all over the place.

Ruth liked fussing over men who were gay, or impotent, or for whatever reason not interested in sex with her or anyone else. 'He's not a threat in that department,' she'd once described one of them.

'Threat?' Max had roared. 'We are not all mass rapists you know! Most women . . .' his tone of voice implied that his sister, even though she was in her seventies, was abnormal, 'enjoy being with full-blooded men with a bit of life still in them.'

'His name is Aubrey Greville,' Ruth said now and Philip could swear her pale skin took on a pinker hue. 'And I once knew him long ago.'

'A long lost lover?' Stella perked up. 'How fascinating, do tell.'

Ruth drew herself up as if she had been accused of a perversion. 'Of course not, just someone I used to know who needs somewhere to live while he gets back on his feet. He'll pay rent, he's not short of money.'

'That's a relief, tell us all about him? Is he good-looking, how old is he?' Stella was transformed into a girl again.

Philip's growing acceptance of having a new member of the household was now nipped in the bud. A moment ago he'd tentatively welcomed another man into the house, now he wasn't so sure.

She was being far too needy, Cinni told herself sternly. Just because Julian had dumped her and she was pregnant with a dead man's baby did not mean she had to expect another man to take care of her. It was a selfish attitude anyway, why should a man who had nothing to do with her predicament pick up the pieces? Falling pregnant with an eighty-year-old man during one bout of lovemaking was an appalling misfortune, but it had happened, as did earthquakes and fraudulent firms misusing their investors' money, or being struck by some accident or deadly disease and she must make the best of it. She was having a baby that she would love and hopefully would love her. Surely that was better than losing everything you owned or being diagnosed with some dreadful illness. She told herself all this to try to bolster her spirits when, in the isolation of the night, her fears attacked her with the ferocity of a pack of rabid dogs leaving her wrung out and weak in the morning.

But at least she'd been saved from making a fool of herself over Lucian. She could not stand arrogant men, people who thought they were too superior to mix with normal mortals. Lucian was not her type at all so why should she mind that Emma – who had come from some hothouse school for young ladies – had ensnared him? Anyway, why would he want her? She was older, less slim and sexy than Emma – and pregnant. If only she had not told him about that, but he had goaded her with his arrogance and she could not stop herself informing him that she was even worse than he had imagined.

Yet there had been something about him when they had sat together over breakfast that had touched her. Something that signalled to her that he too had hidden sufferings, but perhaps that was just her imagination. Here she was – for the first time in her life – alone, without family or friends around her. It was hardly surprising that she homed in on anyone that took even a momentary interest in her. It was pathetic behaviour and she must put an end to it. What was the point of being an independent woman if the first sign of trouble had you running around like a headless chicken looking for a man to lean on?

It was difficult to make friends in her situation now. She was only out here for a short time and apart from picking someone up in a bar – something she never liked doing away – she had little chance of a social life. Pascal was charming when it suited him and she liked Colette, but they had families and busy lives of their own outside work and had no time to spend with her. Any clients who came into the office were already set up with their family or friends and saw her only as someone who worked for Magical Villas, there to help them, not to socialize with – apart from, of course, Helen Mitchell. At least Sue was coming out next week and though her stay might be a minefield of revenge aimed at Gerry, they would have some fun together. She had arranged a couple of days off while she was here. She'd be out of the office though 'on call' in case one of the villas blew up or flooded or whatever. She was looking forward to that.

Emma, having done the brochures and decided that she'd rather have pale lavender toes instead of blue ones, repainted them and disappeared, no doubt to hang around Lucian.

Colette came in just before lunch; her mother had arrived to care for the sick child. Colette explained her complicated childcare arrangements with many sighs and shrugs that made Cinni wonder what on earth *she* was going to do when her baby appeared. She had no mother to rescue her. When she could get a word in she told Colette that Emma was setting sail almost at once with her millionaire.

'Pascal will be *furieux*,' Colette said with feeling. 'I do more work cleaning up after 'er than I do for myself, but 'e thinks we cannot do without 'er. What sort of *famille* does she come from? Many servants who run behind 'er tidying up as she goes?'

'I don't know, she is very lazy but quite sweet and this is her first job and she hasn't a clue how to go about it. But I do agree it is quicker to do things oneself than to ask her to do them.' She was about to tell Colette that the millionaire Emma had found was Lucian whom she had met at the Mitchells' the other night when the door of the office opened and Lucian came in. To her horror she felt herself blushing as if she had been caught saying terrible things about him. He nodded to Colette and came and stood by her desk.

'I was just passing and I remembered that you worked here. I wondered if you would like dinner tonight. My villa is quite a trek in this traffic and if you can come I'll stay around here until you've finished work. If you can't I'll head back now.' As he addressed her he appeared not to care either way, in fact he might far rather prefer to return home at once but as he was here he might as well ask her.

She fought to control her feelings. Of course she wouldn't go. She said, 'But are you not off on your yacht?'

He frowned. 'Yacht?'

She forced a smile, said in a jokey way, 'Emma, who is meant to be working here, said she was going with you on your yacht.'

He laughed. 'I don't have a yacht more's the pity, but I have found someone to charter one that belongs to a friend of mine. I did meet a girl, young, pretty with blonde hair who said she could cook.'

'Cook?' Colette, who had been pretending not to listen, burst out. 'She can't make a cup of coffee, she can't do anything but 'ang around looking pretty, but maybe that is what you want.'

He turned to her in dismay. 'She said she had a Cordon Bleu diploma.'

Colette shrugged. 'Maybe she 'as if she took it in England. Cooking is different there.'

'Nonsense,' Cinni laughed, feeling peculiarly light-headed. 'The French had such bad quality meat to start with that they had to invent wonderful sauces to cover it.'

'I'll look into it further,' Lucian sighed. 'I've seen her hanging round the marina and someone told me she was looking for work, so I asked her if she had any experience on yachts. She said that she had and could cook or do anything. Was she exaggerating?' He looked worried. 'I must have an experienced cook, the clients have paid a good price and will expect one.'

'She wants to sail away with a millionaire and she thought she had found one in you,' Cinni said as she busied herself with her computer so as to seem completely uninterested.

'She's been mistaken. It belongs to some friends and as I was down here they asked if I could find someone to charter it. I have, but now we're missing a cook, I'll have to go and find one.' He hovered round her desk. 'I'd better get on with it, can we meet later?' He added this as an afterthought, as if having once mentioned it he could not go back on it.

Cinni would have liked to go out to dinner with him. She'd like a good meal and was bored with her own company in the evenings, but now he was preoccupied with finding a cook and taking her out would interfere with that and she'd be made to feel a nuisance. She said, 'Look, ring me when you're free. I finish here about six.' She passed him one of her cards that lay in front of her on her desk. The cards she gave to clients with the name and number of the company and her mobile in case of emergencies.

He took it. 'Thanks,' he said. 'I'd better go to an agency that deals in such people. I was just trying to save my friends some money.'

'I can give you one or two names,' Colette who Cinni thought was taking far too much interest in this, in Lucian himself, broke in. He turned to her eagerly.

'Proper cooks?'

'They are qualified; we use them in the villas if clients want a dinner party, some want cooks all the time. 'Ow long is this trip?' She was leafing through the spiral address book on her desk as she spoke and though it was an ordinary action and one she did many times a day, this time the motion seemed almost sensual. She smiled at Lucian, her eyes soft yet businesslike.

'Two weeks leaving at the weekend,' Lucian said going over to her desk and standing with his back to Cinni.

So much for dinner, Cinni said to herself, annoyed at the stab of envy that lodged itself under her ribs. It didn't matter that Colette was married. She and Lucian could have a bit of fun together and it wouldn't mean any more, perhaps even less than a round of golf, or a rubber of bridge. She wondered why she hadn't suggested someone herself. She had the same names and numbers of people who mended things, cooked or cleaned or whatever any of the clients needed. She could have looked up someone just as easily as Colette, but she hadn't.

Colette picked out someone and curling her hand round the telephone receiver as if it was part of Lucian's anatomy, she dialled the number. ' 'Allo, George, is Stephanie there?' She sounded as if she was asking for a seductress rather than a cook. Some minutes later Stephanie was pronounced free and she handed the telephone to Lucian to make the arrangements.

'Thank you so much,' he said warmly. 'For a moment I was really worried I wouldn't find anyone in time. Perhaps Emma could do the cleaning if she really wants to go on a trip?'

'*Non*, she cannot. She will make too much mess 'erself, but if you want someone pretty to lie about in a bikini then she will do well.' Colette smiled at him as if she was sorry for him if he had to make do with Emma when she herself would be a much better choice.

'No, the wives would not want that,' he said.

Colette gave him a secret smile. Cinni felt sick, Colette had never behaved like this with any other man who had come in the office. In fact she had been rather stand-offish as though she had far better things to do with her life than put them in villas, show them where things were and be on call should they need anything. Oh well, she thought, let her have him. She was in no position for a fling herself, not that she wanted one. After Julian, loving him, being with him all those years she did not want to have an affair just for the sake of it. She knew friends who, after they had broken up with someone, had thrown themselves straight back into the mating game as if to prove that they were still attractive or just to have someone in their bed again. But she would feel lonelier after such a night. Just as she had once shared with Julian, she wanted love, affection, laughter and the easy comfort of two people who were happy and content with each other. That was the difficult thing to find and for her she would rather be alone than go through sexual hoops without it.

The act with Max had been an aberration, but he'd been so tender and caring that she had felt as if she was giving him the present he'd wished for. In the end it was he who had given her the present. She put her hand on her stomach; soon she would not be lonely, the love for her child would surpass everything, or so friends who had children had told her.

Lucian turned towards her, then back to Colette taking a few steps as if he were dancing, unsure which one of them to choose. Cinni was about to 'remember' a sudden engagement. She was certainly not going to be either turned down in favour of Colette – though Colette might have to rush home to her sick child – nor was she going to be with him if he was secretly wishing he had chosen Colette over her, when Lucian said, 'I'll go and find Emma and tell her the score, then if you are free I'll pick you up in about an hour?' He glanced at the clock but it was not clear which of them he was talking to.

Colette said, 'I will deal with Emma, she will come in soon.'

Lucian smiled at her. 'No, thanks all the same. I think it only fair that as I offered her the job, I should explain why she can no longer have it. I will be tactful of course.' He went to the door and opened it, turned with a devastating smile to Colette. 'Thank you so much again for solving what could have been a very nasty problem.'

Colette returned his smile and Cinni, caught in the middle, felt she was in danger of being electrocuted.

# CHAPTER NINE

CINNI was called out to a villa to deal with a break in. The family could not speak French and anyway Magical Villas were there night and day to be of assistance. The incident took a long time, not helped by a ditzy woman who could not remember which jewellery of her large collection she had brought with her. She was the type of woman that really got on her nerves – her only interests seeming to be herself and her image – a dyed blonde whose toned body was beginning to turn to scrag. Cinni became so exasperated with her it was all she could do to keep her temper. She refused to admit that these feelings might be exacerbated by missing her date with Lucian, who probably would not contact her anyway. By the time she finally got away the office had been closed some time.

Lucian did telephone, Colette informed her the next morning. She sighed and shrugged and said with an air of boredom that did nothing to fool Cinni, ' 'E made me late 'ome, but what can you do? We are meant to please the clients and 'e was very grateful for my warning about Emma and finding Stephanie.'

'I didn't know he was a client,' Cinni said, not adding that she was not aware that sexual shenanigans were part of their contract.

' 'E might be, you never know. Anyway it would 'ave been rude to turn down 'is invitation. 'E was so grateful, 'e is lonely, I think.'

Cinni tried to ignore the jolt of jealousy that went through her heart. Had she become so embittered over her situation that she cared if Colette went out with a man she didn't even like? What a relief that Sue was arriving this Saturday even if her arrival brought its own hazards. Her mind buzzed with fanciful tales to prevent her from confronting Gerry. The Mitchells had gone home already/moved resorts/disappeared in a yacht.

To stop Colette elaborating on her date with Lucian, Cinni launched into a description of *her* evening. 'The idiots at Villa Azure left the garden door open when they went to the beach and someone got in. They turned the place over a bit but nothing was broken, no smashed windows or doors. But they took the television and the video and various cameras, jewellery and money. I think Pascal better deal with it as it was their fault but of course they are demanding compensation.'

'Tell 'im when 'e comes in,' Colette said and to her relief he did almost immediately so that if Colette had any more juicy details to reveal about Lucian she had to keep them to herself.

Emma flew in resembling a crazed stick insect, all golden limbs and hair whirling. 'Why did you tell Lucian I couldn't cook? How do you know I can't?' She blazed at both of them. Unfortunately for her Pascal was outside on the little terrace behind the office having his coffee and heard her. He came in, his face twisted with impatience like an old wash cloth. He pointed to his office door saying he wished to speak to her. She had come here to work and as far as he could see she had done very little. She sloped in after him and ten minutes later she emerged, looking chastened and started to type up some papers he had given her.

Depression like a damp blanket wrapped itself around Cinni and vainly she tried to claw her way out. Everyone but her seemed to be happy in a relationship with someone. Colette was married and probably playing away with Lucian. Pascal had a wife and a mistress. Emma whispered to her that she did not really mind much not working for Lucian as she had met a boy who was also looking for a long, free holiday under the guise of work.

Cinni was relieved to get out of the office and go to arrange for a new television and video machine for Villa Azure to replace the ones stolen. When she'd dealt with that she left the shop planning to take a walk by the sea to cheer herself up, when she bumped into Helen Mitchell.

'Hi, how are you?' Helen was dressed in well cut shorts and a pink shirt, her face glowing with a tan.

'Fine, thanks, and you?' Cinni was pleased to see her despite herself. She was craving a kind face, a friendly person she could relate to.

'We are all fine. Gerry has taken the children sailing, I'm meeting them later. I get hopelessly seasick even before we've cast off. I'm just about to have lunch; it would be great if you could join me, my treat.' Her face was ruefully expectant.

Warning bells rang in Cinni's head, she must refuse. She could not get involved with the Mitchells knowing what she did about Gerry. Sue would be here in a few days and unless she could stop it there would be some sort of showdown. She did not want to witness Helen's unhappiness or, she admitted, make her think that she was part of the deceit and was perhaps spying on her to report back to Sue.

Helen saw her indecision. 'I hate eating alone in restaurants, feeble of me I know, but I always feel lone women are despised by the waiters.'

'Not so much now, there are so many woman happy to be alone.'

'Oh, I'm sorry. I didn't mean to imply that being alone was somehow . . . some sort of failure.' She struggled with embarrassment.

'I understand, but I've got to get back to the office, thanks so much though.' The last place she wanted to be was in the office. The day was bright and clear – she wanted to be outside among the people, among life and not stuck in that room with only dreary tasks to do.

Helen looked disappointed. 'Don't you have time off for lunch? We needn't be long, just have a sandwich or something quick.'

She could hardly say it was not encouraged to fraternize with the clients as she had already been to dinner there. Surely half an hour couldn't do any harm. In fact, it might be a good thing, for when Gerry's lies and betrayal to both women were revealed, she might be able to be a support to Helen as well as Sue.

'I do have time for that, thanks,' she said. 'Where would you like to go?'

Helen's delight made her feel worse, but it was too late to get out of it. They went to a small bar in the old town that did wonderful salads. Cinni ordered mineral water to drink and when Helen urged a glass of wine on her she said she couldn't while she was working, it made her too sleepy. Helen accepted this excuse but ordered wine for herself and after a few mouthfuls began to confide in her.

'It's so nice to be with Gerry, us all together as a family. He works so hard, I don't see much of him back home.'

Cinni's heart sank. No wonder, he was always with Sue. What made a man with a caring, attractive wife like Helen and three great-looking children, sleep with another woman and lie to them both? And what was even stranger, what was it about Gerry that made two such nice, attractive women like Helen and Sue fall in love with him? Though not nearly such a colourful or amusing character, he reminded her of Max Cavanagh. Women loved him; even after he had broken their hearts they forgave him. But Gerry was not as charismatic as Max. Was it his forcefulness? Did he control them? Was he great in bed? Sue had certainly loved him, been prepared to give up ten years of her life to wait for him and Helen seemed happy with him and now that she knew the ages of their children and had seen them together they obviously still had some sort of love life together.

As Helen talked about their family life it was clear that she was a straightforward, trusting person. She loved Gerry and willingly ran the house and family for him. He was often with her but also had to be away working to earn money for them all and she did not question it, or suspect him of seeing someone else. 'I would downsize if it meant we had more time together,' she said at last. 'I work part-time with a friend who has a children's clothes company. I don't earn much but I enjoy it. If I had to I could find something more lucrative.'

'Then you'd be away working while he was at home,' Cinni said, feeling she had to contribute something to the conversation even though she knew what Gerry was working at.

Helen smiled. 'There's always something isn't there? A price for everything? But you, Cinni, do you have a good life?'

She looked so interested, so concerned sitting there quite close at the small table they shared, smiling with such warmth that Cinni found herself telling her about her break up with Julian and her pregnancy, even about Max's death – though she did not go into the details or mention his name or age. She realized as she came to the end of her story how much she had missed a good heart to heart with a close girlfriend, and how valuable her friends were to her. But here she was far from home without any of them and she had succumbed to Helen's caring nature, adding even more complications to the situation. If only Helen was not married to Gerry she could see them becoming great friends.

Helen listened and though Cinni could see she was shocked, she did not remark on it. When she had finished she said, 'So you are going to be alone bringing up this baby? Do you think, well, I suppose it is too much to ask, but might Julian help you?'

'I'd never ask him to. He no longer loves me and once love has died you have to let it go,' Cinni said with more vehemence than she meant. How she had longed to confide in Julian, hoping he would say he'd made a mistake and wanted her back, would look after her and the child – but that was just foolish fantasy and she had to resist it. She had got herself into this muddle and somehow she must get on with it.

'If I can be of any help please let me know. I couldn't do much in the way of babysitting and such but if you want to talk.' Helen put her hand over hers and Cinni almost burst into tears. She wanted to hug her, tell her she was there for her too in case her happy home life was ever blown apart. If only she could warn her, try to minimize the shock, but what could she say? It was Gerry she must speak to, she decided suddenly. She must confront him, make him sort it out. But how could she get to see him alone? She must think of a reason to get him to call into the office. His payment for the rent had gone through, there was nothing else she could think up which would lure him there. If there had been any queries she could have asked Helen while they lunched. They finished their meal and Cinni said she had to get back to the office.

'I'll walk with you,' Helen said. 'Gerry will be back soon.'

She could not refuse or think up an excuse to stop Helen coming with her so suggested she could browse through their pictures of other villas in case she'd like to come back next year.

Emma was not in the office, nor of course was Pascal, tucked up no doubt with his mistress. When she saw her arrive, Colette said, 'Now you are 'ere I must go out. I 'ave to meet someone.' There was an annoying little smirk playing round her mouth, which dug into Cinni's heart. Let her go out with Lucian, it was none of her business. She was sick of the way these people behaved, married to one person, sleeping with another. If that was the way the world was going it would be a relief to remain celibate, alone at home with her baby.

The telephone rang and she dealt with it a complaint about the cleaner leaving the bathroom worse than before she had cleaned it. Helen sat on one of the chairs in the window put there for customers and immersed herself in the glamorous pictures of the villas on their books. Her mobile suddenly went off and Helen scrabbled in her handbag to answer it. 'Hi, darling, good time?' Helen smiled lovingly into the phone. Cinni heard that Gerry and the children would drive past and pick her up.

She had to corner Gerry now. She might never have another chance. She must tell him Sue was coming out here and that being her friend she knew about his treachery to both women. His car arrived outside and Ben jumped out to fetch his mother. She went to greet him, her face glowing, throwing eager questions at him about his day. She turned to Cinni, her hand on Ben's small shoulder.

'Thanks, Cinni, I so enjoyed seeing you. Come up and have supper, or join us if you ever get a day off. We'd love to see you.' Her voice was warm and sincere as if she really meant it and was not just saying it out of politeness.

'I'd love to.' Cinni watched her walk to the car, get in, then she rushed out. I'm so sorry, it quite slipped my mind, all this sun. I wonder if you could just check something on your form, Gerry, as you're here? I want to be sure about the dates.'

He frowned, looked impatient. 'We have the villa until the end of the month, isn't that so?'

Helen who had not closed her door moved to get out again. 'I'll check, darling, sorry, I could have done it while I was waiting.' She said it cheerfully, not seeming at all surprised that Cinni had just remembered it.

Cinni stood firm by the open door, blocking her exit. 'No, it has to be Gerry as it's his signature. It will only take a moment, but Pascal is very strict and can't read a certain figure so if you wouldn't mind, I'd be so grateful.' She smiled though her heart was beating so fast she thought Helen might see it pounding in her chest.

'Oh, all right, if I must,' he said ungraciously, switching off the engine and getting out.

'Thanks.'

He followed her into the office and she shut the door behind him. 'It's in here,' she said going into Pascal's office. She was going to faint, her breathing was too fast but she had to go through with it.

'OK, where is this form?' His voice was impatient. He seemed huge in the small room and she almost lost her nerve.

She said quietly, 'There is no form but I had to see you alone. Sue Harwood is one of my best friends and I know all about your affair, your difficult wife, how she hasn't slept with you for years.'

At every word his face became whiter, tighter with strain. 'How dare you?' he burst out and took a step towards her as if he would throttle her. 'Have you been filling my wife's head with these lies?'

For a moment she wavered, had she made a dreadful mistake and there was another Gerry Mitchell out there after all? 'I have told her nothing, but Sue might. She's coming out to stay here with me next week. I had to tell her you were here in case we bump into you and I told her that as far as I could tell your wife was a warm and lovely person and that you have a third child so—'

'Shut up!' His hands were clenched by his sides as if he were having trouble keeping them from throttling her. His face twisted in anguish. He glared at her. 'So, how much do you want then?'

'How dare you insult me,' she cried out. 'I'm only telling you because I cannot bear to see how much you have hurt Sue. She's waited for you for ten years, believing you would marry her in a couple of years' time and she could have your child. And Helen, how can you betray her and your children?' She was shouting now, throwing some of her pain with Julian's desertion at him for good measure. 'Now go,' she said, fed up with the whole sorry mess. 'You must sort this out with the least damage to everyone.'

He turned, a great bear of a man diminished. At the door he turned. 'When is Sue coming?'

'On Saturday, she's staying with me. She does not know where you are but I expect she'll soon find you. Why did you hurt her so? Why tell her such lies and how could you cheat on Helen and tell such appalling lies about her?'

'I love them both, call it greed, living two lives. I don't want to lose either of them,' he said defiantly, but the fire had gone from his voice.

What would she have given to have a loving father and secure family life for this child that was coming? What would she have given to have had a strong supportive father in her own life? One she could call on now. 'You may lose them both through your greed and selfishness,' she said, looking over his shoulder through the glass door to the car outside where Helen was laughing with their children.

# CHAPTER TEN

How she wished that she were not going to the South of France, that she could stay here and pretend that everything was the same as it had always been. Since he'd been in France, Gerry had rung her twice. Each time he'd sounded so warm with love, saying how much he missed her, and how he would try to slip away and return to London to spend a few days with her.

She'd listened to him that first time, hardly able to speak in case she burst into tears. Halfway through the call he'd been called away and she wept as he rang off, imagining him with his loving wife and children. Before he rang again she'd half-convinced herself that Cinni had somehow got it wrong, that his wife had been on her best behaviour and gave him hell when they were alone, but when they spoke again she felt stronger and said, 'You do love me, Gerry don't you? Will make a home with me in a couple of years?'

She'd heard his quick intake of breath. 'What's brought this on, darling? You know what I said, of course I will when the time is right.' Then he'd had to go again and promised he'd ring her, but he had not done so for over a week now. She did not ring him; she knew the rules, what if his wife or children picked up the telephone?

Her lukewarm optimism for their future together died. The thought of Helen made her wretched. Cinni would not lie about Helen's character to try to hurt her. She was straight down the line was Cinni; at school she'd stood up for her friends even if it meant she would get into trouble or be unpopular with other people. A sob escaped her, she loved Gerry, she couldn't help it even now and she could have sworn that he loved her. Perhaps he was just a clever actor, using her, preferring to be loved and fussed over by her than having to stay in a soulless hotel if it was too late to go to his home in the country.

She didn't talk it over with anyone, not able to bear their outrage. Maddie, the work colleague she got on with best would say, 'Dump him, how can you allow yourself to stay with such a man?' Maddie guessed something was up, but she wouldn't speak of it.

'I'm just tired, looking forward to my week away,' she said.

'You know you can tell me anything,' Maddie had looked at her with a mixture of anxiety and curiosity. She was getting married in a month's time and fortunately her mind was two-thirds occupied with that.

'Thanks, but it's nothing.' She attempted a smile but it came out more like a grimace.

She went through the motions of packing, had her hair done, legs waxed and set out for the airport. Maybe she wouldn't see him at all and she might even enjoy herself, she owed it to Cinni to try to anyway. But as the plane heaved itself into the sky, she knew she would spend the whole time searching for him wherever she went.

Cinni picked up Sue from the airport at the same time as she picked up her incoming clients. Sue looked dreadful as if she was suffering from some terminal disease, which in a way she was, a broken heart. A wave of affection swept over her as she hugged her friend. How pleased she was that she was here. Over the last few days she'd caught herself wondering if Sue might chicken out of the holiday – she well might have done had she been in her shoes. But how good it was to be with such a friend again, experience the easy companionship, feeling comfortable together. Love was never like that. However well it was going you were always looking over your shoulder, watching out for danger.

'Wonderful to see you. We are going to have such a good time,' she said with perhaps a little too much enthusiasm, causing Sue almost to burst into tears. 'Look,' Cinni said, her arm still around her, 'we are going to enjoy ourselves despite everything.' She said it with more conviction than she felt. The place was beautiful, the sky a sizzling blue, the sun pouring over them like golden syrup but she hadn't got an amusing collection of friends, a string of parties – not even one – to take Sue too.

Sue said bravely, 'Yes, we will have fun. It's great to be here, away from London for a while.'

Cinni made sure her notice announcing 'Magical Villas' was easy to spot. People peered at her, some hopefully as if she was there to look after them then moving on to find the person who had come for them. Some of them were disappointed and asked her if she knew where such and such a holiday rep was. She was used to this; not all the travel firms were reliable. It was almost an instant sacking offence if anyone from Magical Villas was late or did not turn up.

Then her clients appeared. A frazzled-looking woman who seemed as if she needed a holiday from taking a holiday, a slightly balding man rather self-conscious in over bright clothes obviously worn only when he was 'abroad' and a collection of children all squabbling and sulking. The woman, Nina, greeted Cinni with relief as if she could resolve all their problems.

Gaston who had been having his cigarette and a glass of something came to take the suitcases and they all piled into the minibus, the children pushing and shoving one another, motivating their parents to entreat them feebly to behave. Sue and Cinni exchanged glances, both longing to demand that each child shut up and sit down quietly. It later transpired that Rob and Nina, both divorced, were on their first holiday together with each other's children. Neither seemed to dare to reprimand their own offspring in case their children felt picked on in favour of the other children, or daring to reprimand the other's child. It boded ill for a happy holiday and Cinni hoped that she would not be called in too often to reorganize the villa to keep them apart. One time during her first week here, a small boy preferred to sleep in the garden in a tent than share a room with his stepfather's son.

It saddened her. The children were only behaving like this because they were unhappy and resented the fact their respective parent was not taking them on holiday as the family they used to be. Having another parent thrust upon you was bad enough, but having their children too must be torture!

She wondered if Sue was thinking about this as she stared out of the window. If she had married Gerry and had his child how would it all have fitted together with the children he already had? Cinni wondered if her own child would mind not having a father? Despite the fact that her parents did not live together for long – her mother had stuck it out until she was twelve and it had all gone wrong when her grandfather died – she had seen quite a lot of her own father during her early years. He'd been more like an older brother, romping and playing with her like another child, though his toys were sports cars, alcohol and women. She'd loved him then though as she matured she wondered why he too had not matured. He gradually eased out of her life, disappearing – apart from the occasional scrawled postcard – until visiting her mother just before her death. She barely saw him now, hadn't for over two years and then it had been a rushed meeting. When he'd disappeared during her childhood her mother had said it was because faced with a growing daughter he could no longer pretend he was so young. She hadn't missed him that much, her life had been full with love from her mother and, for a while, her grandparents as well as lots of interests and friends. How she still missed her mother. The tears rose in her; if only her mother was here now, she would have supported her in anything.

Cinni had always been against women thinking it 'their right' to have a child without the father being part of their lives, and chasing sperm over the Internet or in expensive clinics to get their wish. There were so many unwanted children already in the world to give a home and love to, why did these single women who longed for a baby not enrich their lives with these?

In the first desperate weeks without Julian she had even thought of adopting a child herself if she never found another man to settle down with.

For the first time as she sat there in the back of the minibus with the children muttering and seething in front of her, she thought of her child as a living person with feelings and opinions like everyone else. Babies were not babies for long, to be tucked away out of sight. She was about to embark upon a lifetime of responsibility on her own. The thought was terrifying.

She would find out all she could about Max, get photographs of him and of some of the pictures he painted and put them everywhere so that their child would know about his father Although she had resolved to tell Ruth – her child's aunt after all – she worried that she, who had always been annoyed with Max's 'carryings on' as she called them, might want to have nothing to do with it.

'You all right?' Sue said. 'You look, well, different, spaced out. Are you tired, this job must be quite a strain?' She eyed the children in front.

Sue did not yet know about the baby. 'It is exhausting and I've masses to tell you. When we've dropped this lot off we'll go home, we can eat there or go out and I'll tell you everything that's happened.' They arrived at the villa, a pink concoction standing in a small, rather dark garden, the sea gleaming like a metal ribbon in the distance. 'Here we are, give me a moment to settle them in; come in if you want.'

'Looks great, I'd like to see it,' Sue said.

Sue turned out to be a great asset, arranging the children in rooms away from each other and managing to persuade two of them that the downstairs shower was far more cool than the upstairs bathroom, so each set of children had their own bathroom. At last, Cinni feeling like a squeezed out rag, slumped back in the minibus. Gaston dropped them back to her car parked at the office.

'So,' Cinni said, 'out to dinner or shall we go home, well, what passes for home anyway? I have got some food there but it won't be as good as a restaurant.'

'Let's go to a restaurant. You don't want to cook after coping with that lot. Goodness I don't give their relationship long, both having to tread so carefully with each other's children. But can we go somewhere not too slow? I know good restaurants cook freshly for each person, but I don't want to go somewhere where you feel they have gone out to catch it as well.'

Cinni laughed. 'I know, I hate that too. You always end up drinking too much or eating too much bread so you've lost your appetite anyway. I know a great place, just fish.'

'Let's go there, then.' Sue smiled. 'It's so good to be here with you. Life's been hell, but I feel much better now I'm here with you.'

'Good, I've missed you too. There's no one I can talk to here, have a laugh with.' Then guiltily she remembered Helen and felt like a traitor.

Cinni parked outside the fish restaurant and they went inside. She often came here when she couldn't be bothered to cook and they always greeted her warmly and certainly did not despise her for being a woman on her own.

'*Bon soir*, Stefan,' she greeted the owner, who waved to the waiter who showed them to a table on the terrace beside the road. Their table was shielded from the road by a row of flower boxes stuffed with a profusion of plants. It was dark now, the place discreetly lit by lamps and candles. The place was crowded. The waiter asked how they were, welcoming Sue to France. When he had settled them with the menus he brought them each a glass of Kir 'on the house'.

'This is lovely, I feel on holiday,' Sue said, holding her glass up to Cinni. 'To life,' she said before she drank from it.

'To life,' Cinni echoed, taking a tiny sip and putting it down.

'Don't you like it?' Sue said. 'I think it's delicious.'

'I . . . I'm not drinking.'

'Since when?' Sue sounded incredulous. 'I mean you never overdid it but you certainly enjoyed it and being out here with all the lovely local wines, how can you keep off them?'

'I know, it's just . . . well work and . . . I was going to tell you but I thought. . . .' She stalled, she'd forgotten how observant Sue was. She had planned to tell her in a few days when she had relaxed a bit, not bombard her with everything as she arrived battered and bruised from the journey.

'Tell me what?' Sue looked worried.

'Let's order, the fresh sardines are scrummy,' Cinni said, as the waiter approached. When he had gone with their order she said, 'You remember that eightieth birthday party I went to, Max Cavanagh's? The night before I came here?'

Sue nodded.

'It's hard to explain, sounds incredible, but we made love and he died and now I'm pregnant.'

Sue's mouth dropped open, her eyes wide in disbelief, then she laughed. 'You're winding me up. It couldn't possibly have happened. I mean, men of eighty need an overdose of Viagra before they can do anything anyway, and as for making babies. . . .'

'It is true although I know it sounds mad. He might have taken Viagra, I don't know, and maybe I came along just as it took effect. Maybe he was waiting for someone else, but he was so tender and sweet and I was feeling so lonely after Julian leaving me so I thought, why not? It was a sort of birthday present. I didn't mean him to die though.'

'So, when his sister rang me to say he'd died that was why?' Sue frowned. 'But does she know? No, you're wrong Cinni, he might have died afterwards, too much excitement in every way, don't beat yourself up about it.'

'He did die then. I'm sure of it. I kept telling myself he was just asleep, but I know that's not true. I should have said something but I was, perhaps in shock, I don't know. I just ran out on him, I feel terrible about that. I should have rung them but I came out here and then I didn't have their number and time went on. . . .'

'At least it was a good way to go. Do you think they guessed?'

'I don't think so, I tidied him up, but I suppose if he had a post mortem they would have found out.'

'I didn't hear anything, only that he'd died. But, Cinni, are you sure you're pregnant? I mean, it's not guilt or anything making you think that?'

'Yes, I am sure now. For ages I put it down to being tired, travelling, missing Julian, anything but that.'

Sue looked most concerned. 'You'll keep it?'

'Yes, Max was so full of life I couldn't do that to his child, and Mum was caught with me and she kept me. Anyway . . .' she paused, realizing her next remark would hurt Sue so she decided not to say it, but Sue said it for her.

'It might be your last chance to have a child.'

Cinni put her hand over hers. 'I'm sorry, I know how desperate you feel about that.'

Sue took another drink, then the food came and more wine. Cinni asked for water. 'So, you're back in two weeks, what will you do? You know you can stay at the flat as long as you want to.'

'That's great, I'd love to, but when it is born I'll have to go somewhere else. There's a lot to be done, telling Max's sister, hoping my job will pay maternity leave. I haven't been there very long.'

Sue said that as this baby was probably the nearest she'd ever get to having her own now that Gerry had turned out as he had, she could stay as long as she wanted to. She wept a little and then started on about Gerry and it was not until they reached the coffee stage that Cinni began to glance about the place and there, three tables away, she saw Lucian and Colette. They were both engrossed in conversation, the candle stuck in a bottle between them throwing shadows on their faces. She looked away surprised at the pang that pinched her heart. Why should she care if he took Colette out? She barely knew him and what business was it of hers if Colette was cheating on her husband? Had he seen her, she wondered or did he only have eyes for Colette?

Sue noticed her concern and looked round in alarm. 'It's not Gerry?'

'No, no one, well a girl I work with who is married but out with some-one else. She might be embarrassed if she sees me,' Cinni said knowing that on the contrary Colette would get pleasure from showing off her catch.

'I must see Gerry,' Sue said in a tone of voice that suggested she was volunteering for a suicide mission. 'I want to see him face to face and ask him why he lied to me for so long.'

Her voice was flat, without vitality, the voice of someone coming to terms with shattering news that had changed their life. Cinni knew how she felt after losing Julian, wondering how she would fill that terrible void yawning before her. But at least Julian had been honest about it. It might have been harder to accept at the beginning but better than hiding behind a web of lies, trying to persuade herself things would work out when they most patently would not.

'You know where he is,' Sue went on, 'so please tell me.'

Cinni did not know where to start. Should she say she liked Helen and that she had been betrayed as much as Sue had? Now knowing that Lucian was there in the darkness she felt she was on show, though why should she care what he thought? But she could not help it, she was aware that she was sitting straighter, turning her head a little to catch the flickering candlelight. What a fool she was, he must be feeling relieved that he had avoided taking out a woman, pregnant with a dead man's child, who might set a trap for him and lure him in to look after her.

Rather lamely she said, 'Let's sleep on it and decide what to do in the morning.' She did not tell Sue about her confrontation with Gerry. She had wondered if he would disappear but so far she had not heard that he had. Since she'd confronted him she'd half been expecting a call from Helen saying he had been called away on urgent business.

'OK, but I am not going to leave without seeing him,' Sue said.

'We'll work it out,' Cinni said, squeezing Sue's hand. She glanced again towards Lucian and Colette. Lucian was staring at her, he looked quickly away. They both stood up to leave, Lucian went inside the restaurant. Colette saw her and gave her a smug smile as she came over.

'We 'ave business, 'ow 'e makes 'is villa smart enough for us to take on,' she said, her eyes on Cinni's hand still covering Sue's on the table. '*Alors*, your *petite amie* is here, *bon soir*.' She smiled at Sue and then left them walking back to the entrance that led to the street. Lucian reappeared, nodded to her as he passed her but made no attempt to come and speak to her. He joined Colette and they both left the terrace and walked down the road beside them. Cinni heard Colette say to him in French, 'That must be her great friend, the woman she loves. It explains the strange story she told me of carrying a dead man's child. It is a surrogate baby made without a man touching her. It will make them a family.'

Only the arrival of Stefan asking if they had enjoyed the meal stopped

Cinni springing up and refuting Colette's remark. Thank goodness it had been in French and Sue did not understand, but now Lucian would think she was gay and show no interest in her at all.

# CHAPTER ELEVEN

THE two women slept late and when they surfaced they took their breakfast on to the small patch of roof above the flat. It held two plastic chairs, a wooden wine box that served as a table and a pot holding a sick-looking plant. Someone had once tried to make an effort with the space.

'I could easily get used o this life,' Sue said, tilting her head to the sun. 'If I were you I'd be tempted to stay out here; won't Magical Villas keep you on?'

'No, I don't think so. The man I've taken over from until he recovers from whatever he has, is apparently a wizard at keeping the villas full. Anyway, beautiful though it is I want to come back to my friends, the way of life I'm used to.'

'Once you've been here awhile you'll make friends.' Sue sighed. 'I'd love a new start, go somewhere comply different and meet new people.'

'I know how you feel, after all I couldn't stay in Scotland when Julian left me, but you are doing so well at your job and you have your flat. When I get back we'll go out and meet new people. London has so much to offer and probably has far more fascinating people than you'd find here, apart from the locals that is and goodness knows how you meet them, or get accepted by them.'

Sue said sadly, 'The pathetic thing is I don't want anyone but Gerry. Even after finding out how he lied to me, I'd take him back tomorrow.'

'You can't.' Cinni thought of Helen, then seeing Sue's puzzled reaction to her tone of voice, said more calmly. 'You cannot waste your life waiting for him, he wants you *and* his wife, but it means you'll never have a home with him, and if you have his child you'll be on your own.'

'You're on your own, so was your mother most of the time and you've turned out all right.'

'My pregnancy is a complete accident, it's the last thing I wanted, or expected, but I'm going through with it because I couldn't bear to deprive it of life. I wouldn't have known if my mother had got rid of me, but I'm jolly thankful she didn't. Anyway she and my father loved each other and they did marry although my father was not much better than a spoilt child himself. I had grandparents until I was twelve and my mother's friends.'

'My parents are still alive and very active – they'd disapprove at first if I got pregnant, but I know they'd relent when they saw the baby. I get on well with my sister and her fiancé, my brother and sister-in-law, and Gerry would be around, I'm sure of it,' Sue said defiantly.

'Last week you were seeking revenge for his selfish, despicable behaviour and I would have helped you. Cutting holes in the crotch of his best suits, putting raw onions in his smart shoes, but suddenly now you want his baby?' Cinni was incredulous, before remembering how she wished she'd had Julian's baby, snitched it off him as a permanent part of him. How much, she wondered now, was this yearning for a child a last cry of dwindling fertility or a way of keeping a part of the errant lover?

'I know, I did want that, but now, hearing your news has made me think. We are the same age and although your pregnancy is strange to say the least, it has happened and soon you will have a child to love. I've always wanted children, I adore my brother's children but I've always thought I'd have a baby with Gerry. He promised he would marry me when his last child finished university and we would have one.' Her voice wobbled and a tear ran down her cheek.

'But he lied to you, Sue,' Cinni said gently. 'By the time Ben finishes uni, you will be fifty-something. OK, by then medial science might find a way of prolonging women's fertility into their eighties – they seem to manage it in Italy – but Gerry may be past it, or even dead. Far better find someone else.' She smiled encouragingly though she knew from her own experience that was not easy. There seemed to be a dearth of decent men willing to settle down with women their age. They either panicked and escaped like Julian or preferred younger women. The only choice seemed to be older men and they came complete with baggage and often a string of impossible children.

'But he loved me,' she said. 'I know he did.'

Cinni remembered Gerry saying when she confronted him that he loved them both and was greedy. But it was not fair to have a child like that, though Sue would not be the first woman to do it. Some of her married friends had 'accidentally' found they were having another child when their husband had only wanted one or two, or when they wanted their man to commit.

'He loves himself more,' she said, 'and what about his wife and the children he has already? How would they feel?' She thought of Helen so trusting and happy with Gerry but then she wanted Sue to be happy too. But why had she let herself be hoodwinked this way? Wasting all those years waiting for a man who would never leave his wife. He'd seemed content with Helen when she'd seen them together; they were comfortable in each other's company. Max had loved women; he'd always said that one was never enough. He liked the facets of their different characteristics, depending on his mood. Gerry seemed to enjoy family life and yet he needed more, the frisson of a mistress, forbidden sex. The practice was as old as time. It was a sad fact of life that most women preferred to make their nest with one person while some men – perhaps all men though it wasn't always feasible – liked a choice.

Sue wiped her eyes and sat up straighter. 'How will they feel if they find out that he has been with me for ten years? What if I'd had a child? I had a few scares and if one had turned out to be true I would have kept it. Ten years, Cinni, we have been together, longer than some marriages. We have a strong relationship.'

'But based on deceit. He told you he was unhappily married to a cold, demanding wife who had not slept with him in years. In reality she is warm and loving and their youngest child is about ten,' Cinni said, feeling mean as she saw Sue's tears start again, but it was true and having his baby was only going to make things worse.

'I want to find out why he did it,' Sue said. 'I'm sorry to hurt his wife but there must be something missing for him to need to be with me.'

'He's just greedy,' Cinni said darkly. 'Now come on, let's go out, forget him for a while.' She felt exhausted, she had not slept well. Lucian had loomed in her dreams but when she had stretched out to him he had melted away. She was angry with him for ruining her sleep and angry with Colette for implying that she was gay. But what did it matter what he thought? He was no doubt having a rip-roaring affair with Colette and she was well out of it.

They drove away from the coast and the snake-like traffic jam, and headed up into the hills. The light was strong, enhancing the vivid colours of the flowers and the bright villas. The sun baked down on them and toasted the earth. They stopped for a late lunch then wandered round the shops. Sue bought a cheeseboard made from olive wood and some lavender soap for her mother. Cinni bought bags of herbs and tisanes. For these few hours they enjoyed themselves, there was an unspoken pact between them to leave men and love out of their conversation and they both felt the better for it.

I may be pregnant and alone but I can still get pleasure from life, Cinni thought, pottering around this beautiful place with a good friend, wandering into shops rich with the scents of flowers and herbs or cheese and pâtés. The idyll was shattered by her mobile ringing. The divorced couple with the squabbling children she had settled in yesterday were in trouble. One of the boys had broken a window and they dare not leave it open all night in case an intruder got in.

'God, these people. Sometimes I wish someone would get in and tie them up and gag them for their entire holiday,' Cinni grumbled to Sue. 'But let's have a drink before we go, they can wait a little longer.'

'What can you do about it?' Sue said, sitting down at a table in the square, arranging her bags of shopping around her feet.

'I have to go and see how bad it is and if necessary get someone out to mend it. As you know it is almost impossible to get anyone to do anything in France in August but we have a string of people we have to pay over the odds to do it.' She ordered a *citron pressé* from the waiter.

'So does Magical Villas pay for it?'

'Initially, but we get it out of their deposit. What a bore, we were having such a lovely time.'

'Must you go? Can't that colleague we saw at the restaurant go instead?'

'No, I'm on duty. Pascal didn't want me to have any time off – well I'm only here a couple of months and it is high season – but he agreed I could if I stayed on duty for any dramas.' A hideous picture of Lucian and Colette too busy to answer the call, entwined in a bout of frenzied lovemaking almost made her choke on her drink.

'Well, it won't take too long to sort out, then we'll find somewhere nice for dinner,' Sue said.

Reluctantly they set off to the villa. They passed her studio room so she could drop Sue off. Sue became very quiet and when Cinni questioned her she just said she felt tired after all the sun. 'I'll have a sleep, and then I'll be ready to go out. I do feel sorry for you having to go and sort out those tiresome people instead of resting in this heat.'

'I'll be fine,' Cinni said though she did feel tired now and would have loved a cold shower and a lie down on her bed.

It took about fifteen minutes to get to Villa Jasmin. Both Nina and Rob appeared tight with tension. The children screamed from the direction of the swimming pool.

'I'm so sorry, it was an accident,' Nina said.

'Hardly an accident, it was a deliberate act of bad temper,' Rob seethed.

Nina looked as if she wanted to roll up and crawl away out of sight. Would they last this week together, Cinni wondered as they led her to the shattered window? Relationships were difficult enough with two people but an assortment of children from different relationships seemed like a disaster of Titanic proportions.

The space where the glass used to be was large and square, giving enough room for a whole regiment of thieves and rapists to enter. Had it been smaller she would have patched it up with a piece of wood until the morning, but this needed professional help, to be boarded up if the new pane of glass could not be fitted at once. She took the measurements and rang the glazier. He took some time to answer, sounded very bored but finally agreed to come in a couple of hours. Cinni told them to ring her when he arrived and set off back to her flat to shower and rest before dinner.

She entered the flat quietly so as not to wake Sue but to her surprise Sue was sitting on the sofa looking anything but sleepy.

'So, sorted it?' she said cheerfully.

'Almost.' Cinni explained what had happened. 'So, we'll go out in about an hour; there's a nice restaurant near them and I can nip up and see to it.'

'That's fine.' In the short time she had been away Sue seemed to have been rejuvenated. Cinni's heart sank. Unless she had met some delicious Frenchman on the stairs, which was unlikely, she must have been in touch with Gerry.

'So,' she said sinking down on the chair. 'What's up?'

'I rang Gerry . . . and before you say anything I know what I'm doing. I rang his mobile and he was able to talk. He's so unhappy and wants to see me; he said that he loved us both in different ways, and does not want to hurt any of us.'

'Hurt himself, you mean,' Cinni said darkly.

'He is dreadfully upset,' Sue went on, 'and wants to meet so we can talk. I've arranged it for tomorrow as you're working. I won't see him again this week and we'll see what happens when we get back to London.'

'I don't know what to say to you,' Cinni said wearily. 'I think you are making a terrible mistake, you will get hurt and so will his wife and family. I know you love him, can't imagine life without him having invested so much in him. It is hell thinking of starting from scratch with someone new – if you can find one.' She smiled ruefully. 'I know that too well. But Gerry is only thinking of himself and that is not good for you, nor is it really love.'

She saw that her remarks had crushed Sue. Deep down Sue knew Cinni was right but could not face it. She would rather stay with the only man she had ever loved, on his terms, than be without him. Cinni understood that. Whatever she said Sue would not listen so if she wanted to enjoy this week she had better leave them to it.

'Oh, sorry, almost forgot, there was a call for you too,' Sue said. 'Lucian Fielding, you know, the writer who writes books on art history and the lives of artists.'

To her annoyance her heart leapt. 'The writer? I didn't know he was a writer.'

'I know he is because I'm in the art world. He's written some well-regarded books on various contemporary artists. He says he wants to get in touch with you as he's been commissioned to write a book on Max Cavanagh, and he's just found out that you are the daughter of one of his muses.'

Cinni was too stunned to say anything for a moment and was crippled with an inexplicable disappointment. Lucian was not interested in her at all; he only wanted to know about Max. Then the knowledge crushed her further. Think how he would crow over his scoop when he found out that she was carrying Max's child.

'You didn't tell him that I'm having Max's baby? You didn't, did you, Sue?' Cinni cried out in panic.

Sue looked pained. 'Of course not. That's up to you to tell him or not as you think fit. He sounded charming, said he'd met you at a dinner party and had no idea you were Fiona's daughter.'

'However did he find out then?' Lucian had obviously not told Sue he had met her at the Mitchells' or she would have skimmed over Lucian's request in her eagerness to hear every minute detail of the dinner party.

'He's in touch with Max's sister. I suppose he asked who else he could interview and your name came up. Apparently they knew you were working out here. Lucian only found out about it this morning.'

'I did write to them about Max and I probably did say I was working at Magical Villas in Nice.' Panic fluttered in her like a flock of birds.

'I said you'd ring him back.' Sue picked up a piece of paper by the telephone and handed it to her. 'We might have him round, he sounds . . . amazing, I can't think of another word. He had such a sexy voice and he sounded so interested and genuine.'

'Go for him then instead of Gerry,' Cinni retorted feeling jittery with anxiety. How could she talk about Max to someone who was writing a book about him and who would no doubt be delighted to grab her story and twist it into goodness knows what salaciousness to promote his book? She pulled herself out of the chair, if only she could curl up somewhere out of the way and hibernate until all this was over.

'I'm going to have a shower then we'll go out.' She moved to the door.

'Ring him first, I said you wouldn't be long,' Sue said.

'I can't deal with him today, I want a shower,' Cinni said and stumped into the bathroom strewing her clothes as she went. She turned the water on full blast, all of a few dozen spluttering drops, and stood under it, her feelings in turmoil. How could he be a biographer? But like Gerry Mitchell it couldn't be a coincidence. Two Lucian Fieldings, one who wrote art books and one who hung about looking like Darcy, too arrogant to speak to anyone below the level he had set himself. Two Gerry Mitchells, one who was cheating on his charming wife and lying to one of her best friends and one who was married to a bitch and longed to leave her and make a home with Sue.

When she was dressed and ready to go out, Sue reminded her again to ring Lucian, dangling the piece of paper with his name and number written out in her neat hand under her nose. She pushed it away. 'There's no time, I want to be settled in the restaurant before those wretched people ring me when the glazier arrives.'

'You can ring him on your mobile when we get there,' Sue said firmly slipping his number into her bag.

'If you want to have an affair with an arrogant man who will only notice you when it suits him, be my guest, in fact I'll gift wrap him for you,' Cinni said. 'I'll tell you a few things about Mum and you can pass them on. I don't want to get involved with him and for him to find out about the baby. I don't want everyone – anyone at all – to know who the father is. I want privacy for me and the child. At the right time I'll tell the child about his father, I'll tell Max's sister, Ruth, but I don't want it plas-

tered all over the gutter press so he can sell his book.' She shot forward
in the car narrowly missing a cyclist, making Sue cry out for her to take
care.

'I'm sure he's not like that,' Sue protested, as Cinni drove more carefully. 'He wants to know about Max's life, the people he painted, detail
in his pictures. He's a serious writer not some hack trying to make a
living from lurid gossip.'

'I don't want to talk about it,' Cinni said with vehemence. 'There are
plenty of other people he can talk to. Philip Gardener, who lives in the
house with Max's sister, for a start. He loved my mother, nursed her
through cancer. Max half admired him for that and half resented him for
doing it because he could not do it himself. He hated illness and ugliness.'

'I'm sorry if I upset you, Cin. I am just curious to meet him. I know
some of his books but I've never met him.'

'He was at the restaurant last night with Colette, thought we were a
couple of lezzies,' she said, causing Sue to gasp, which made her laugh
and explain.

'Some men fancy them; think they will be the one to change their way
of thinking. Some women think the same about gay men,' Sue said,
laughing too.

'He does not fancy me, he just wants to muckrake about my mother,'
Cinni said. 'Anyway, please forget that Max is my baby's father. I should-
n't have told anyone, even you. You are to tell no one at all. Even if a
friend asks, just say you don't know, or it's a French man, or the man in
the moon. But please, please . . .' the events of the day suddenly overtook
her and she found herself near tears, 'keep it to yourself.'

'Of course I will,' Sue touched her arm, sounding aggrieved. 'What do
you take me for? Haven't I kept quiet all these years about Gerry?
Anyway, I'm sure Lucian is a professional, serious writer and your mother
will only be a small part of a very detailed, informative book about Max's
work.'

'That's what I'm afraid of,' Cinni muttered, knowing the nausea she
was experiencing came not from her pregnancy but from this new anxiety of avoiding Lucian.

Once settled in the restaurant and determined to eat her dinner before
Nina and Rob rang to insist that she return to their villa to deal with the
glazier, Cinni said, 'I suppose now that you've spoken to Lucian and you
are so keen on meeting him I'd better tell you that I met him at a dinner
party given by the Mitchell's.' As Sue opened her mouth to interrogate

her she went on, 'It was pretty dreadful, they had some other friends there and they all talked and laughed about things they had done together, completely excluding me and indeed, Lucian.' She remembered his dark, brooding expression. 'I don't think they meant to but they did. I got Colette to ring and pretend there was an emergency in one of the villas so I could leave early.'

'You must tell me what she is like. Really, keeping nothing back,' Sue said stoically, as if preparing herself for some catastrophe.

'I've told you, she's warm, attractive and just the sort of woman I would like as a friend, and you would too under different circumstances. The children seemed nice and normal too, not like those brattish ones in Villa Jasmin. I'm sorry Sue, but that is how it is. You will, I hope, always be one of my best friends but I will have nothing whatever to do with what you and Gerry get up to. I'm not going to arrange anything or cover up for you, anything else but that.'

Sue's face tightened with strain. She said at last, 'Fair enough, but don't let's fall out over this. I thought I could give him up but I can't. I've been out with other men over the years, but they were nothing compared to him. I don't want to hurt Helen but at least she has his children and after all, we have been together for over ten years now.'

'Still doesn't make it right,' Cinni said.

'It can work though. Look at the Bloomsbury Group who all loved each other.'

'Maybe it works in some circles,' Cinni said. 'Max was rather like that, but as far as I know he never lied to any of his women, not lies like Gerry has told you of being unhappily married to a cold bitch of a wife.'

'I'm sure he didn't mean it,' Sue began, then was interrupted by Cinni's mobile and the waiter bringing their calamari.

'Damn, that glazier must have arrived, what bad timing. Hello?' Cinni answerered with ill-disguised irritation.

'Cinni, Lucian here.'

She snapped off the phone and said furiously to Sue, 'How's he got my mobile number?' Then she remembered she had given him her business card the night he'd come into the office.

A few minutes later it rang again and she had to answer it in case it was the glazier. It was not.

'I'm sorry, we got cut off,' he said.

'I cut us off, look, I've got your message. I don't want to talk to you, there are plenty of other people who'll tell you what you want to know.'

'Cinni, please, can't we just meet for a drink? You often saw Max when you were a child. I just need to build up a picture of as much of his life as I can.' His rich voice made her feel warm. She must not be so stupid as to succumb to it. Had she not heard somewhere that good interrogators made you think they were your friend so you were seduced into confiding in them?

'Look, I can't stay on the line, I'm waiting for an emergency call,' she said.

'I'll call round at the office tomorrow, take you to lunch,' he said firmly and rang off.

'I'll take the day off. I feel a headache coming on,' she said but knew she could not or Pascal would not let her take any more time off while Sue was here.

They finished dinner then the phone rang again and it was Rob telling her that the glazier had just arrived, 'And it's so late and we want to go to bed,' he grumbled.

'Should have dealt with your children better then,' she said, when he had rung off.

The glazier, a small pointy man who reminded her of a ferret, was not in a good mood having to come out so late, though he could have come earlier but Cinni did not want to go into it. He took more measurements for the glass – obviously not trusting hers though she was pleased to see they were exactly the same. He boarded up the hole until he could cut the glass.

'Will you come tomorrow?' Cinni asked, wondering if she could spend the day here waiting for him and so not be in the office when Lucian came.

The ferret shrugged and mumbled and shrugged some more and Cinni said sharply, 'If you can't do it, I'm sure we have someone else on the books who will, so if it is not done by tomorrow I will find someone else, OK?'

With much sighing, grumbling and shrugging the ferret said he'd see what he could do. Nina, who looked even more exhausted than when she had arrived, said, 'Thank you, that seems to have sorted him out. Will we have to stay in until he comes, only we made a plan for tomorrow?'

Cinni said, 'I'll try and find out when he is coming and see that someone is here, but please could you try and see this sort of thing does not happen again?' She might not have said that had she not felt so annoyed and fearful of Lucian discovering her secret. She felt mean about it when she saw Nina's face. Poor woman, Cinni bet she was wishing she had not come on holiday with their combined children. It was a pity that Sue had not come out of the car and seen this too. It might make her change her mind over Gerry. You needed a very strong love indeed to take on someone else's children.

Back at the studio later Cinni said, 'Look why don't you come to the office tomorrow at lunchtime then if Lucian turns up I can say we were lunching together and he can either take us both out or arrange to see me later. As you know, I return home soon so I might be able to escape him completely.'

'I can't tomorrow,' Sue said quietly. 'Don't you remember? I said I was meeting Gerry.'

'Oh, Sue, is that wise?' Thinking so much about Lucian she had forgotten that Sue was meeting up with Gerry. This irritated her, not only because she thought the affair must finish in the circumstances but also because she did not want to be alone with Lucian.

# CHAPTER TWELVE

WHEN the alarm clock shattered her few minutes of deep sleep, Cinni burrowed herself back into bed feeling as if she had spent the night being tumbled and bruised in a washing machine. She had tossed and turned most of the night fired up by the problems of Sue and Gerry, the terror of her own pregnancy and, worst of all, Lucian stalking her to worm out salacious snippets for his book on Max.

She would not meet him for lunch or at any other time. It was lucky that she had been warned what he was up to. In ten days she would be gone, be back in London and she could escape him. Once she had told Ruth about Max's baby and warned her that Lucian's book might well upset her with its gory details, Ruth would take charge in that imperious way she had and send him packing. There was plenty of available information about Max and his painting – which should surely be of more interest to art lovers than his love life – elsewhere.

Sue was subdued at breakfast. Her bravado at meeting Gerry had waned in the night. She was now tortured with the fear that he only wanted to see her to end their affair. Cinni sympathized with her then wondered if somehow she could get her together with Lucian and so get him off her back. They would probably get on very well; after all, they both worked in the same world. He could take her out to lunch instead, lured by possible titbits about Max, which of course Sue would not divulge. But somehow she felt reluctant to suggest it. That was hardly surprising, she told herself – ignoring a nudge of possessiveness – for even the best, most discreet friend might let something slip under the influence of a little too much wine in a warm ambience and an inclination to please.

Cinni arrived at the office early with plans to leave mid-morning to go to Villa Jasmin to oversee the glazier. She would go anyway whether it was to be done that day or not. She would leave the office well before lunch and somehow get tied up and not appear back until the afternoon. But when she arrived she found that Pascal was in the office already, which was unlike him, and to make it worse he was in a bad mood.

'Who do they think they are these clients?' he grumbled. 'I found three of them on the answerphone. One wants a light bulb changed, another can't cope with a glazier and another has flooded out the place with the washing machine. However do they cope at home? Or do they have servants to do everything for them?'

Cinni grunted sympathetically, deciding not to quote back to him his slogan that Magical Villas looked after your every need to give you a complete holiday. The clients certainly paid for a whole team of people to fix the light bulbs, water the garden, mend and mop up everything even if they didn't use their services at all, so there was always money in the kitty to pay that bit extra to persuade people to work during the holiday month.

Colette arrived rather late and seeing Pascal was already there threw a mini tantrum over the driving skills or lack of them of the tourists who clogged up the system. It was obvious it was only done to excuse her late arrival in case Pascal scolded her but he, in full tilt now on the stupidity and idleness of rich people, just reinforced his grumbles.

Cinni did not want to go to any of the villas at this moment; it was far too early, which would make her get back to the office by lunchtime when Lucian called. She could of course offer to see to all three and be out all day. When Pascal paused for breath she told him about Villa Jasmin and how she would go up there a little later when she had finished things here.

'Finished what things?' Pascal demanded. 'Paperwork can wait. Colette, you go to Villa Jasmin, it's that old charlatan Serge who will charge a fortune if we don't keep an eye on him. I will get Gaston to change the light bulb and, Cinni, you can go and deal with the washing machine.' He glared at her as if daring her to defy him, quite the little turkeycock with his quiff of mouse-brown hair quivering with self-importance in the middle of his round little head.

'I will stay here and man the office.' He made it sound as if he had pulled the short straw and was making a huge personal and dangerous sacrifice. 'You must leave at once, Cinni, as the plumber is on his way and he will do it as quickly as he can and it will only leak again. Go now.' He sounded like a commander giving orders for one last assault.

Perhaps she could spin it out, Cinni thought, taking her car keys out of her bag again. Pascal was now harassing Colette, who told him to calm down and if he was so worried about the glazier cheating them why didn't he go himself and she would stay in the office?

Cinni left them bickering, relieved to be outside in the clear air, still quite fresh before the onslaught of the baking sun. Then she had to go back inside to ask which villa she was meant to be going to.

'Rose, didn't I say?' he waved her away dismissively.

'Rose? I can't go there,' she protested in horror. It was the Mitchells' villa and she'd see Gerry sloping off for his secret rendezvous with Sue. Helen would be there, kind as ever, and all the time she knew what was going on. If the truth came out, Helen might even think Cinni had engineered it so that Sue and Gerry's meeting could take place. She was torn between her loyalty to both women, Sue, one of her oldest friends and Helen, a decent woman who didn't deserve such treachery from her pig of a husband.

'Of course you can go,' Pascal fumed at her.

'Would it not be better if I finished off at Jasmin? After all, I was there last night and I've already seen the glazier, he's expecting me.'

'Non, non, Colette must go. She knows how to deal with him. Now hurry up and get on your way.' He flapped his hands at them as if he could not bear their presence a moment longer.

Colette grumbled that she needed a coffee before she could function but Pascal would have none of it and the two women left the office together.

Cinni had one more try. 'Let me do the glazier,' she said to Colette.

'Non, when Pascal is like this it is better not to antagonize him. His wife is coming that is all. She likes to see that everything is in order; she put some money in the business and she likes to be sure she will get some back each year.'

'I see. I haven't met her. What is she like?'

Colette shrugged. 'She is very particular, keeps an eye on him and he does not like it. Maybe his girlfriend will ring or even come in while she is there and it will make complications.'

'I thought that marital infidelity was just another sport here.'

'Maybe, but if you are found out there has to be a row about it.' Colette threw Cinni a pitying look at her naïvety.

'Anyway,' Cinni said, 'I do feel awkward going to the Mitchells' villa knowing what is going on there. Are you sure we can't swap?'

'No, we cannot. Serge always tries it on but I know how to deal with him, you do not,' she said mysteriously and got into her car.

With a heavy heart Cinni drove slowly towards Villa Rose. Perhaps Helen would not be there, had taken the children out somewhere leaving Gerry free to meet up with Sue. She felt ill with anxiety, wondering how on earth she could behave towards Helen if she saw her, knowing that her friend had no intention to stop her affair with her husband. And Gerry, how would he behave knowing she knew he was about to go off to meet Sue?

She turned into the small space in front of the villa and saw there was only a corner to park in. The plumber's van was there and another car she did not recognize but perhaps Gerry had changed the car he'd hired. Her insides contracted with tension, dreading his reaction when he saw her. Dare she speak to him again about Sue? It must have crossed his mind that she would be the one to come out and cope with the flooding machine so no doubt he was prepared for it and would brazen it out.

Bracing herself for the encounter she got out of the car and rang the bell. After a moment Helen came to the door.

'Oh, Cinni, I'm so glad it is you, Gerry's not here. I think the whole discharge pipe has had it, but the plumber only wants to patch it so it is bound to go again.'

'I'll see to it.' Her words came out sharper than she intended but she felt like a traitor standing here with Helen obviously so pleased to see her and not just to rescue her from the plumber.

'Fine, this way.' Helen still smiled but her smile had lost its sparkle. Cinni followed her through the villa to the kitchen and there was Lucian haranguing a man whose bottom – vainly trying to escape from a tight pair of jeans – was sticking up in the air while he toiled with the machine.

She felt she might faint; he was the last person she thought she would – or wanted to – see here.

'You know Lucian Fielding? Helen said pleasantly. 'Fortunately he rang to ask if he could return some books Maggie borrowed and he's supervising the plumber. My French does not stretch much beyond ordering a meal in a restaurant, certainly not the technical stuff to do with plumbing.'

'That's OK, I'll deal with it now.' Cinni ignored Lucian, fighting to hide her shock at seeing him, addressing the plumber in a stream of furious French. She insisted on knowing exactly what the trouble was, expecting no nonsense at having it patched up but having it properly repaired with a new hose. Her tone of voice surprised everyone especially the plumber who muttered about seeing what was in his van and scurried off to fetch the new hose, which he knew was there but could not be bothered to fit.

'Very impressive, I wouldn't want to be on the wrong side of you,' Lucian said.

'Just doing my job,' she replied ignoring a surge of pleasure at the admiration in his eyes.

It's good to see you. Perhaps when we have finished here we could go and have a drink before our lunch. Get the work over first.'

Before Cinni could answer Helen broke in, 'You can stay here, stay on the terrace. I won't disturb you. Gerry's gone on some errands and taken the boys to the beach, Sara is still in bed. I think she overdid the sun yesterday, so we're staying here.'

How would Helen react if she knew that Gerry's errands included meeting Sue? But maybe Sue's premonition would prove correct and he was meeting her for one last time to tell her it was over? Poor Sue, what agonies she'd suffer. Cinni still hadn't got over Julian and something silly, like the snatch of a tune, a smell of a certain aftershave, would bring her anguish flooding back. But cheating on a decent wife after so many years was a different situation. In truth, however much it hurt Sue, Helen had more claim to him. But perhaps when – if – she knew the whole story she would chuck him out straight into Sue's welcoming arms. Whatever the outcome it would be painful all round. No doubt she would be swept up in it, but now she had to deal with being faced with Lucian when she was determined to avoid him.

Helen went on, 'It's so exciting, Lucian's book about Max Cavanagh and your mother being one of his favourite muses. Isn't life full of coincidences?'

Lucian said, 'Absolutely. And thanks, Helen, it's lovely here on the terrace, quiet too, but it's up to you Cinni, where would you feel most comfortable?'

'I . . . I won't be able to do it today. I'm sorry, I've got another villa to go to after this, kid broke a window,' she said, hoping it sounded genuine.

The plumber returned holding a piece of grey hose in his hand as if it would infect him with some nasty disease. With much mumbling he got back on the floor and started to fix it.

Lucian had on his arrogant look. 'It won't take long. I've done quite a bit of your job identifying the problem with the washing machine, you can surely spare me a few minutes.' He looked with distaste at the half-exposed bottom of the plumber. 'I'll probably need more than one meeting anyway; this will do as a starter.'

'You must do it, Cinni. I adore Max's work; he is so sympathetic towards women. Did you meet him?' Helen looked almost star-struck as if Cinni were famous herself, which if Lucian got his way she soon would be, well, infamous at least for hastening Max to his death.

'I met him a few times,' Cinni said.

The bottom unfolded and the plumber knelt up swearing. 'This machine is too old, you need a new one. The hose won't fit.'

'Nonsense,' Lucian said. 'This machine may be old but it is far better made than the modern ones. If you fix that pipe it will be as good as new.'

Cinni felt too exhausted to carry on with the plumber and Helen seeing this insisted that she sit down and have a coffee.

'I'd love some tea,' Cinni said, finding coffee difficult to digest at the moment. She felt as if she could see a huge wave of disaster looming above her that she had no hope of escaping. Helen and Lucian knew she was pregnant. In some perverse way to shock him she had told Lucian that the father of her child was dead – might he not piece the story together? What if Philip or Stella or even Ruth inadvertently let slip that Max had died after making love? A good journalist would soon work it out.

She sighed, slumping down gratefully on a chair in the part of the room used for eating. Helen sat down beside her saying quietly, 'You're doing too much; I expect you feel ill with all this heat and dashing about in your condition. I never felt well in the first few months of pregnancy. Can't you stay here in the cool and rest for a little?'

It was a great effort not to burst into tears and agree. Chuck in her job, escape Lucian's invasive questions and the torturous knowledge that Gerry was hurting two such nice women. But the longer she stayed here the more difficult it would be to extricate herself from the situation.

Having got the plumber to persevere with the hose and get it fitted properly Lucian joined them. 'We were having lunch together,' he said, 'so we can take things easy, just cruise through a few questions.'

'I haven't time for lunch,' she said wearily. 'When I got to the office this morning I found all these problems to deal with. I hardly know anything about my mother's life with Max anyway, it happened before I was born.' She did not add that one of his pictures of Fiona shown at the summer exhibition had made her father seek her out. It had been a deep love affair while it lasted. One of her favourite photographs was of the two of them on their wedding day, so young, glowing with love and passion, her mother in a cloud of white and her father laughing into her eyes. Such images caught fleeting moments and held them for ever but time moved on and that moment passed never to be recalled.

She realized that Lucian was watching her with unconcealed interest. She pulled herself back to the present, threw him a forced smile. 'So, I know nothing really. I'm sure there are other people who could tell you more. One of his ex-wives still lives in the house.' She felt a bit disloyal divulging that, but Stella often dined out on her days with Max.

'I know. I've been there. His death was very sudden and they are all still very shocked.'

'Was it a heart attack?' Helen asked with interest.

Cinni thought she'd pass out. She got up slowly and went over to the washing machine and the plumber's bottom and began to ask him how it was going. Any moment Lucian would work out that she was carrying Max's child and then he would never leave her alone.

'Yes, apparently he had a bad heart but he hadn't told his family. Wanted to ignore it and just get on with life. I suppose that is one way of dealing with it,' Lucian said, coming over to her.

'He died at his own birthday party. I believe you were a guest there. I quite understand if you don't want to talk about it yet, it must have been a terrible shock. Did it happen while you were there?' His voice was kind but she sensed an undercurrent of determination to find out the truth.

'I wasn't there then,' she said, holding on to the kitchen worktop to stop herself falling. 'But I don't want to talk about it, after all it is nothing whatever to do with his life or his work.'

'I disagree, death is the end of a life, and sometimes the manner of the death is all important.' His eyes looked into hers as if he could see deep into her heart and read the secrets there. He knew, somehow he knew about her role in his death. The washing machine was mended and the plumber protested at how difficult it had been and how sick he was at wasting time mending machines that should have been on the scrap heap years ago.

Cinni dealt with the bill trying to ignore Lucian's brooding presence. When the plumber had gone she followed him out, calling out, 'Goodbye, must dash, so much to do at the office.'

'I'll be there at lunchtime,' Lucian said firmly.

'Probably can't manage today,' she said.

He followed her out to her car. 'I don't want to be in a rush if you haven't got much time for lunch. How about after work? You finish about six don't you? I'll call for you then.' He smiled and turned back into the villa before she could protest.

'No way,' she said to the deserted drive. She got into her car, worn out with the fight but she could not allow herself to give up now. Lucian was dangerous and she must keep away from him.

# CHAPTER THIRTEEN

THE spirit of Max haunted Cinni as she drove down the winding road back to the office. How could she have behaved so badly? Panicked like that? She should have owned up to Max's death at once and now she had got in so deep it would be impossible to extricate herself with any honour. She supposed she deserved to be punished, but it was just sod's law that someone as arrogant as Lucian Fielding would uncover her deceit.

She was aware that writers today had to sing and dance and do anything else, however shameful, to draw attention to themselves and their latest book to generate sales. The manner of Max's death was a bull's eye. She could imagine him laughing in heaven or wherever he was. What a joke, the climax of his life ending with the climax of lovemaking. But you left more you old roué, she muttered. This child, what am I to do about it? If I keep quiet about its father I'll deprive it of at least knowing where it came from. If I tell anyone the means of its conception the truth will come out and Lucian will see that it is smeared all over the place as publicity for his bloody book.

Perhaps she ought to terminate the pregnancy after all. There was still time. Would it not be kinder for the child than having it run the gauntlet of all this scandal? School. God, she felt sick thinking about it. She'd been bullied because some little madam in her class had seen the pictures of her mother swathed in material.

'Was it because her body was horribly deformed, so ugly she had to hide it?' Sybella had jeered. All these years on she could still hear her sharp little voice, still feel the echo of the jagged pain deep inside her. She'd told her mother who had laughed, hugged her and said the bully was just a sad little girl who was jealous of her, but it hadn't helped. She didn't want her mother to be famous, see her picture used all over the place. It had been used in an advertising campaign for a cosmetic company, suggesting that by using its products one's mysterious hidden beauty would be revealed. Even some of the teachers resented it, the headmistress remarking whenever she was in trouble, 'Just because your mother's picture is all over the place does not mean you can talk in the dormitory/draw attention to yourself in class/not help with the domestic duties.'

Cinni could not bear her own child to suffer in the same way and yet was that a valid excuse to end its life? Was she just being selfish in keeping it because it might be her last chance of having a child at all? She knew what her mother would say if she were still alive. 'Life – live it, love it, it is always too short.' She had said that as she lay dying, her body eaten away by the cancer but still her eyes burning bright. Her life had been short, far too short, but she knew how precious it was. She had not taken the easy route and got rid of her although all of Theo's family had risen up in horror at the idea that the second son of a baronet should marry an artist's model from – in their view – an inferior background. Cinni would keep this child and somehow try to protect it or anyway teach it to cope with sneering remarks.

But what, the thought struck her as she parked the car outside the office, if she approached the problem from a different angle? If she confided in Lucian, appealed to his better nature – if he had one – and begged him to say nothing? To leave out all reference to the child and apart from saying Max had died of a heart attack at his birthday party say no more about it? But then the story would not be so exciting and would Lucian really forego masses more sales just to please her? She doubted it. She sat in the car a moment, her hand unconsciously on her stomach. She'd first visited Max with her mother when she was five. He'd frightened her a little, there was so much of him, he was never still, darting this way and that, his eyes forever scrutinizing things, turning his head to study them from another angle, catch them in another light.

'What a beautiful child.' His voice had been quieter than she'd expected. 'Like you, Fiona, and yet I can see her father there and Theo is almost more beautiful than any woman.' He'd put his arm round Fiona and pulled her to him and she had laughed and snuggled her head on to his shoulder, small and slight against his bulk. She could see the two of them now. Fiona had never had an affair with Max, though the newspapers had often insinuated otherwise. So had girls at school. 'An artist's model is just another word for a tart,' Sybella had jeered.

'I never slept with him. I was quite a prude, being a convent girl and all,' Fiona had said when she'd asked her. 'I was, am still, very fond of him though I never fancied him that way, besides, I hate sharing men, and women swarmed round him offering themselves up like sacrificial virgins.'

Oh, Mum, why did you go and die? Misery swamped her. I need you now to help me deal with this. I feel so alone in it all, you'd have known what to do, stood by me.

Fiona wouldn't have believed it, she almost laughed at the thought of it. She'd have been aghast at such a predicament, her own daughter pregnant by such a famous artist whose picture had catapulted her into the limelight and arguably been responsible for getting her married into one of the oldest aristocratic families in the country.

Pascal came out of the office, walking fast as if he had a train to catch. He caught sight of her and came over. Cinni sniffed furiously, thankful her sunglasses would hide her tears.

'Alors, Cinni. Where have you been? The telephone never stops ringing and I have an important appointment.'

In bed with your girlfriend, Cinni mutterered to herself, reluctantly getting out of the car. It was so hot, too hot, how she longed to slip into a pool of cold water. If she had stayed at Villa Rose she could have done just that, spent the day there pretending that the washing machine had taken all that time to get mended.

'Will you be away long?' she asked, irritated that he would be enjoying himself while they worked and that he would later get the credit for it.

He threw her a look to say it was none of her business and got into his car. She walked quickly into the office craving the coolness of the air conditioning.

Emma, who had parted company with the boy she had met, was staring at her emails on the computer screen; she blushed, hastily closed it down then saw it was Cinni. 'Thought it was that randy old goat. Why does every man think you are longing to sleep with them?'

'Do they?' Cinni sat down at her desk. Emma was wearing a sleeveless T-shirt with no bra and a minuscule skirt. 'I expect it's the message you give out,' she said. 'So much tempting flesh on show.' Her own flesh, she thought darkly, was fast losing its charm and would do so even more when her stomach swelled with this child.

Emma giggled. 'But this is the South of France and it's so hot, what am

I meant to wear?' She spoke with the arrogance of someone who assumes they are the only person affected by the heat.

'So, where is Colette?'

'Not back, some trouble with the glazier I think. Still, I can answer the phone. At least all the clients speak English.

The afternoon passed slowly and uneventfully. Cinni had to force herself to keep awake, though her anxiety about being grilled by Lucian at the end of the day tortured her. He wrote about artists, how their lives affected their work – no doubt he was a master at winkling out their secrets. She'd be no match for him, he'd find some way to persuade her to tell the whole story. The thought of him made her heart beat a little faster. Oh no, she was not going to allow that old trick to influence her at all. He was arrogant – first impressions are usually right, she counselled herself – and no doubt he assumed he could seduce it out of her even though Colette had suggested she was gay. He was only interested in her because she might hold some tasty information for his book. And yet, she thought of how he'd been at the flower market before he had known who she was. There had been something deep in his eyes that had touched her heart. But she'd probably imagined it, wanted to find something to bind him to her, as she was feeling so lonely and wounded without Julian. She must be strong now, for her child's sake and not give him any information. She'd leave the office before time, she'd have to, she could not be alone with him.

Probably knowing Pascal would be away some time, Colette came back late, then Pascal whirred in looking purposeful, but on finding all had been quiet went into his own office and closed the door. Each time the phone rang Cinni expected it to be Sue. Either she'd be in tears over the end of the affair or upbeat having been persuaded by Gerry that he loved her and would somehow make a life with her. Whichever way it had gone she would suggest that they meet at some bar out of the way so she could escape Lucian. But Sue did not ring, and she did not have the heart to ring her on her mobile. If Sue wanted her she would contact her, wouldn't she? But Cinni told herself that she must stop jumping to conclusions. If Gerry had ended it, Sue, who was half-expecting it, would hardly throw herself in front of a car in the Promenade des Anglais, or drown herself from the quay. She would suffer terribly but would probably be walking on the beach trying to come to terms with it knowing Cinni was in the office and could not see her until the evening. But still Cinni worried, surely Sue would ring, even if she couldn't speak for tears?

The clock clicked on to six. Pascal came out of his office, his face flushed as if he had been asleep, preventing her leaving early. Cinni willed someone to ring from a villa, giving her an excuse to escape from her drink with Lucian. Her body tensed, any moment he would come in and she must think of a way to get out of it. She wondered if Emma might be persuaded to distract him but before she could ask her, Emma threw her a furtive smile and slipped out of the office before Pascal could think of a reason to keep her back.

The telephone rang and Cinni pretended to be searching for something in her bag. Colette, wanting to leave, answered it with unconcealed boredom. Then her face changed. 'Lucian, 'ow can I 'elp you?' she purred, her eyes on Cinni.

Cinni jumped up to leave, snatching up her bag but her car keys fell out and she had to go down on the floor to retrieve them from under her desk.

'Disappeared? Gerry Mitchell?' She heard Colette say. ' 'Is wife is distraught, 'as there been an accident? I 'ave not 'eard of one. Where did 'e go?'

Gerry disappeared? Had he and Sue legged it to some secret hideaway? She felt sick, thinking of Helen's anguish and hadn't she said he was going to take the children to the beach? What had happened to them? She got up and slumped back down on her chair. She knew where Gerry was and she would have to tell someone; in the circumstances Lucian might be the best bet. But before she could signal to Colette to pass her the phone so she could explain, Lucian rang off. Then her mobile rang and it was Sue.

'Oh, Cinni, where are you? We need you desperately.'

# CHAPTER FOURTEEN

THE plan Sue and Gerry had made was for her to meet Gerry outside Cinni's flat. It was outside Nice and it was unlikely anyone would see him there. Gerry was to leave the boys on the beach, meet her and then pick them up again. Sue did not ask what story he had concocted for his wife; she was determined not to think of it. For ten years Gerry had made up stories of his whereabouts for Helen, he must be a master at it now. He had also – the thought was like a knife in her – been making up stories for her. A marriage to an unloving wife and the existence of a third child years off going to university.

And yet she loved him. In the long nights she interrogated herself far more intensely than Cinni had done. Was it the fear of being alone, of never finding another man to love her that kept her with him? Gerry was the pole star in her life, he ruled her thoughts, gave her life a sparkle it would not have without him. She knew it was wrong to sleep with a married man and she'd taken a long time to be persuaded into his bed. But he'd told her his marriage was dead, cold and unloving and she had believed him, or, she thought shamefully, wanted to believe him. She had given him love and comfort, wanting to care for him, to smooth away the hurt of this painful marriage and yet according to Cinni he was not hurt. Helen was warm, loving, a woman that they both in other circumstances would welcome as a friend. Why had he lied to her? Had he other women he lied to as well as her? The thought was so frightening she suppressed it. She must not overreact.

She waited outside the building, sitting on the whitewashed wall of the two flats. She would not allow him to come in. He would start being affectionate with her and she would not be able to resist him and it would not be fair on Cinni knowing he had been in her space, making love when she so disapproved of him.

Beside her stood a huge earthenware urn baked dry by the sun holding the pink bougainvillea that snaked up the building. The bulging belly of the pot made her think of Cinni's pregnancy. How strange was its conception. With anyone else she might not have believed it, thought it a fabrication to hide a more sordid truth, the result of a one night stand with a stranger. Not that she'd have judged her, even the smallest hint of affection offered momentary balm to the bleakness of loneliness.

A car whisked up the hill and stopped. It was Gerry. He got out slowly, coming towards her with a hesitant smile on his face as if afraid of her reception. She wanted to tear him to shreds for hurting her so and yet she wanted him to hold her, swear he'd never leave her.

'You look lovely.' He stood before her, holding out his hand then dropping it, searching her face with his eyes.

'You don't,' she said, the tears rising up in her. She bent her head to hide them and he was beside her, holding her, his arms round her, his body bent over, his head on hers.

She must be strong, tell him he must leave, she would have no more of his deceit, but she could not. The familiar scent of him, the familiar feel of his body trapped her. She would live any way he wanted as long as he still loved her.

A man walked by with his dog who ran up to them and sniffed at them. The man called at him lazily to come away.

Gerry straightened up. 'It's too public here, can we go inside?'

How she yearned to feel his skin on hers, his kisses and caresses. She would not be able to stop him. But it was Cinni's flat and she would not do that to her.

'No.' She pushed him away. 'We must go somewhere else, away from here. How long have you got?' She felt as if he were going away to be killed in battle, that this might well be the last time they were together.

'Most of the day. Where shall we go?'

'Let's go inland, it's so lovely there, less crowded than the beach.' She did not add, 'and less risky'.

She got into his car and he eased it back up the road. They sat in silence for a while. She knew she must say something, not let him think she was weak and things were still all right between them and could go on as before. 'Cinni says your wife is very nice, not at all how you described her.' She steeled herself for his anger.

'She is,' he said. 'It was just that we were going through a bad time, she was busy with the children and her sister was ill and she was work-

ing and she didn't seem to have time for me. Then I met you.' He gave
her a rueful smile as if it was not his fault at all. 'And I fell in love with
you. I thought it would work out.'

'Work out how?' A hollow, dead void was opening inside her.

'That I could have it all.'

'And what would I have had in this? You know I wanted marriage and
children, you led me to believe I would have that with you.'

He had the grace to look embarrassed. He drove a while in silence. 'I
thought you'd meet someone else and it would end without trouble.' He
stopped the car beside a field, turned to her and took her hand. 'I'm
sorry, I really am. It just got out of hand, became a habit – a nice habit, a
wonderful habit – and I did not think of the consequences.'

'But you promised to marry me, give me a child.' The pain was so deep
now she felt she would shatter like frozen glass. It hurt to breathe; her
hand lay limp in his. This was the end, he was trying to extricate himself
from her and she could not bear it.

'I would if I could,' he said. 'I love you, I do love you, Sue, but I love
my family also. I don't know what to do.' He bowed his head and looked
so miserable that she lay against him. 'Let's get out,' he said, 'it's so
uncomfortable in here. I'll park the car.'

He turned off the road on to a dirt track, one side bordered with trees,
at the side of the field. They got out. He would make love to her and she
wanted him to. It would be the last time and she must remember it and
keep it with her for the rest of her life. Perhaps she would get pregnant,
she thought, for she had stopped taking the pill since Cinni had told her
about Helen. She felt spaced out, too sad to care. This would be their last
day together, she would not think beyond it.

She clung to him on the dry earth, the car shielding them from the
road. 'I do love you,' he said, 'and don't want to lose you, but I cannot
offer you marriage . . . unless. . . . He clamped his mouth shut, his eyes
wild and she knew he was going say 'unless Helen died or left me'.

'I want you both,' he said, burying his face in her breasts.

They lay in the shelter of the trees a long time, talking and making
love. Gerry had some water and food in the car he was meant to be taking
back to the villa and they picnicked together, leaning against each other,
feeding each other. The sun was hot, scorching them and the earth, now
and again a car passed on the road but no one disturbed them. The sun
caught the dial on his watch dazzling him a moment but making him
remember the time. It was past five. He jumped up, his bottom half

naked. 'Oh God, the boys. I'm meant to pick up the boys.'

Her heart sank, he was now another man. Gerry the father, Gerry the anxious husband. Gerry the lover had evaporated in the heat.

'Quick,' he said, pulling on his clothes then hiding the remains of their picnic in the bushes, 'we must go. I said I'd be back by three.'

He jumped into the car and she got in too, still dressing herself. She was fighting back tears, an urge to plead with him to stay. He put the key in the ignition and turned it, nothing happened. He did it again, this time more roughly, then again.

'Bloody hell, the battery's dead. I must have turned the lights on or something by mistake.' He snatched at the light lever. 'No. Damn, the radio, must be something wrong to make it drain so quickly. What are we to do?' His face was ashen, the fear tightened in her. He was going to blame her, hate her for getting him in such a predicament. With rising panic he searched his pockets then the glove box and the pocket in the side of the car. 'Where's my mobile, where in hell's name is my mobile?'

'I've got mine,' she said, his furious anxiety upsetting her. She had never seen him like this before. But the boys, he had left the boys so long. Would they be safe? But they were not both small children, the older one would be more than capable, she reminded herself, but if anything happened to them she would blame herself even though it was more Gerry's fault than hers. 'Oh, God,' she prayed silently, 'let this end all right.'

'Give me yours.' He was rough with panic. 'Oh, I can't ring from it in case . . . Helen will see it's not my number. I'll have to say mine was missing and I borrowed one. Oh hell, what a mess.'

He was so distraught she said, 'I'll ring Cinni, she'll rescue us.' She dialled her number and Cinni answered at once.

'Where are you? Lucian's just rung here and said Gerry was missing, Helen's in a terrible state.'

'The battery on the car has gone. Can you come and get us, or get him? Perhaps we could jump start the car, and his boys, he's really late to pick them up from the beach.'

'They took a taxi home. They tried to raise Gerry on his mobile but it was turned off.' Cinni sounded exasperated and Sue couldn't blame her. 'Look tell me where you are and I'll come for you, but can't you ring the breakdown service used by the car company? It should be in the info somewhere in the car.'

Sue put this to Gerry, who said, 'We'll ring them but if Cinni could come and fetch us that would be wonderful.' Sue relayed this back to Cinni.

'I'll come because it's you, but somehow the car's got to be mended and explanations as to why it is where it is, given, but I'm having nothing to do with that.'

'Thanks, Cinni.'

'So, where are you?'

'Just close to Grasse outside the town by a field. About a mile away from a honey place.'

'I think I know where you are; there's a very exclusive villa that we sometimes use about a mile ahead. I'll be there as soon as I can.' Cinni rang off.

The warm feelings of love that Sue had been feeling for Gerry such a short time before were now suffocated with anxiety. It devoured the optimism that had slipped into her that their love would never die and would somehow keep going. It had not died, she saw it in his eyes as he looked at her, but it could not flourish any more. She knew he felt this too. His love for his children would stop it, the terror of thinking they were in danger while he, their father, who should be protecting them, was making love to another woman. It was that one fact that decided her, made her see that their affair had come to the end.

'Why did you not tell me you had a younger child, who won't go to university for at least eight more years?' She demanded having not questioned him before as she did not want to sour their time together.

'He was an accident, after a drunken New Year.' He did not look at her.

'But you still could have told me about him.' She was tempted to ask if he had never intended to marry her at all, but she knew she could not stand the pain of watching him trying to justify himself, so she let it go.

Gerry got out of the car and paced around, hands in pockets, feet scuffing up the earth, his face set, thinking, no doubt, how he would explain this to his wife, wondering if he would get away with it. Sue felt icy calm as if she had been poleaxed by some shattering news. She'd felt like this when she'd been told that her father needed heart surgery, calm yet terrified, determined to get him through it. It had been hard but she had done it and he had recovered. She must face this too and get over it.

To her surprise the frantic pain and fear of losing Gerry she'd experienced at the beginning of the day had left her. His anxiety, his thoughts only of himself and how this would affect him peeled off one of the layers of their love. What about her sitting here in a field? What about her feelings? He seemed to have forgotten about her he was so bound up in the worries of his own predicament. She expected that any moment he would start blaming her for them. Perhaps when you fell in love, she thought, you painted a picture of the person you wanted to see. Only truly great love faced and accepted the failings as well.

Neither spoke until at last Cinni arrived. Gerry rushed to meet her. 'Thank God you've come, have you jump leads?'

'Yes, but if they don't work, you'll have to call the garage,' she answered curtly, taking them out of her car and handing them to him. 'There's just about room for my car beside yours.' She got back in and positioned it.

Sue got out of the car and threw her a grateful smile. Cinni sighed. 'What are you doing out here? No, don't answer that, but everyone is frantic, why did you go so far away and stay so long?'

Gerry was fixing the clips of the jump leads to his car. They kept slipping and he swore, his anger making him clumsy. Sue saw that Cinni seemed amused by this but she pretended not to notice, ignoring her instinct to help him.

'I know, we were meant to be back ages ago, but we lost track of time, then the car wouldn't start. Is . . .' she could not say Helen's name, 'everyone all right?'

'Well the boys are, fortunately they found a taxi and got back to the villa, but Helen is frantic and who can blame her?'

Sue said nothing, what could she say? Cinni opened the bonnet of her car and then sat in the driver's seat ready to turn on the engine. Gerry attached the clips and the engine jumped into life.

'Thanks so much,' he said, leaving the engine running while he dismantled the leads. He glanced at Sue and the pain in his eyes echoed in her heart. If only she could hold him one more time but she knew that in front of Cinni he would not touch her.

'I'd better drive back alone,' he said. 'I'll be in touch.' He turned his face from her and got into his car and began to back out but becasue of the angle of Cinni's car it took a little time.

Sue crept into the back of Cinni's car, exhausted suddenly by the heat and her whirling emotions. She lay down on the back seat huddling into herself, trying to keep her tears in check. Cinni opened the boot to put back the jump leads. There was the sound of another car approaching; it stopped abruptly as the driver saw them. She heard the car door open and slam and a man's voice saying, 'Cinni, whatever are you doing here in this field with Gerry?'

# CHAPTER FIFTEEN

LUCIAN'S expression of anger bordering on disgust stunned Cinni. Trust him to turn up and add to the complications. Had he brought Helen with him? That would be the end. Fearfully she glanced at the passenger side of his car but no one was there. Unless she'd already got out and was attacking Gerry, which he certainly deserved, but she did not see her. She could not have borne to see her misery, especially if it was directed at her. What a mess it all was. She shut the boot and got into her car, she was not going to say anything, just ignore him and drive away.

Sue still huddled down on the back seat said, 'Who's that?'

'No one of any importance, stay down until we hit the road.' She turned on her engine and began to reverse. Gerry was on the road now and Lucian was in her way parked on the dirt track running beside the field. She touched the horn and he got back in the car and reversed out violently, almost crashing into Gerry. This gave her the room she needed and she swept out and sped up the road away from them.

Would Lucian now think that she and Gerry had had an amorous rendezvous even though according to Colette, she was meant to be gay? She had told him that she was too busy to see him and would he assume this was the reason? He would think her the worst sort of bitch, a woman who slept with another woman's husband while pretending she liked her. Well, what did it matter? It might keep him away from her and she could keep her secrets safe. But then, the uncomfortable thought hit her, her behaviour might urge him on, make him think it would add spice to his blasted book. The daughter of one of Max's most famous models, who unlike her mother, was some sort of sexual predator and liked women as well as men. She minded what he thought; the pain twisted in her. What a fool she was to care what such an arrogant man thought of her.

Sue sat up, blew her nose. 'Did whoever it was think that you were with Gerry?'

'It doesn't matter.' What a mess her life was in. She'd inadvertently killed Max, was carrying his child and now was most probably being branded a bi-sexual adulteress.

'Of course it does. I suppose it will all come out now and I can't have you taking the blame. Who was that man? Do you know him? Will he tell Helen?'

'It was Lucian Fielding. I don't know why he turned up, or knew where we were.'

'Oh Lord, he might jump to all sorts of conclusions.' Sue was shocked.

'Surely. Slut who sleeps around, kills off one man, snatches another while he's on holiday and don't forget Colette told him I was gay. I'd laugh if I didn't feel so miserable.'

Sue sniffed. 'I'm so sorry, I seem to have fucked up so many people's lives. I'll tell him it was me with Gerry, don't worry.'

'I wouldn't say anything unless you have to. Maybe Gerry will be able to convince Helen that he was seeing a man about a dog or something and broke down.'

'I think it's over.' Sue's voice wobbled. 'I wanted to keep it going whatever the cost but now I see that I can't. Somehow in London it worked, Helen was busy in the country and I could kid myself that she'd never find out. Anyway, I thought he was unhappily married and would soon be leaving her for me.'

'He is a shit,' Cinni said with feeling, including Lucian in her description. What sort of person was he to jump to the wrong conclusions so quickly? How would that characteristic come out in his book about Max, especially if he ever found out the truth about the baby?

'But I still love him.'

'But he is no good for you. He's standing in the way of you meeting anyone else and having a chance at having a family. But maybe you'll be relieved it's over when the pain subsides. I don't know what I'm going to do when this baby is born, how I am going to cope without a father for it.'

'I'll help you, I'm hardly a father, but somehow you'll manage. At least it's something to look forward too,' Sue said sadly.

They went back to the flat and sat out on the roof terrace. The violet light shot with the pink and apricot of the dying sun surrounded them. The air was still warm, heavy with the scent of flowers.

'This is beautiful, romantic but we only have each other to share it with,' Sue said bitterly.

'I know, maddening how often one is in a romantic place alone or with a girlfriend or one's parents or something.'

'Pity Lucian didn't turn out as a lover. I do hope he doesn't make trouble for you. You will tell me if he does, won't you? I don't want you to be blamed for anything I did.'

Cinni felt her heart tighten – this was a place for love – but life being what it was love did not always turn up in the most romantic places. In fact had she fallen in love out here she would have had to disregard it until it had been tested in a cold, wet climate of soulless high-rise flats and dirty streets. 'I'll keep you posted. How I wish I were coming home with you! Still, only another week. I'll keep clear of him until then and he'll never find me when I'm in London.'

'He will if he wants to. He'll go back to Max's house and ask there. You'll have to go and see them, tell them about the child. It will be tough on you but you said you'd do it, and I think you're right to.'

'And so I will.' She sighed, the magnitude of the deed overwhelming her. 'Perhaps I ought to write, warn them. Or confide in Philip; after all, he was almost like a father to me, my own having the mentality of an adolescent. What do you think?'

Sue poured herself some more wine and topped up Cinni's water. 'I think you should tell his sister first, the baby will be her niece or nephew. She might not want anyone else to know, might be so shocked she'll want nothing to do with it. Have you thought of that?'

'No, not really.' Cinni thought of Ruth, tall, skinny like a bird, forever swooping around as if she would take flight. She'd heard her scold Max often enough about his women, his obsession with young nude bodies.

'Always women, couldn't we have a man or two? I understood that the male body was the most perfect, but I suppose that might be too difficult for you to get right,' she'd said once, making Max roar at her.

'Then no doubt you'd criticize me for going through a gay stage. I'll paint what I like. Don't forget, the bills have to be paid here and I don't notice you contributing much.'

Cinni had noticed his obsession with money the few times she'd seen him in the last years as he had aged. Perhaps he was not making so much and everything did seem to get more and more expensive. But when she was young and Fiona was alive she remembered his generosity, the way he took everyone out to eat, his friends, his family, anyone who was about, sometimes even asking any neighbours they passed on the way to the restaurant. Then later he'd begun grumbling about the cost of things, the cost of housing his sister, his ex-wife and Philip.

Ruth might well be shocked, might not believe her, think that she too was trying to cash in on whatever money Max had left behind. The thought chastened her; it would be bad enough telling her the news but to be labelled as a scrounger would be even worse.

The next day Sue said she'd hire a car and go to visit the medieval villages in the hills that she loved. Cinni also suspected that she wanted to get away from the possibility of seeing Gerry or his family and be by herself to reassess her life. She dropped her at a car hire office having already made a reservation for her. They agreed to meet up again that evening.

Cinni breezed into the office as though nohting had happened. There was a man she had never seen before going through her desk.

'What are you doing?' she cried out. He was bent over one of her drawers, rifling through it.

He stood up; he was tanned, lean-faced with grey hair cut *en brosse*. He smiled. 'Excuse me, I am André Riqueur. This is my desk, you are only borrowing it.' His English was impeccable. He came forward his hand outstretched to take hers. He dragged one of his legs.

'Oh, sorry, you had the accident.' He was the man she'd been covering for. She took his hand, it was smooth and cool and he held hers a fraction too long, his clear brown eyes looking into hers. A surge of warmth infused her. Don't you start again, she scolded herself, you are in enough trouble. She took her hand away and said briskly, 'So, you are back? Shall I go home?'

'No, I am not working full time until September. I just came in to see how things were. Pascal was here and ah, here is Colette.' The door opened and she came in, her face lit up when she saw him.

'André. *Comment vas-tu?*' They kissed each other, jabbering at each other in excitement. Then Pascal appeared and the three of them continued talking and joking together, Pascal slapping him on the back with obvious delight leaving Cinni feeling excluded. Should she just sit down at her desk and carry on with her work or was André going to sit there?

Was she needed here at all today? If only she'd known she would have gone with Sue and had a wonderful day out exploring the villages in the hills. She made some excuse of going to buy some breakfast and went out into the street and walked down to the quay. Everything, she thought now, had a feeling of coming to an end. Sue had finished, or said she had, with Gerry, and was returning home the day after tomorrow, her job here was ending and ... well, nothing had happened between her and Lucian so she could not pretend there was anything there to finish, but if he had been interested in her – as herself not as Fiona's daughter – and she'd felt that he had, he would be so no longer after that scene yesterday with Gerry. But maybe Gerry had put Lucian right? Told him about Sue.

After twenty minutes she returned to the office. André greeted her with a smile. 'I'm sorry if I made you feel unwanted. I am only here to see how things are going. You sit at the desk. I will share with Pascal – he is going out anyway.'

'Thank you, if you're sure.' She liked his manner and his face, open and smiling. What a pity it had not been Pascal who had had the accident and she had taken over from him.

Colette called out, 'Oh, that man came in, all in a fuss, wanted to see you.'

'What man?' No doubt it was Lucian bent on embellishing her story to jazz up his book.

'The man who's rented Villa Rose – he is coming back – oh, here he is.' She shrugged and got back to her work though Cinni suspected her antennae were quivering with curiosity.

Gerry marched into the office, homed straight in on her. 'Ah, Cinni,' he said as though he had come across her unexpectedly. 'Just the girl I want to see, can we talk?'

Lead pellets seemed to be lining her stomach. She was aware of André regarding the scene with amused interest. 'Something wrong with the villa?' she asked, going over to her desk and sitting down.

'No, nothing like that. I'd like to speak to you in private if I may.' His face was tight, eyes boring through her as if he expected her to obey him.

Glancing at Colette who was now on the telephone, and watching André's back retreating into Pascal's office and shutting the door, she said, 'This is private enough. I have a lot of work to do, what can I do for you?'

He put both his hands on the front of her desk and leant over like some huge monster trying to intimidate her. She experienced a shiver of apprehension but ignored it. What could he do to her here with Colette sitting there and André and Pascal within shouting distance? Had he bullied Sue, did he bully Helen? Well he wasn't going to bully her.

He whispered harshly, 'You know what it's about.'

She looked up at him. 'Do I?'

'Of course you do, now listen. Helen thinks I was with you, not that we were having an affair or anything,' he added hastily, 'but it would be easier if she thought that. She doesn't know Sue exists and it's better that way.'

She could not believe what she was hearing. 'It's only better for you. I like your wife and I'd hate her to think I was carrying on with you behind her back. You must tell her the truth.'

Anger fuelled by panic rose in him. 'She would not understand and what have you to lose? She'll never see you again, and anyway she won't think that.'

'I bet she does. If our so-called meeting was above board why didn't you tell her about it beforehand? Women hate that sort of secret – it makes them suspicious. Anyway, I care about my reputation and I will not take the blame for your behaviour. What's more, if I have to I'll tell her what you asked me to do.'

He flinched as if she'd hit him. He said with some shame, 'Please, Cinni, I want to save my marriage and not hurt Sue.'

Did he hope to pick up with Sue again after a decent interval? She leant back in her chair and regarded him. Sue had said she must accept that it was over – unless,' she had added, 'his marriage broke down over it then she would insist that he marry her and give her a child.' Cinni had not pointed out that this might be a rather shaky start to a marriage. Sue had suffered enough and it might be better to say nothing and see what happened. But here he was apparently desperate to cling on to his marriage.

'I will not be part of your shady love life,' she said. 'I came to help when your car broke down because Sue called me. She is a great friend and perhaps in some strange way I wanted to help Helen, save her from pain. But I do not want to help you. I despise you for the way you have behaved towards both of them. Sue has been hanging on for years hoping you would marry her. She could have played dirty and got pregnant, blowing the whole affair out of the water, but she did not and now she might not find a nice man in time to become a mother.' Cinni got up and walked round the desk and into the body of the office. Colette put down her telephone and pretended to look through her papers though obviously fascinated at the scene.

Gerry seeing this, hissed, 'I want to continue this conversation outside.'

'Why, will you hit me?'

'Of course not, I just want you to see how awkward this is for me . . . for all of us.'

Lucian's expression when he had caught sight of her in her car beside Gerry loomed back in her mind. She'd been upset that he had jumped to such a conclusion about her though later she had reassured herself with the thought that Gerry had put him right, but now she knew he had not. Gerry had let Lucian believe, perhaps even reinforced it, that it was Cinni he was seeing – not Sue. Lucian did not know Sue's place in Gerry's life. It would be easy to make people think Cinni was the one he was involved with. She saw by his expression that he guessed her feelings.

'I'd be so grateful, I'm sorry, really I am, that things got so out of hand. I thought it would be all right, but I suppose it was too much to hope for. I left my mobile behind and the car battery ran down, if that hadn't happened. . . .'

'But it did and it all came out. But I won't take the blame for it – you owe it to Helen to tell her the truth.' But even as she said this she thought of Sue and how loyal she had been to him over the years, believing him when he told her he would marry her soon. She would not see the Mitchells again, she was leaving here in a few days and no one in this office would care. If Helen thought it was just a one-off she might forgive him and her marriage be saved and the family not be broken up. Sue would not have to go through the agony of being cited in a divorce, which, she suspected would not end in her marrying Gerry.

'I want you to leave and never speak about this again,' she said. 'You have deceived two wonderful women and you don't deserve either of them. If you can keep Sue out of it, well and good, but tell no more lies about me.'

Relief flooded his face. He stretched out his hand to take hers but she moved away. 'You've saved my marriage, how can I thank you?'

She saw the gleam of tears in his eyes, crocodile or what? she thought coldly. 'Just leave and let Sue get on with her life,' she said and turned away. Helen could never have been her friend in these circumstances anyway, so all she had to lose was Lucian's admiration – if she'd ever had that in the first place. She ignored the stab of pain in her heart, she was just being fanciful and what did she want with a man like that? He was not her type at all.

# CHAPTER SIXTEEN

'THE Mitchells have left,' Colette greeted Cinni when she went into work on Monday. 'Is he following your friend?' She said it with a smirk on her face as though she thought the whole story of Sue having an affair with Gerry was just a cover up for the two of them being gay. To Cinni's relief Colette did not seem to know that Lucian thought Cinni was the one caught with Gerry.

'Gone?' Cinni couldn't hide her surprise quickly enough. Sue had gone home at the weekend and she had only another week here herself. She was determined to keep her head down and see no one.

'Yes, they rang Pascal over the weekend and said they had to go home. You can see that the villa is cleaned, made ready just in case someone else wants it for their last week, or you could have it yourself; the rent is paid.'

'Did they give a reason?' Relief was seeping through her shock. At least she would not run the risk of running into Helen in the street, have to face the nightmare of her thinking Cinni had seduced her selfish husband. She'd suffered agonies over this; no doubt she had a terrible reputation by now, pregnant with a dead man's child, sleeping with the husbands while they were on their family holiday – if she could have thought of an excuse to go home she would have taken it.

'I don't know, it was sudden. Perhaps someone died. You must ask Pascal.' Again that smirk as if to say, 'You English, so prudish about sex having to weave such excuses and elaborate stories all the time to excuse your behaviour. No wonder you're meant to be so bad in bed, all your energies go in the subterfuge.'

Cinni put down her bag and sat down at her desk. 'Colette,' her voice held a command, 'I want to know exactly what happened on Friday. Did you tell Lucian where I had gone with the car?'

Colette glanced at her sharply but Cinni detected a slight uneasiness in

119

her manner. 'He rang me – he is a friend.' She smiled smugly. 'Though maybe he rang my number instead of yours. You know he said that Gerry Mitchell had disappeared. Then your phone rang and I heard that someone had broken down and you repeat how to find them. I told him maybe he was there, that is all.' Her voice was defiant. 'Did I do wrong?' Her look of pained innocence made Cinni want to slap her.

'Gerry did not ring me. It was Sue, my friend. Their car had broken down and she wanted me to come with some jump leads and sort them out. All I did was go there to help them, nothing else, is that quite clear?' She'd broken into English her voice rising in her distress and Pascal, coming in at that moment, frowned at her in disapproval.

Seeing him, Colette relaxed. 'I did my best, you English are too complicated.'

'What's happened?' Pascal barked, his head turning from one to the other like a manic bird. Cinni would have laughed if she hadn't felt so angry.

'Nothing, just a misunderstanding,' she said, not wanting to go through it all again.

'I hope it will not affect your work. Ah, Emma, you are always late. We will not notice when you have gone home, you do so little work.'

Relieved that Emma had come in and unwittingly defused the situation, Colette said, 'She has been here but went to post some letters.'

Emma threw her a grateful glance and Pascal went with a loud sniff into his own office and shut the door, only to come out again immediately and say to Cinni, 'The clients in Villa Rose had to leave suddenly. I want you to go up there to see the state of it, check nothing is missing or broken and see that it is cleaned. I have someone who might take it for a few days.' He went back in, shutting the door.

'What's the betting he and his lady love will take it,' Colette said, picking up her phone and dialling a number. 'Ring that cleaning agency,' she gestured towards Cinni, 'and go and do the inventory. The keys should be in the safe.'

To Cinni's relief, her telephone rang and she answered it. A client wanted a babysitter, but the issue was complicated and Cinni took some time to resolve it. By then Colette had gone out and Cinni decided to cope with the Mitchells' villa later. She could not face it now.

Sue had been very subdued on her last day, knowing that her long affair with Gerry was over. 'Something in me has changed; I can't go on with it, though I still love him. Or maybe I love the man I thought he was,' she added sadly.

'You've just faced up to reality,' Cinni told her. 'He was cheating on you both.' Cinni did not tell Sue that Gerry had begged her to keep up the misconception that it was Cinni, not Sue, with whom he'd had a quick fling. Sue had enough to cope with in trying to start her new life without him. It upset Cinni that Helen would think so badly of her but Sue had been her friend since they were eleven years old, both new and shy at boarding school together. She could do this for her.

André Riqueur had saved the day by suggesting that they all go out to supper together. At first Cinni had refused saying she had a friend stay-ing but André had insisted that Sue come too. The evening had been a success. Everyone liked André with his easy manner. Emma flirted with him outrageously, Colette obviously knew him well and even Sue managed to throw off her misery and enjoy herself.

'Pity you're not staying; he seemed to be quite keen on you,' Cinni teased her on the way home.

'He is fun,' she said, 'but I'm not ready for anyone new yet.'

'But at least he's shown you that you are still very attractive to men and you won't be alone for long. You'll find a decent man who is avail-able, this time.' She did not add that Sue was free while she would never be again with this baby coming.

Sue had laughed and though she was far from over Gerry, Cinni suspected that the evening had sparked the first light in the long, dark tunnel of her recovery.

Pascal came out of his office and came over to her desk, leaning over it and saying quietly, 'Have you been to Villa Rose yet?'

'No, I've had a lot to do here.' She did not want to go there and vainly tried to think of an excuse to pass it on to someone else. The inventory had to be done and no one liked doing them. If only Emma was not so idle and disorganized she could have done it. She scowled at her, annoyed that she was so unreliable. Emma, endlessly texting one of her friends did not see her expression.

'Well, go now. Ring the cleaners and tell them to meet you there. I might have someone ready to move in this evening.'

'Do you know why they left so suddenly?' she asked, tensing herself for his answer.

'No. Mr Mitchell didn't say. I don't know how he got *my* number.' Pascal looked aggrieved as if he were far too important to have been disturbed during his weekend. 'Weren't you dealing with them? I don't know why he didn't ring you. Anyway,' he sighed as if his entire life had been interrupted by it, 'he rang yesterday. He said he had to go, would leave the keys in the drawer in the kitchen table. He knows we have spare ones here. We have his credit card number and his deposit so if he has cleaned the place out we should get some money back.'

'So you didn't see him?'

'No, but could you go now and check it out, and see it is cleaned?'

There was nothing for it but to obey. She rang the cleaning agency and was told someone would turn up within the hour. With dire threats to Emma to do it properly Pascal put her on telephone duty, but then Colette returned so there was no excuse for Cinni to remain in the office. With a sinking heart she got in her car and drove up the steep road to the villa.

She hoped that the cleaner might have arrived before her so they could go in together and disturb any ghosts lurking there to provoke her guilt, but there were no cars in the small driveway. She sat in the car a moment thinking of the first time she had come here with the family and how much she had liked Helen and how angry she'd been with Gerry for his deceptions. She got out at last and unlocked the front door and went in. She looked about dispassionately as if inspecting the state of the place as she did in all the other villas when they were vacated. This one had a cleaner who came in twice a week.

There were a few dishes in the sink as if someone – probably Helen – had started to tidy up then stopped. The cushions on the chairs were dented from people sitting on them; a copy of *Hello* magazine lay on the floor. An empty Coca-Cola bottle was on its side by the sofa. It was not particularly untidy. She went upstairs, the beds were unmade, a pile of towels on the bathroom floor. She went into their bedroom. Had Helen really not known that her husband had had a lover for ten years of their marriage? Could a man – or woman for that matter – in a close relationship really keep such a thing hidden from their partner? And Sue, had she really believed that Gerry had an empty, unloving marriage? Perhaps we don't want to rock the boat if it is sailing straight, she thought remembering Julian becoming quieter and quieter before he finally told her he did not love her any more. We want to keep our lives on an even keel, not look beneath the surface because most of the time everything seems fine, or at least we can persuade ourselves that it is.

Tiny particles of dust danced in the rays of the sun that streamed through the window and touched on something on the floor that glinted. She bent down and picked up a silver earring resembling a shell with a pearl in the centre. It looked expensive. Had Gerry given it to Helen to relieve his conscience? Helen would be sorry to lose it, or would she? Might she now throw out all the expensive presents he'd given her, knowing they were payments for his infidelity? She put it in her pocket. She would leave it in the office saying she had found it in the villa.

The doorbell rang and she went downstairs. Two women who looked like mother and daughter introduced themselves as the cleaners.

'We know this villa,' the mother said looking round. 'Leave it to us. It will be done in a couple of hours.'

Cinni started on the inventory – nothing was lost, nothing was broken. She was tired, the cleaners would soon be finished so she would sit out on the terrace and enjoy the sun, leave the office to get on without her for a little longer. There were a few books on the shelves mostly in French and a few paperbacks obviously left by previous holiday occupants. There was a colourful book on the region and this she took outside to the terrace to browse through it.

It was hot and still. She pulled up a sun lounger from beside the pool, its once bright pink cushion now faded to almost white, only its seams still held the old colour. She lay on it in the shade under the awning on the terrace and looked about her. The grass round the pool was brittle and dry but the plants in the overflowing pots were rampant. Someone must have watered them, for this villa did not have an automatic watering system. She leant back; she'd hardly had any time to enjoy the beauty of this place. Friends grumbled at how lucky she was to spend so long in the south of France, but it had been hard work. It would have been wonderful to have stayed out when her time at Magical Villas was finished for a week's holiday but she had no one to holiday with, with Sue gone, and besides, she had this baby to face up to, not to mention telling Ruth about it.

The reality of it hit her like a sledgehammer. Being out here had been a kind of escape. She knew her body was changing, her breasts swelling, the feeling of nausea in the evenings and feeling tired, but she'd managed not to dwell on it, unconsciously telling herself to put it aside until she returned home. Well, now the time was almost upon her, she would be getting larger and she would have to face up to it. She dreaded telling Ruth and the rest of them at the house, but perhaps, she thought optimistically, after they got over the initial shock they would be pleased that this tiny Max would be born. She began to paint a picture in her mind, Ruth, Stella and Philip all loving this child, supporting them both with their love and their interest. The child growing up as a part of this eccentric yet loving family.

'Whatever are *you* doing here?' His voice made her jump and drop the open book on her lap on to the flagstones.

Lucian strode on to the terrace, his face contorted with anger. 'Haven't you caused enough trouble, without coming here to gloat now that they have gone?'

# CHAPTER SEVENTEEN

'H E'S written a very nice letter, at least he has good manners – so rare these days,' Ruth said, as they sat together drinking a sherry before lunch.

'I suppose he'll want to interview me, after all I was married to Max for five years,' Stella said, unconsciously patting her hair and sitting up straighter in her chair as if Lucian Fielding was sitting with them too.

'He says he is interested in his work and it is definitely not a kiss and tell,' Ruth said sharply. 'It is a serious work. I will not give my permission for one of those vile, gossipy books written for the sort of people who wouldn't know the difference between a Rembrandt or a Picasso.'

'Max would not be mistaken for either,' Philip said quietly. Unlike the two women, he dreaded any intrusion into the part of Max's life that affected him. Fiona had been the only woman he had ever loved, he would never love another and would not want anyone to sully his memories of her. She was perhaps Max's most famous model, her calm, still beauty giving out such mystery, those eyes watching you yet hiding secrets, giving the impression that you, the viewer, might be the one she would choose to tell her secrets to. Their love, ending with her premature death, was something precious, something to be held close and not laid out like wares in a market for people to pick over and comment on.

'Of course he wouldn't,' Ruth said sharply. 'But I want this book to be a serious book about his work, not sidetracked by some cheap thrills – and God knows there were enough, culminating in his unseemly death – to pander to the lowest type of person.'

'I don't think being married to me comes into that category,' Stella said archly. 'I had a good influence on his work. In fact,' she preened herself, 'during the time he was with me I think he produced some of his finest work.'

'That is debatable,' Ruth retorted. 'He was no good with women; he was never satisfied with any of them because all he thought about was sex. I think I, as his sister, had the most lasting influence on him. I gave him a home, security. I gave up my life for him.' She lowered her eyelids in an attempt at modesty at her great sacrifice.

'Nonsense,' Stella retorted. 'You didn't have anything much to give up. A few dreary men who would have killed you with boredom. I could give him everything, my body and my soul.'

Ruth puffed herself up like an adder but before she could release her venom Philip intervened. 'Come on girls, don't let's squabble over this. I think this book is a bad idea and it is far too soon to think about it. Let's tell this chap we'll leave it awhile, then he'll get bored and go away.'

'But we don't want him to go away,' both women chorused. Ruth went on. 'Max is now fresh in people's minds. With all that is happening in the art world – the penchant for dirty beds and dead animals – he might get forgotten. Now is the time to get a book out while people are interested in him. We must bring him to the attention of young people, show them what real art is. What real talent, honed over years of hard and dedicated work, really is. The standards today are far too lazy and sloppy. Just throw a few things in a pile and call it art. We need to raise them.'

Philip cringed inwardly. He was no match for these woman, was no match for Max either. Max had been jealous that Fiona had loved him, made love with him while she had refused Max but also Max had been grateful to him for nursing Fiona through her cancer, holding her in his arms while she slipped into death. He and Max had been bound together in an uncomfortable relationship.

'I just don't want him to write about Fiona,' he said miserably, 'when she is not here to defend herself.'

'But he can talk to Cinni. She won't let him write anything nasty about her own mother. Not that there was anything nasty,' Ruth said reasonably. 'It's not Fiona we are worried about; I mean she was the only woman who did not sleep with him. The only one who knew how to behave, had some sort of dignity. Self respect. I mean the others . . .' she rolled her eyes, 'alley cats the lot of them.'

Stella, who wondered if she was included with these alley cats, said darkly, 'Max was hardly an innocent man led astray by oversexed women. I'd say if there were any alley cats he was the king of them all.'

Afraid they would start squabbling again Philip suggested lunch. The joint of lamb would be dried out and they all so much preferred it 'rose' like the French did. This did distract Ruth and they all processed into the kitchen to fill their plates and push them through the hatch into the dining-room. This Sunday ritual was very important to them, 'keeping up standards' as Ruth called it, after wondering if they were the only people in the country who still sat down to a properly laid table and ate a good meal together at home.

The new lodger, Aubrey Greville, was out. He was not, as far as Stella and Philip were concerned, a success. Apart from long heart to hearts with Ruth in the drawing-room some evenings with the door firmly closed he did not join in with the rest of them. Ruth hinted that he was 'getting over some tragedy' but what that was, neither Philip nor Stella knew. They had both – though both denied it – tried to listen at the door but their hearing was not as sharp as it used to be and all they could pick up was a low mumble. No one seemed to know where he went out to, or who with, but his money was a help and saved them having to stump up more towards the expenses.

It was a sunny afternoon and after lunch – leaving the dishes neatly stacked for Mrs Tadger in the morning – Ruth suggested that they take their coffee into the garden. Philip said he wanted to go to the National Gallery, praying as he said so that neither woman would profess an interest to go with him. To his relief they did not. He enjoyed wandering through the vast galleries, the pictures were like old friends whom he never tired of seeing but more importantly they bought him closer to Fiona for it was there that they had first met and he had rescued her.

He had been lost in his fascination with Experiment with an Air Pump by Joseph Wright of Derby. He never tired of that picture, the candlelight looming from the darkness exposing the faces of the watchers of the experiment; the young girl in tears at the fate of the bird, the old man contemplating his past life, the lovers looking forward to theirs to come. He'd heard a sniffing, a little sob and turned to see a woman, furiously dashing tears from her eyes. Drawn to her beauty and thinking her over-come by the picture, he said gently, 'It's very moving isn't it? Depicting so many stages of life.'

She frowned; he'd said the wrong thing. He apologized. 'Sorry, I thought you were moved by the picture. I'm so sorry.' He attempted a smile and took a step away, reluctantly because now he knew she cried for another reason he had an overwhelming urge to put his arm round her and ask if he could comfort her.

'It's all right. Thank you for asking.' She'd thrown him a watery smile that smote his heart. 'I'm fine, I'm going to find a handkerchief, stupidly I haven't got one.'

'Have mine,' he handed her his spotless, white linen one, his mother had trained him to carry.

'I . . . couldn't, but, well, thank you.' She took it, blew her nose and wiped her eyes. 'I'll wash it for you, send it back. It's a good one, Irish linen, I can see that, you won't want to lose it.'

'It's fine, please keep it. I have so many, Christmas presents from aunts.'

'And socks?' She smiled.

'And socks.' He smiled too and felt his heart lift and sing. She had long fair hair and large grey eyes that regarded him with honesty and interest. 'Would you like a cup of tea?' he asked tentively. 'Or something stronger?'

She'd looked at him a long time, her eyes gently going over his face as if assessing him, wondering if he were safe, or interesting enough or could be trusted, he didn't know which. He felt he knew her and yet he did not. He said as if it would help her make up her mind about him, 'My name is Philip Gardener.'

She smiled, held out her small fine hand. 'I'm Fiona, Fiona Langley.' The tears welled in her eyes. 'Well, I was. I suppose I'm Fiona Cameron now.'

'You mean . . . you are. . . .'

'Yes, the woman who held secrets,' she laughed. 'That's what the press used to call me after that picture. Stupid really can't keep any secrets and anyway I did lots more work apart from that, photographs for *Vogue* and things, but Max Cavanagh's picture of me wrapped up like a kind of mummy is the only one people remember.'

She'd had tea with him and then told him that her husband – a Peter Pan kind of man who would never grow up – had left her and their daughter and gone off somewhere in Asia to discover his inner self. He owed money all over the place and his family were sick of bailing him out, or rather Simon, his brother, was. He had recently succeeded to the baronetcy on the sudden death of his father and he had offered her and her daughter some tiny hovel on their estate, but how could she find work there? She wanted to return to London but was not even allowed to sell the hovel – although no one but a homeless pig would want it – to put down a deposit on something in London.

Thinking of that time Philip walked up the steps to the gallery and made his way to the Experiment with an Air Pump and stood there look-ing at it, his mind so occupied with Fiona he almost heard that little sob, almost convinced himself that if he turned he would find her behind him, the love of his life.

At that time his mother had recently died leaving him what was left of the lease on her rather dreary flat in Cadogan Gardens. There were three bedrooms there and two bathrooms, a large living-room and kitchen. He'd moved in while he decided what to do with it. What was the point of paying rent when he could live for free? He felt he was rattling round on his own. Friends had suggested he sell it; find something more modern. He'd offered Fiona a room for her and her child.

'I'll pay rent,' she said. 'I wouldn't take it for nothing. You've saved my life but I won't take advantage of you. I'll get back to work and pay what-ever rent is the going rate.'

Cinni, her daughter, was at boarding school – paid for from a trust from her errant husband's family. Fiona had lived there a year before she and Philip became lovers. Although she'd been out of the limelight for a while she'd got plenty of work modelling for magazines. She never brought anyone back except for Cinni – though sometimes she did stay out all night.

It had been Christmastime – their first Christmas together. She and Cinni had been invited over to friends, he had gone out for the day with some relations. Cinni had stayed over, Fiona had come back alone. She had tried to be cheerful – he loved her for that – however sad she was she tried hard not burden other people with her feelings. He had not seen her that morning and he hugged her, friendly affectionate, a Christmas hug. But she stayed in his arms, and when he kissed her she did not move away.

'You are the kindest, nicest person I have ever known,' she'd said later in his bed.

'I love you,' he said, 'and have from that first moment.'

She'd held him then, he could feel her arms round him, her skin against his. He felt such an ache now, a longing for her, he felt his own tears well up and he turned from the picture catching the glances of others looking at it, thinking he was moved by it.

# CHAPTER EIGHTEEN

L UCIAN'S furious entry on to the terrace like a rhinoceros in full charge almost made Cinni burst into tears. He was the last person she expected to see here. Pascal yes, slouching in with his lady love and telling her smugly to make herself scarce, but not Lucian.

She had taken off her shoes and was half asleep. She dropped the book, struggled to get up to escape him, hating him even more for making her feel so clumsy. Seeing his expression of disapproval she blushed with shame, which added to her torment. Of course, he thought she was having an affair with that toad, Gerry. She was overcome with weariness. She really could not be bothered to try to explain the true story. She did not need to impress this man; she never wanted to see him again. She wanted to have Max's baby in peace and bring it up without having its conception bandied about for all to pick over in Lucian's wretched book.

Perhaps there was something about the sight of her scrabbling for her shoes that made him soften his voice, but only slightly. 'They felt under the circumstances that they had to leave. Helen told me I could stay here their last week as our villa is being painted and it's difficult to work with all the mess there. Why are you here?'

She was standing now. She pulled at her skirt, which she realized had crept up to the top of her thighs, pushed back her hair and said, 'I am here to do the inventory, supervise the cleaning so, I suspect, my boss can move in with his amour. If you want to stay here I suggest you tell the office unless you want to share.' She walked past him, head high. She would go back to the office, maybe even say she had a migraine and go back to her flat and cry.

He looked disconcerted, raking his fingers through his hair. 'I'll ring them now; I've got a deadline for the proofs of my current book. I must finish them this week.'

'Fine, bye.' She walked through the living-room, which now looked spotless, cushions plumped up, rugs in line. She liked the villa; it was old and shabby in a comfortable way, curtains gently faded by the sun, wood warm with age. She hated some of the modern villas, beautiful yet soulless, usually done up in white and white and white again, minimal and dead.

He came after her, his voice flat, insistent as though breaking bad news, but news that had to be faced and dealt with. 'I need the interview about your mother.'

'I'm not giving one,' she said, as she walked on. No doubt he was not so disapproving of her supposed affair with Gerry to let that go. 'There are plenty of press pages and things about her, I have nothing to add.'

'Please, Cinni? I want to know about how you perceived Max. You saw him often when you were a child, didn't you? I just want his life from all perspectives.'

Her heart did a funny jump at the tone of his voice. How dare it behave so stupidly? She was afraid of this man, disliked him with his arrogant ways and worse still, his sin of jumping to conclusions about her behaviour without even asking her about it. What would you think if I told you about his last moment, making love like a Trojan before dying, leaving me with his child, she thought, the pain of the incident digging into her? The thought of it suddenly brought tears; she was glad she had her back to him. She fished about in her bag for her sunglasses and put them on.

'I can't remember him at all,' she said, and called up to the cleaners that she was going and could they drop the keys off at the office. If Lucian wanted keys he'd have to make his own arrangements. Then she remembered that the Mitchells' set of keys was in the kitchen drawer so she went in there to get them. The drawer was empty save for instructions for the kitchen appliances. She took off her sunglasses to make sure they were not hiding in some corner, but they were not there.

A shadow passed over the table making her look up. Lucian was standing in the doorway blocking the sunlight, blocking her exit. He held up the keys. 'I have them. It's all right, the villa's paid up for another week and I won't trash it.'

Unless he moved out of the way she was trapped in here. She said briskly, 'I suggest you ring the office at once if you don't want roommates. I must get back, so much to do. Excuse me.' She came close to him expecting him to move away. His eyes were on her face, she could see the flecks of topaz in the pupil, they were beautiful, and then she pulled herself up. She was feeling decidedly peculiar. No doubt it was hormones. Perhaps her body was subconsciously looking for a man to look after her. Well, it had got its wires crossed with Lucian. She frowned, said more sharply, 'Excuse me, please. I must get back.'

'I am so disappointed in you, in your behaviour,' he said, standing away from her as if she were contaminated. 'I've known Helen a long time and you couldn't find a more loyal, decent woman. She didn't deserve this.'

She could not speak, clamping her mouth shut in case she broke down altogether. She was past him now, almost through the living-room. The sound of the vacuum cleaner hummed above them so he had to raise his voice. 'Is it a perk of the job, sleeping with the husbands?'

She swung round and slapped him right on the cheek, she saw the surprised pain in his face, saw the marks of her hand first white then red on his skin. She jammed on her glasses and ran out of the villa towards the car, her tears blinding her. She slipped, fell awkwardly but struggled up, determined to get into her car, even if her legs were broken, to get away from him.

She swept down the road, the sea like glinting metal on one side of her. What an odious man. She could imagine the perverse pleasure he would get in writing of her child's conception, how he would write her up as a slut who slept around, preying on other people's men. Her leg stung and glancing down she saw her knee was grazed and blood was running down into her sandal. She swerved, almost hitting an oncoming car, the driver hooted and shook his fist at her. Her heart beating with fear she forced herself to slow down, breathe deeply. Would the fall bring on a miscarriage? The thought of it terrified her. Please God, she found herself praying, don't let me lose the baby. She pulled over and sat awhile in the car, her hand on her stomach, stroking it as if to reassure the child inside. If she did lose it how much easier her life would be, but now she knew with fierce conviction that she wanted this baby and could not bear to lose it. She telephoned the office and got on to Colette.

'I've seen to the villa, it's being cleaned now, but Lucian Fielding has moved in for the last week. The Mitchells said he could. I have such a migraine, I must go home and rest I'll try and come in later.'

'Lucian? Is he alone there?' Colette sounded excited.

'I've no idea,' she lied, attempting to squash down the jealousy that inflated like a mushroom inside her. 'I must go and lie down.'

'Do, and take the rest of the day off, I'll manage Pascal,' Colette said ringing off, obviously delighted at her absence as she could use it as an excuse to go up to check on Villa Rose and the new occupant herself.

Cinni drove carefully home and went inside to inspect her injuries. The blood on her knee had dried but she had bits of gravel in the graze, her hand hurt as she had used it to break her fall and she thought she felt a dull ache in her lower back. Should she go to a hospital? Get checked out by a doctor? She didn't know one, though the office did. She had a shower, washed her knee well and lay down on the bed concentrating on her body. The ache in her back remained, not much of one but it was there. She kept pulling down her pants expecting to see blood. If only Sue were still here, or her mother was not dead, or Julian still loved her. How she wanted someone who cared for her to give her comfort. The tears came now, coursing down her face unchecked. She was so alone, she had no one here to ask for help, should she go to hospital after the fall or was it insignificant? It was hardly falling down a cliff. She was just shaken up, had fallen badly, surely the baby was too small to have been hurt? Yet she knew of people who had miscarried falling. Better to be safe than sorry. She'd ring the office and ask for the number of a doctor.

Pascal answered the phone, he sounded angry, no doubt irritated that Lucian had taken over his love nest. 'But why do you need a doctor with a headache? Take a couple of aspirins and lie in the dark. Then it will go. It is the heat and perhaps wine. I will see you tomorrow.' He rang off. Never had she felt so desolate. Here she was, possibly in the first stages of a miscarriage, and there was no one she could call on.

This is what it is going to be like, she realized starkly. If this child lives you will both be alone, there will be no one to share the good times with or the bad. Ruth would probably be so angry and shocked she would ban her from the house, besides she was in her seventies and knew nothing of children; she could not be expected to be much help. Philip would be kind but useless. Sue would be supportive but like her knew nothing of childcare. You will have to make all the decisions about him or her on your own, she told herself bleakly.

Helen came to mind. How happy she had been on holiday with the husband she loved, the father of her children, a man who was cheating on her but had still been there with her, interested in the children, sharing a life with her even if it was not as rosy as it appeared. Gerry might be a rat but he did care about his family, she'd seen that. She would not have that. Others coped alone, but would she? Did she want to?

Her mobile rang and she snatched it up as a lifeline from her lonely pit of misery. Pascal must have told Colette that she'd rung to ask for a doctor just for a headache and Colette being a woman and knowing about her pregnancy would know that something had made her concerned about the baby.

'Hello, Colette?'

'It's me, Lucian. I'm sorry; it was unforgivable what I said to you. I was upset. Are you all right? I saw you fall, but you so obviously wanted to get away from me I didn't come after you. I hope you are resting after it because of your pregnancy.' His concern stopped her breath. He went on anxiously, 'Are you all right?'

'I . . . I don't know. I'd like to see a doctor,' she managed to say at last.

'I know a very good one. Do you want the address? Take a taxi, or shall I come and get you?'

She could not believe his kindness and for a split second she felt herself weakening, wanting him to come, to take her arm, perhaps even slip his arm round her waist to steer her to the car, then her strong resolve kicked in. He wanted to interview her and in her state she might be lulled into saying anything. She must not be with him. She might be silly and lean on him and then feel she ought to repay him by telling him too much about Max, even admitting that he was the father of this child. But then the real reason she did not want to see him loomed in on her. She didn't want to see the disapproval, dislike even, in his eyes when he looked at her. Strange that, when she did not like him at all.

'Just give me the address,' she said, 'and thank you for your concern.'

# CHAPTER NINETEEN

IT had been one of the most difficult weeks of her life. Now she was back home Sue felt Gerry's loss more keenly. There were too many memories of him here in her flat. That green chair that he liked so much, sitting there, his legs stretched out, a drink in his hand and a word of love, or more probably lust, on his lips. The large squashy sofa brought from home where they had often made love, or curled up together watching a video or something on television. Those were the times she'd liked best, just the two of them, shut up here away from the rest of the world. And the bed, she'd never felt it was so large before, so empty without him. She'd slept alone more often than with him but then she could remember with joy those love-filled nights; now the memory of them burnt into her, racking her with pain.

Had he really loved her, she tortured herself, as she lay sleepless in the dark reaches of the night? Or was it just a sexual excitement, a bit of naughtiness on the side to make him think he was still young and good in bed?

She'd been a fool to allow herself to have played his game for so long. The reality that she'd ignored with excuses and platitudes was now there stark before her. So many friends had warned her that she would come off the loser in such a relationship, quoted her dire statistics that married men rarely left their wives after a certain time, but she had not listened. She had not wanted to. Their love was different; Gerry wanted to spend the rest of his life with her. But now she knew he did not, not without Helen too.

It was good that Cinni was coming back on Sunday. Only three more days and she would be here. She'd offered to meet her but Magical Villas were sending a car for her, or rather it was already to be at the airport having dropped off clients and would give her a lift back to London.

It had been Cinni telling her how nice Helen was, how in other circumstances she would have liked her as a friend, and the thought of his children, that had finally opened her eyes. Quite a few married men had made
a play for her over the years. She'd always refused, been shocked that they
thought so little of their marriage vows. But Gerry was different; they'd
met at a viewing night at Christie's and a group of them had gone on to
supper. They'd talked all evening about art and life and when he'd
dropped her home, he'd kissed her chastely on her cheek and said he
hoped to see her again. He had at another preview, then another, then
they'd had dinner alone where he had hinted at his unhappy marriage.

She had genuinely believed Gerry when he'd told her he was unhappily married, had a shrew of wife who had turned him out of her bed,
when in reality she was a warm person and they had made another child
together that he had not told her about. His predicament told in short,
sad bursts, had unleashed her caring, sympathetic side. She wanted to
ease his hurt, love and protect him and he was happy to let her – but now
knowing that her love had been given under such false pretences
increased her agony.

Cinni rang her most days. 'How are you getting on?'

'Fine,' she lied, telling her about something that had happened at
work, or a film she'd seen with a girlfriend. 'How are you?'

'Busy, but looking forward to coming home. I had a fall.'

'No, are you all right?' She tensed herself for news of a miscarriage.

'Yes, saw a very nice woman doctor, she reassured me. But said I
should be seeing a gynaecologist, get booked in somewhere for the birth.
I suppose I ought to, but I'm not sure where I'll be living then.'

'I hope here.' The words slipped out and she meant them. Of course
she did. Hadn't she half hoped that that last time she'd made love with
Gerry, when she was no longer on the pill she too would become pregnant, and the two of them would raise their children together? But of
course that had not happened.

'For a little while I would love to, get myself sorted out, but when the
baby is born I must find my own place. Your flat is too small for three of
us especially one who will scream half the night.'

Sue sensed Cinni's fear under her bravado, assured her they would
cope, but deep down she knew that Cinni spoke the truth. She'd worked
hard for her flat, spent time and money on decorating it just as she liked
and a baby, however sweet, would not fit in here. She knew from her
nephews that they hardly stayed tiny babies safely imprisoned in their

beds for long. It would be up and running around, breaking her precious things, making her pale furnishings grubby with snot and sticky fingers, not to mention puddles and worse from the other end. No, Cinni was right. Had she had Gerry's baby she would have been forced to change her way of life but now she need not. She looked round at her sitting-room, pale cream and dove grey with touches of cherry pink. A small round table stood in one corner with her collection of glass paperweights carefully arranged on it. The glass fronted cupboard held her collection of Russian painted boxes, each with a scene so tiny, so exquisite, it took your breath away. All these things would have to be packed away and yes, she thought, looking at her pictures and the carriage clock and Staffordshire houses arranged on the mantelpiece, she loved these things, had scrimped and saved to buy them over the years. They were her children and would give her infinite pleasure and she could not bear for them to get broken.

Gerry had liked them too, complaining that they couldn't have such precious things at home as some child would surely break them. Was it this that had drawn him to her? Peace, a haven from his world? Had she built herself a nest that signalled to men that she did not want children? And yet she had wanted one, wanted Gerry's. She remembered that pain, that anguish of time passing but perhaps her idea of motherhood was a dream, an illusion of happiness like her love with Gerry had been.

She was just about to sit down to supper, a bowl of soup and an orange – she'd had a good lunch out today with a client – when the bell went. Marion, her next door neighbour had pushed a note through her door saying she had taken in a parcel for her and would drop it in when she got back from her bridge session. Marion was divorced and struggling to make a new life for herself. There were too many attractive women left stranded in their middle years. She'd ask her in, share her supper or anyway a glass of wine, ask her about the bridge club, may even join herself.

She opened the door, a smile of welcome on her face. Gerry stood there, smiling at her sheepishly. It was raining and his hair and shoulders were damp, his hair dripping down into his neck. Her heart soared before she remembered her resolve.

'Gerry, you can't come in, you know it's over.' She could not look at him, afraid he would see her desire, her need of him in her eyes. How easy resolutions were in the cold light of day when the addiction was not dangled in front of you.

'I want to talk to you. We parted so quickly, there is so much I want to say.' His hand was on the door jamb and if she shut it she would crush it.

'You can't be here, it is over, you must go back to your wife, to Helen.' She said her name firmly to remind herself that Helen was real, not an imaginary appendage she'd previously been able to disregard. Then the thought hit her and her heart leapt. Perhaps she had chucked him out, and he was here to tell her he loved her, wanted to marry her. He saw her hesitation and pounced.

'Let me in, darling. I'm soaked, I don't want to die of pneumonia on your doorstep.' He pushed himself into the tiny passage that held two doors, one open to her flat the other closed for the upstairs one. The occupants of the top flat were away on holiday so unless Marion came by now it would be hard to get rid of him.

'No.' She put her hand on his chest pushing him away though she longed to slip her fingers between the buttons of his shirt and caress his chest. 'It's no good, Gerry. It's too late.'

He snatched up her hand and put it to her lips. 'You must let me in. I've been in hell without you. Just for a minute, just to talk, I swear I won't. . . .' He pulled her into her flat and shut the door behind him.

She longed to throw herself into his arms, to tear off his clothes and hers and pull him down on the sofa and make love as they had so often before. Frantic, greedy for each other, she felt faint thinking of it. But she must not. Unless he was free to marry her, she must not start the affair up again.

'Darling,' he said, pulling her to him, kissing her on her neck.

Oh, the scent of him, the feel of him. She felt his hands stroke her back, run down to her bottom and with an enormous effort she jumped back. 'No,' she pushed him away. 'It is over. You told me too many lies. You made me think your last child was about to go to university and we would soon be together and . . .' she held up her hand to stop his protests. 'You said your wife was cold and unkind but Cinni says she's lovely, she—'

'Cinni?' His mouth curled. 'What's Cinni to do with it? She's just making trouble, jealous of you having a man in your life when she does not.'

'That's not true.' His blaming Cinni for pointing out the truth to her cooled her ardour. She looked into this face, the face she'd loved, seen in so many guises, and did not like what she saw. He was weak, a spoilt, greedy man who would not take responsibility for his actions. He would not admit that he had cheated on a wife who was, as Cinni had told her, a decent person. He had made up lies about her to glean her sympathy and she had fallen for it.

'It is true. Cinni is not as good a person as you think she is. She strings men along like a praying mantis. No doubt she'd eat them if she could.'

'Oh, nonsense,' she almost laughed.

'You don't believe me?' He looked hurt and she was stabbed with uncertainty.

'No, I don't.'

'She was after a friend of ours, Lucian Fielding, playing hot and cold with him.'

'He wants to interview her; he's writing about Max Cavanagh and her mother was one of his most famous models.'

'He didn't know that until well after he had first met her and . . .' he eyed her carefully, 'she made a pass at me. Desperate she was.'

This could not be true. Cinni had constantly said she did not like him, had warned her he was using her and should stay away. Gerry sensed her uncertainty.

'My wife is difficult; it's not her fault, she suffers from depression. Has to take pills for it, she has mood swings which can make life very hard. From the moment we got there Cinni tried it on with me and with Lucian. She's one of those women who feels inadequate without a man by their side, are jealous of other women having one, so they try and seduce them, just to score points.'

'I don't believe you.' Of course it was not true. But then there was that strange story about the baby. An eighty-year-old man, impregnating her and then dying. Had she made up this story to cover the true story of her child's conception? It was not Julian's that she knew from the dates, but had she had a one night stand, seduced someone she shouldn't have done and got caught and was now so ashamed she had made up this story about Max? She had known Cinni since she was eleven, though it was true she had not seen much of her these last few years, but she was not like that? Surely she was not.

Gerry read her expression and gently took her into his arms and held her to him. He kissed her and stroked her, whispering words of love and contrition into her ears. Her body was starved, dry and brittle as a parched river bed. His kisses and caresses getting ever stronger surged through her, bringing her life and energy until she could no longer resist him.

# CHAPTER TWENTY

How good it was to be back in London. The South of France was undeniably beautiful but it was so crowded and noisy at this time of year with the never-ending buzzing of the motorbikes that sped along the coastal roads like annoying insects. But her pleasure and relief at getting back without having encountered Lucian again was tempered with dread. Now she had to face up to having this baby and breaking the news of it to Ruth.

They turned into the street and Cinni told the driver the number of the house. Sue had sounded strange the last time Cinni had rung her. She had been out most of the times Cinni'd telephoned which had irritated her as Cinni wanted a friend to chat to, but on the other hand she did not grudge Sue as she knew Sue was trying to restart her life. Though it was odd she had not rung her back when she came in.

'See you Sunday,' Sue'd said rather flatly. 'You have your key if I'm out though?'

'Yes, I have.' Cinni'd waited for Sue to elaborate on where she might be as she always did: go to work, followed by a grumble, or see a friend, then she'd mention their name and if Cinni did not know them follow with a brief description of them, but she said none of this. Now here Cinni was in front of the small house that held Sue's flat. The driver took out her case and she unlocked the door, calling, 'Hi, it's me!' But there was no answer.

'I expect she'll be back soon,' Cinni smiled at the driver as he deposited her case in the living-room. He left her and she looked about the room; there would be a note propped up on the mantelpiece saying where she was and when she'd be back, and some jokey message. But there was not. She looked in her room in case there was a note on the bed but there was nothing. She tried to ignore the cold loneliness that sprung at her. She was tired after the journey and the last madcap days when she had finished up her work and handed it back to André. Why shouldn't Sue go out and enjoy herself? She'd obviously forgotten to write her a note; any moment she would ring or come bouncing in flushed with welcome and apologies for not being here when she arrived, but she did not come.

She must banish these feelings of rejection; really, she was getting too emotional these days. She unpacked, went out, bought some food and had a bath and changed her clothes. Still there had not been a word from Sue. At nine o'clock Sue came back and the minute she walked in Cinni sensed that something was wrong.

'Sue, good to see you.' Should she hug her as they usually did? Sue looked awkward, dancing a little on the spot, not able to look at her.

'Oh, Cinni, you're back,' she said as if she had not expected or even wanted her to return.

'Yes, you knew I was coming back today, didn't you?'

'Of course, good flight?' she asked as if she had to fill this yawning space between them.

'What's happened? Is it not convenient for me to stay any more? Just say and I'll find somewhere else.' Perhaps she'd found a lover who'd moved in. Pretty quick going for anyone, especially Sue, but it could be someone who'd reappeared from the past.

Sue bit her lip, could not meet her gaze. 'You can stay until you find somewhere else. I wondered . . . well, you said it was a big house, if there might be room in that artist's, Max's, house for you. If you are having his child surely they would take you in.' She threw her a glance, ashamed, unhappy yet defiant.

Cinni sat down, stunned by Sue's unexpected mood. 'What has happened?' she said, looking at her. 'If you have someone else you'd rather share with at least tell me, or . . .' the thought curdled her stomach, 'has Gerry come back?' She saw at once that she had hit home. 'It's up to you how you behave,' she said wearily. 'I will move out as soon as I can.'

Sue's expression tightened, she looked as if she might cry. Cinni guessed what had happened. Gerry had told Helen that he was having a quick fling with Cinni, hoping of course that Helen would think it her fault that Gerry had been seduced by such a predator and forgive him. Perhaps he had told Sue Cinni had seduced him to discredit her and stop her supporting Sue in her resolve to give him up. It hurt that Sue believed him, so if Sue believed him and Lucian believed him there must be something about her that enforced this idea. Was it her pregnancy and the extraordinary story that preceded it?

She said, 'I want to know why you don't seem pleased to see me. It's something to do with Gerry. You owe it to me to tell me.'

Sue sniffed, sat down too, sniffed again, dabbing at her eyes with her sleeve. 'Gerry says you tried to seduce him and Lucian.'

'Oh really, wishful thinking or what?' Anger rose in her throat like vomit. 'Not content with cheating on his own wife, a decent, far too nice woman for him, he cheats on you, then being caught out tries to shift the blame on to someone else – me in this case.'

'That's not really true,' Sue bleated.

'Yes it is, because he told me that himself. Remember Lucian found us in that field when I came to rescue you when your car wouldn't start? He only saw me and thought it was me with Gerry. Gerry wanted to keep it that way so Helen would think he had – completely blamelessly of course – been seduced by me. Poor weak man that he is – high up in some prestigious company, a grown-up boy who travels by himself all over the world and pulls off important and difficult deals – can't help himself having sex with a pregnant woman nearing forty. You are a fool if you believe him, Sue.'

Sue looked as if she'd been slapped and Cinni felt so angry at the way both Sue and Lucian had believed the worst of her without asking her first that she stomped out to her room and slammed the door. She would move out tomorrow, even if she had to go to a hotel.

She barely slept and did not come out of her room until she heard Sue leave for work. By the kettle was a note written in her neat hand: 'I really am sorry for not believing you, or at least not listening to your side of the story. Will talk to you tonight, Love Sue.'

This went some way to mollify her feelings but Gerry's accusation had left its poison. Would they ever get back to their relaxed, easy friendship again? She had the day off and had to go back to work the next day. She had to ring Ruth and go to see her. The thought of the ordeal ahead made her feel too sick to eat but she forced herself to drink some juice. She dressed and then made the call. Philip answered.

'Oh, Cinni. Haven't heard from you for ages, how are you?' She heard the surprise in his voice. And something else, a kind of guarded awkwardness, or was she being paranoid?

'I'm fine, hope all's well with you? Should she mention Max? She didn't dare but ploughed on. 'I'm just back from a couple of months working in the South of France. I wondered if Ruth was there?'

'She's out, she and Stella. I'm working from home today.'

'I wanted to come round, today if possible.' She must do it now before her nerve went.

'She's back for lunch and then she said she wanted to tidy up the conservatory, shall I get her to ring you? Or tell her you're coming this afternoon?'

'Tell her I'm coming,' she said, dread taking away all her energy.

Ruth was pleased to see her, so were Stella and Philip who stood in a sort of reception line in the large drawing-room. Cinni kissed each one. The two women enthused about her sun tan. Then she saw there was another man there hovering by the bookcase. He was small and slender with greying hair and a neat beard; he must be one of their friends and her heart sank. She could not talk to Ruth if he were here.

'You don't know Aubrey Greville, our new lodger,' Ruth said, flushing a little and holding out her hand to beckon him into the group. He came, shuffling slightly, his eyes reminding her of a cunning animal checking her over in case she had anything of use to him.

'So, you are the famous Fiona's daughter?' His small mouth smirked with self-importance as though she should be grateful to make his acquaintance. Mechanically she took his outstretched hand but her body revolted. She did not like him. It seemed that Philip felt the same; he made a sudden excuse and left the room.

'Oh, Philip leave that dreary work and come and join us for tea. It is so nice to see Cinni again,' Ruth said leading her into the garden where there was a small table covered with a flowery cloth and a rather lopsided sponge cake residing on a cake stand. 'I'm sorry you can't stay, Aubrey,' she went on to Cinni's and, Cinni suspected, Stella's relief. 'Perhaps Cinni will stay for supper, then you can get to know her.'

'That would be nice,' he said but Cinni quickly excused herself, inventing an evening at the cinema with some friends.

'A pity, another time then,' Aubrey said and slipped away.

Ruth guided her to the table, Philip now returned, hovering about uncertainly on the edge of the group. Now she had to say something about Max. It touched her that Ruth had obviously made a cake for her and it made her feel worse about her imminent confession. Perhaps none of it had happened and any moment Max would stride into the garden, beaming at her. He'd kiss her, complain about his sister, ask what Cinni was up to, if she was in love, He always asked each young woman that, and his presence would affect them all like a huge, annoying yet lovable child, demanding everyone's attention. As Stella fiddled with the tea things and Ruth with the faded sun umbrella, she sensed that they missed him too.

'I miss Max,' she said 'I'm sure you do too.'

'Yes, well, he was larger than life,' Ruth said pursing her lips. 'But just like him to go like that, though I would have thought he'd have waited until after the party. I'll just go and get some tea, or would you rather coffee?'

'Tea will be fine, can I help?'

'No, stay sitting, will be back in a jiff.' Ruth went inside and they could hear the hiss of the kettle and the ring of the lid of the tea tin as it fell to the floor. Philip went to investigate. He seemed more awkward than she remembered and could not quite look her in the eye.

Stella seemed older, her skin slacker on her face, she wore a bright gash of lipstick that drew attention to her pallor. She said, 'He died making love, not a bad way to go. One that would have amused him anyway, but of course,' she laid her wispy hand on Cinni's, 'to the general public we say he died of a heart attack, which he did. He had a weak heart we did not know about, but the truth is, it was that that killed him.'

This was dreadful. Cinni was now going to have to tell them that she was responsible for his death and was having his child. Since she had last been here the house seemed to have become older, more . . . genteel, the word came to mind. There was no longer Max's energy, his rumbustious way of talking about sex and love and life, which squashed out any thought of a quiet, secluded life played out by gentle pastimes and rhythms. How could she bring his child here to shatter the new life they had made for themselves?

Ruth came out now with a small jug of milk, Philip followed her with the teapot. 'You can go back to your work later,' Ruth was saying to him. 'We haven't seen Cinni, or anyone else for that matter for a few weeks; let's enjoy her while she's here. She's so busy she may not be able to come again for ages.'

Philip looked so nervous he nearly dropped the teapot, causing Ruth to ask him if anything was the matter. He blushed and said there was not.

'Not used to pretty young girls, I suppose,' Ruth said archly. 'Now that Max isn't littering up the place with his women, we've been very quiet.'

'Well, not that bad. We had that very attractive man, you know . . .' Stella gestured towards Ruth, who was sitting down now and pouring the tea into the flowery, pink cups before her.

'He was just a man wanting to write a book about Max's life. Not particularly attractive but then you're so frantic to meet men,' Ruth said, passing Cinni her cup.

Cinni nearly dropped it. Was it Lucian they were talking about? Or someone else wanting to write about Max's life. Perhaps that bearded man who had been introduced as a lodger, perhaps he was writing a book on Max. If she stayed here with the child, the whole sorry story was bound to come out. She wanted to leave, go now and not say anything about it, but she could not.

'So. Tell us your news.' Ruth took a contented sip of tea and sat back. 'Oh, the cake, you must have some cake – it's lemon,' she said, leaning forward, cutting and offering it. Cinni took some mechanically but thought she'd be sick if she ate it. Ruth sat back in her chair again, Stella eyed her expectantly like a child wanting a story, only Philip stared out at the garden, but she could see the tension in his body. They all seemed to be waiting, like an audience at the theatre, waiting for the entertainment to begin.

# CHAPTER TWENTY-ONE

THE expression on Cinni's face reminded Philip so much of Fiona it smote his heart. That look she had when she was cornered by bad news – most recently that of her cancer – fear and yet a certain courageous determination to face it despite the difficulties ahead. He could not bear it, he knew what she was going to say, why she was here. She had run away from it but she was too decent, too brave a person to hide from it and hope it would go away.

'What do you think of our new herb pot?' he said quickly, pointing to the fat bellied pot with its little pockets holding herbs that Stella had so lovingly planted.

'Herbs? We don't want to hear about herbs, Philip. We want to hear what Cinni's been up to,' Ruth chastised him as if he were a child. He mumbled something, wishing he could think of something clever and interesting that would draw their attention away from Cinni. He caught her grateful glance and felt a little better, perhaps she would just tell them of her trip, her job, maybe a new boyfriend she had met and Max's death could stay out of it.

Cinni had always had a look of Fiona about her but now the resemblance seemed stronger. She'd filled out, seemed to have found the sort of inner calm that Fiona possessed and yet he saw that she was agitated. She was hardly a girl any more. Perhaps as she aged she would become more and more like her mother. He could not stop looking at her and his heart bled for Fiona.

'So tell us about France, I loved it there, staying in Cap Ferrat at the . . .' Stella was well away. She'd been there with Max and she began to tell them amusing stories about their time there. Philip could see Ruth was irritated by the way she had snatched the attention, but Cinni had grabbed her story as if she'd been thrown a ball and kept asking questions, urging her on until Stella became unstoppable with her reminiscences. The sharp shrill of the telephone cut through her performance.

'Please Philip, would you mind, or maybe I'll go, get some peace,' Ruth said half-rising from her chair.

'No, I'll go,' he said, jumping up, relieved to be out of the way. He wondered how long Cinni would spend with them; maybe she was in a hurry to go on somewhere else and would not have time to say what she'd come for. Perhaps she had meant to confess her part in Max's death but now that she was here felt too daunted. He didn't blame her, Ruth was daunting. She'd always held a rather bitter jealousy over Max's sex life. Well, hadn't they all if the truth be known? Max had not, as far as he knew, crept off to dubious sexual pleasures with prostitutes, but many lovely women had happily jumped into his bed. Surprisingly, there was very little jealousy between these women – he treated them so well, they almost felt it was a privilege to have been chosen. Only one, his beloved Fiona, had not succumbed.

'Of course I love you, you old roué,' he'd heard her say once, 'and I want to stay loving you and you loving me and I think if we stay out of bed that will always happen.' Of course, she had been in love with someone else, that man-child Theo Langley. She'd got pregnant by him and he had at least married her, but he was hopeless and spoilt and it had all ended in tears. Her tears. He went into the drawing-room to the telephone. Shadows from the late afternoon streaked across the room. He could feel her now, feel the weight of her body in his arms, her hot tears wet on his neck. He picked up the phone mechanically.

'Hello. It's Lucian Fielding speaking. Is that Philip?'

'Yes.' It was that writer; he couldn't speak of Fiona now when he felt her loss so keenly. He felt the image of her receding and had an overpowering need to call out, 'Don't go, stay with me!' But he could not.

'I hope I'm not disturbing you but I want to come to see you, see all of you. I'm back in London at the end of next week and I thought I'd make an appointment to come over. Will that be all right?'

'I'll have to ask the others.' He realized his irritation had come out in his voice and he coughed, tried again. 'We have a visitor, Fiona's daughter, Cinni; the others are talking to her. Could you ring back later this evening?' He thought he heard a sort of strangled gasp but it was probably the line; they paid enough to the telephone company but there were still so many glitches.

'Is Cinni there now?'

'I just said she was. Do you know her? Well, of course you must know of her as she is the daughter of one of Max's most famous muses.' He had to say it, bring Fiona back again although it hurt him. He hoped this man was not going to denigrate Fiona's memory, find some sordid affair to smirch her character, to break the dream he had of her as the ever mysterious, loyal woman, the woman who held secrets.

'Yes, I met her out here in France.' He sounded rather bored now, but he supposed it was hard work rounding up all the people whom Max had known. Perhaps some of them, not Cinni, for she was not like that, made a nuisance of themselves pushing their stories at him, wanting to sound more important than Max himself.

'Oh, so you've interviewed her already?'

'No, not exactly.' The voice was curt, and then it softened. 'Do you know her well? I know you were close to her mother?'

'Quite well, yes, but I'll leave you to interview her. Wouldn't like to say anything on her part.' He'd loved Cinni almost like a daughter though he had not seen much of her, but he would always protect her. He was certain that she had been with Max when he died; he had accounted for everyone else in his mind. Eric, his doctor, had let it be known that he had a weak heart that could give out at any moment. It would be disastrous if the truth got out. She must not tell them the truth. The agitation rose in him, he had to go back to the garden and head her off. Max had died, and that was that. Ruth and Stella knew a woman was involved but they did not know which woman and there was no need for them to know now. If they knew they might blurt it out to this man in their excitement of being interviewed. 'Ring tonight,' he said quickly almost throwing down the receiver and running back to the garden. The two women looked at him sharply.

'What drama now?' Ruth said. 'Who has died? At our age people keep dropping off their perches. I suppose we should be thankful we are still here.'

'No one's died.' He sat down, his eyes darting between them to try to gauge if Cinni had said anything about her lovemaking with Max, but they all seemed calm.

'So, who was it then?' Stella said. 'We're all agog, was it a girlfriend?' she teased, making him blush.

'No, it was Lucian Fielding, wanting to make another appointment.'

'Lucian.' Cinni let his name go as if it were poison. She went pale.

'He says he met you in France,' Philip said. What had he done to her to make her appear so agitated?

'Did he come out especially to interview you? I must say these writers have a good life, don't they, swanning about in lovely places professing to be interviewing people or doing research for their books? Put it down to expenses I suppose,' Ruth said with a smile, then she said more seriously, 'You know, think I ought to write the book about Max. After all, I've known him the longest.'

'I could as well. I knew him intimately,' Stella said.

'But you've never written anything longer than a shopping list, whereas I used to write articles for *Country Life*,' Ruth said, with a hint of pride.

'I don't think you can compare Max with the nesting habits of a yellow hammer,' Stella retorted, glaring at Ruth.

'Come on girls,' Philip said, 'Lucian is a well-known biographer. He'll make a good job of it. You can both write your own reminiscences another time.' He was sitting next to Cinni; Stella and Ruth were still on about who should write about Max. He was aware that Cinni had gone very quiet; usually she was amused by the rivalry between Ruth and Stella. He said quietly, 'Don't you like him? Did he make himself a nuisance?' Perhaps she shared her mother's hatred of pushy people.

'I can't bear the hard sell, people who go on and on at you, that you must have or do something which they think is wonderful,' Fiona had said more than once. 'I always feel they are hiding something sinister.'

Cinni said, 'No, well I suppose he did. I don't see why he needs to interview me. I know nothing about Max, nothing about his painting techniques and things like that. I saw him on and off. . . .' She tailed off, her face a picture of misery. He saw the tears in her eyes. He put his hand on hers. 'Don't say anything,' Philip said urgently. 'It is better that some things stay as they are.'

She frowned as if she did not know quite what he meant, then she said. 'Oh, you mean things about Mum? I'd never say anything about her and will sue him if he makes up anything sordid about her.' She clenched her mouth in a hard line and he was about to say he was not talking about her mother when Ruth broke in.

'So, what did he say? Is he coming to interview us?'

'He'll ring later, I told him—' He was about to say that he'd told Lucian that Cinni was here but he had a feeling it would only make her angry so he went on, 'You were busy. Well it's such a lovely afternoon I didn't think you'd want to be cooped up inside talking to him. He could ring this evening; you're in aren't you?'

Ruth nodded then began to tell Cinni about some plans they had for the house, exchanging the ancient kitchen for a lovely one she had seen in B&Q. She had never been in such a shop before and had got quite excited at the displays of kitchens and bathrooms, not to mention the special offers.

Philip breathed a great sigh of relief; he blessed that time he'd taken Ruth shopping and then called into B&Q to buy various small items. She'd come in with him and he couldn't get her out she was so enthused by what she saw there. Kitchens and bathrooms all displayed there, as if you could pick them up and take them home at once with you to replace the shabby ones you had already. She'd talk about this for hours and Cinni's secret would be safe. He'd make quite sure she kept it that way by having a word with her when she left.

'I feel I can plan quite a few changes,' Ruth went on. 'We were worried when Max died that he might have left the house mortgaged to the hilt, or to one of his women, but bless him he left to us and when we're dead it's to be turned into a museum of his work.'

'Unless he had a child, of course,' Stella said, 'then the house would belong to it, but he hasn't so we can all breathe again.'

# CHAPTER TWENTY-TWO

A child! She had to tell them everything now. As the afternoon had worn on in the warm haze of the sun and the sleepy sound of the bees buzzing in the buddleia, she had been lulled into thinking she would wait until the child was born and then, when they saw it, and came to love it, tell them the story. But now, after hearing Stella saying Max had wanted to leave the house to any child he might have had, she had to tell them the whole story. He might well have other children but for her own child's sake she must stake its claim. The house must be worth a lot now and even if there were other children it would produce a good sum to share between them eventually.

Philip was watching her anxiously; he leant forward as if to say something. He'd guessed, she was sure of it and was about to warn her to keep quiet, but she could not put it off a moment longer.

'Ruth . . . well, everyone, or perhaps I ought to tell Ruth first, alone.' She felt spaced out, drowsy in the sun, dreading what she had to say yet forcing herself on.

'Oh, nothing stays secret in this house,' Ruth said, obviously not picking up on the gravity of the situation. 'Tell us all, dear. Have you said something you shouldn't to that writer fellow? I'm sure we can persuade him not to print anything we don't like.'

'No. It's something about Max.'

'Don't let's go into that now,' Philip said sharply. 'You look tired, had a bit too much sun I expect.'

'Nonsense, she's been boiling in the sun for weeks.' Ruth flapped her hand at him as if he was an annoying wasp. 'What is it about Max?' She smiled indulgently. 'Something your mother told you?'

It's about me. On his birthday . . . well.' She blushed, looked down at her hands that squirmed in her lap. 'We made love and he died.'

Ruth started as if she had been shot. She said, her voice cold with disapproval, 'I wondered if it was you, you did come dressed for it – or rather undressed. Like mother like daughter. She, too, eventually took her clothes off for him.'

'So he could paint her. And anyway, you only saw her back view. Fiona did *not* sleep with him,' Philip said firmly.

'Well, that's what she told you but Max had a way with women, could seduce the Virgin Mary if she happened to be passing.'

'That is a disgusting remark,' Philip said.

Stella said, 'Well, at least he went happy. But why didn't you tell us before? Did you think we'd be shocked? After all,' she darted a smug look at Ruth, 'I knew him so well, he loved women, he made love to as many as he could, and you, my dear . . .' there was a tinge of sourness to her voice, 'are a very pretty girl and . . .' she added, as if that was easier to bear, 'the absolute spitting image of your mother at the same age.'

'I couldn't, because of what happened. He fell back, I thought he was dead and I panicked. I'll never forgive myself, I was going to tell you but the next day I went to France and as the days went on—' She felt awful now, she swallowed back her tears. She had behaved so badly, she should have told them about it at once. A kind act had turned into a tragedy. 'I managed to convince myself, until I heard otherwise, that I was overre-acting and he was just exhausted.'

'He was dead, all right,' Ruth said with finality. 'But better you than some little tart with her eyes on the main chance. But don't go telling that writer fellow, will you? In fact, we'll make a solemn pact now never to refer to it again. Agreed?' Her face was grim. Cinni saw the hostility in her eyes and dreaded having to confess the worst part of it.

Philip looked miserable, staring out at the garden as if he did not want to believe it was her, or perhaps Ruth's remarks about her mother had wounded him deeply. Stella looked thoughtful as if she was about to say something of great importance to seal this scene for ever in their minds.

Cinni had to go on with it, she could not chicken out now. She said quietly, her heart beating fit to burst, 'There is more, I am going to have his baby.'

'Baby? Nonsense!' Ruth was the first to speak; the other two seemed frozen in horror. 'Now, Cinni, this is unworthy of you. I'm sorry if you've been foolish enough to have got caught by some feckless young man but you can't, you simply can't try and pin that on Max.'

Philip and Stella glared at her accusingly. Stella said, 'Are you saying this because I said Max wanted to leave the house to any children he might have?'

This was terrible. Cinni had expected them not to believe her, but as she had not known about his wishes of leaving the house to his children, she had not imagined that they would think she was trying to trick them out of the house. Before she could try and explain, Stella went on savagely, 'This is quite preposterous, Cinni. We may be getting on but we're not gaga yet. Max's child!' Her laugh was hoarse. 'He went out of his way to deny any woman a child. I should know, I was married to him.' Her over-painted mouth quivered. 'It's a hurtful, horrid trick to play on us and I think you should leave at once.'

Tears welled up in Cinni's eyes. She wanted to leave, to escape their hatred of her. She could feel it oozing from them like poisonous gas. 'It is true, I promise you, I am as surprised as you are. But I haven't slept with anyone else.'

'You had that boy in Edinburgh, no doubt it is his. Well, he must take responsibility,' Ruth said. 'We will have nothing to do with it. I'm very disappointed in you, Cinni, I was fond of you. I've known you since you were a child. I never thought you'd try this sort of trick on us.'

'But I haven't, it's true. It is his child,' Cinni burst out, sobbing now, the pain of their anger, the pain of everyone thinking the worst of her, Lucian, Helen and Sue, overwhelming her like an avalanche.

Philip said quietly, 'When it is born it can have a DNA test to prove it. You haven't got rid of Max's personal things yet, even a hair from his hair brush will be enough to find out one way or the other.' He put his hand on her shoulder. 'Don't upset yourself, it's bad for you in your condition.'

His kindness saved her. What a decent man he was. She remembered when she was a tiresome teenager, she'd asked her mother what she saw in such a boring, nondescript man and she'd said, 'Kindness. If you find that in someone it is worth far more than good looks and charm.' She leant against him, needing his support. If only her mother were here, she would have sorted this out at once. She could almost feel her, her eyes flashing with anger, saying forcibly, 'My daughter does not lie. How dare you think such a thing of her?'

Stella regarded her sternly. 'That's true, we can do that. I'd forgotten that. In the past you could – many women did, especially when their husbands came back after the war – pass babies off as anyone's, but you can't today. If what you say is true then we'll know, if not, you might as well confess now and put an end to this nonsense.'

'Of course it's nonsense,' Ruth spat. 'Max was an old man and you're not that young yourself. Women's fertility drops after their mid-thirties. An old man and a middle-aged woman, come on Cinni. I've read about fertility in *The Times*, how career women miss out on having children as they put it off too long.'

'Or can't find men to commit, although I've heard,' Stella threw her an icy glance, 'that you can buy a sperm from a catalogue over the internet.'

Her remark made Philip laugh, 'One sperm would not get you very far. Now come on, let's not get too fanciful.' He turned to Cinni, held her close. 'Now, Cinni,' he said quietly, 'tell me the truth, for your mother's sake and we won't hold it against you. I understand you must be feeling very frightened finding you are having a child without a husband.'

Cinni tried to stop crying but she could not. Since she was last here her life had been charged with unfounded accusations. She had lost one of her best friends, was despised as a slut by the well-known writer who was writing a book about Max, hated and distrusted by Helen whom she had liked. Gerry, too, was no doubt blackening her character to anyone who would listen, regaling them with stories of how he was powerless when she had set out to seduce him.

The two women watched her dispassionately. Philip had his arms round her and she was sobbing on his chest, twisted round in her chair.

Ruth's voice could have shattered glass. 'I think this scene speaks for itself. You've made up this ridiculous story about the baby. It couldn't possibly be Max's, we all know that. We are very disappointed in you. When you have pulled yourself together, I suggest you leave, and we do not hear from you again.' She got up from her chair, imperious as a queen. Stella, fired up by the drama of it all, followed rather more reluctantly behind her.

At the door to the conservatory, Ruth turned, her face commanding. 'I forbid you to speak to that writer fellow. I shall tell him myself that you are not to be interviewed as all that sun has obviously addled your brain and you will not make a reliable contributor.'

# CHAPTER TWENTY-THREE

Cinni sat crumpled in her chair as if she had been squeezed out and discarded. Philip could not let her go home alone in this state. He got up and gently pulled her to her feet, taking her arm to steer her through the house to the front door. Ruth and Stella were in the drawing-room. As they passed through he felt their displeasure burning his back as if they were scorching him with flame-throwers.

'Will you never learn, Philip?' Ruth hissed. He ignored her, thinking of Fiona. If only she were here she would know how to deal with this but it was because she was not here that he had to help Cinni. He could not let Fiona down by not helping her daughter.

She was still weeping and he supported her, his arm round her waist. It was the first time since Fiona's death he had been in such close contact with a woman. Cinni was wearing a cotton dress and he could feel the warmth of her skin through the thin material. It disturbed him, brought back images of Fiona, her skin against his. He was overcome by an aching yearning for her which made him close his eyes and hold Cinni closer to him. This alarmed her and she moved sharply away and he released her, hot and bothered, apologizing profusely. Ruth saw it all and said waspishly, 'So, that's how it is? What fools men are.'

He blushed, ashamed and furious with himself, and with Ruth. What a sour old bitch she was. He hid his face from her not wanting her to see this hate. If only he did not have to live in her house, but without her he would have to move to somewhere small and cramped, in an area that would frighten their few friends who would not dare to visit him after dark.

He was moving as if in a trance, as if in a nightmare that wouldn't vanish with the light of day. He'd accepted soon after it had happened that Cinni had been the person who had made love to Max, but to be left carrying his child? Surely that couldn't have happened and yet why would she lie? It could not be because she wanted the house, that she, on a sudden impulse when hearing of Max's wishes in his will, had pretended that the child she carried was his. Perhaps she was not pregnant at all. She did not look pregnant, but then it was still early. He was certain that she was not a liar, a schemer, and yet he did not really know her. Fiona was the most honest person he had ever met and he wanted Cinni to be just like her, a beloved clone come back to comfort him.

He put his hand on her upper arm, feeling the soft skin beneath his fingers and eased her outside the house to his car that was parked a few steps away. He didn't use it that often – that dratted mayor being a non-driver himself was doing all he could to make owning a car in London as difficult as possible – and he'd been seriously thinking of selling it but he was glad he had it now. It was a private space to be in and maybe when they were alone she would confess the truth to him. Tell him that the child she carried was someone else's who had deserted her and she, in the heat of the moment, had pretended that it was Max's.

He opened the passenger door and helped her in. He must not forget her father, he'd never met him but understood from Fiona that he was a selfish man who refused to grow up and accept his responsibilities. Cinni could just as easily take after him as she could her mother.

He got in and turned on the engine. 'Where shall I drop you?' he said.

'I—' She sniffed then blew her nose violently. 'I suppose where I live now, in Fulham. I'm sorry, it's quite a way and you must have other things to do. If we see a taxi you can drop me.'

'No, it's fine I'll take you.' There was a heavy silence and he wondered what to say to her. He could have been her stepfather, perhaps he should find something to say to chastise her and yet she was no longer a child. Perhaps it would be better to leave it.

She said, her voice a little muffled, 'I know it's a shock and sounds so unlikely but it is true. I came to Max's party and he was there outside his study and he pulled me in, but. . . .' She paused; she had turned to Philip and saw his expression. 'He did not rape me or anything, he was loving and kind and I thought, why not? Give him a birthday present. I don't know why I acted so much out of character but I was unhappy, felt so lonely and rejected after the man I loved, had thought I'd marry, had dumped me.' She raked her fingers through her hair, her face troubled as she continued to look at him, making him anxious with her scrutiny. 'I don't know why I did it, and then he fell backwards and I panicked and ran away.'

'I understand that,' Philip said, thinking of a time at school when he had been rushing, late for something, and knocked off a vase that stood on a shelf in the hall. He'd been too afraid to own up and then time had passed and he had never got round to it. It had been fortunate that another school had been over that day to play a match and the headmaster had decided that one of them must have done it because 'his boys', as he thought of them, were far too honest not to own up.

'But it was wrong. If I hadn't left for France so early the following day I would have come round and told Ruth.'

'But you have now and anyway, according to his doctor, he could have had a heart attack any time. He was excited that day because of the party and he'd been teasing Ruth about the number of girlfriends he had invited. Even if you had not made love he might well have died that day. It was just your bad luck it was with you.' He drove slowly, just missing the lights and having to stop, which made the driver behind him hoot angrily. Normally he would not have cared at this show of road rage but now he felt vulnerable and it stabbed at him, adding to his misery. The lights changed and he started off, the driver behind him overtook him, mouthing something at him and shaking his fist as he screeched away. He felt his confidence draining from him; if only he hadn't got himself into this situation with Cinni. He should have called a taxi for her and let her go.

She said, 'I am having his child. I know it sounds far-fetched but it is true. I'd broken up with Julian two months before and Max was and still is the only man I've slept with since then.'

Embarrassment flooded through Philip. He felt uncomfortable talking about such intimate things with women. In fact, Fiona had been the only woman he'd been able to, not that she talked much of such things. But he'd loved her, honoured her body, known it as well as his own and so her female rhythms seemed almost to become part of him. But Cinni, even though she was her daughter, was a stranger and he felt unclean, almost as if he was committing incest to know so much about her.

He coughed, spluttered, 'But the boyfriend, I mean two months before you came to Max's party. It could have happened then.'

She must have guessed about his embarrassment for she said gently, 'Philip, I had my period at least twice between leaving Julian and seeing Max. I could not be pregnant with Julian's child and as I've said, I have not slept with, or even touched another man since.' She blushed, no doubt wondering if he was going to go into more intimate details of how a pregnancy could occur with just foreplay. He guessed this and flushed too; he was not going to go down that road either.

'Ruth and Stella are very upset,' he said lamely, wondering how they would behave when he went back. Just before he and Cinni had left he had heard Aubrey return. Would Ruth tell him what had occurred? He was a strange man, often creeping about in the shadows, so quiet you barely heard him then suddenly he was there, by the coat stand, in the library, behind a tree in the garden. He didn't like him, nor did Stella, but they needed his rent. It was difficult to say anything to Ruth who had formed some sort of attachment to him. Ruth was Aubrey's warm and comforting friend. She had been quite smug about it, telling them with a hint of self-importance that he carried some great weight upon his shoulders and only she could help him deal with it. Max would not have stood for him being in the house but then if he'd still been alive there would be no need for another lodger.

'He'll feel the weight of my boot on his backside as well as his shoulders if I find him snooping around any more,' he could hear Max roar. Max hated weakness, especially in people who used some real or imagined hurt to get special attention from everyone else. 'Attention seekers, all of them,' he'd say. He, the greatest attention seeker of them all, could not bear to be upstaged.

'So where do you live?' he said to break the tension. 'Do you have your own place?'

'No. I share with a friend. It's her flat but I'll have to find somewhere else before the baby comes.' She sounded frightened and again she reminded him of her mother, how he'd found her weeping in the National Gallery as she had nowhere to go with her child. How history repeats itself, he thought, and wondered if Cinni knew the story of their meeting. For one mad moment he wondered if he should offer to take her in, not of course at Ruth's house but to use his small savings – perhaps put them in with what Fiona had left her – to buy them a place. What sort of place and how could he, at his age, put up with a baby? He'd never had anything to do with babies and it was madness to start now and yet he felt responsible for her.

'I wish Mum were here,' she said. 'She'd sort it all out, wouldn't she? It happened to her but then it was different, she married my father and even though he was hopeless his family did help. They paid for my schooling and after the marriage broke up they did offer her a cottage, though it was pretty dreadful. I wonder if it is still there and I could have it? But then, I do have to work and there'll be no work available for miles around.'

'She said exactly that,' he said, seeing Fiona's face, her pride and yet a kind of shame as she admitted that she could not live in such a place.

'She could not bear the loneliness of it, the acres of empty green land. You can't talk to land she'd say. She needed people, life. I was sent to boarding school, that was the deal if the trust was going to pay for my education. My father's family thought they were both dysfunctional parents, but she was wonderful.'

'I miss her so much,' he said, 'and not just because she would have sorted out this mess.'

'You were so kind.' She put her hand on his arm. 'Mum said kindness was more important than charm or money and I think she is right.'

Her words brought a chill to him. He'd always kidded himself that Fiona had loved him but now he suspected that it was kindness she craved, and as Cinni said, he with his flat in London had offered that. She had not needed his love; she had that from thousands of men all over the world who had seen her picture – the woman who held secrets. He wanted to cry, to scold Cinni for shattering his illusion, but as if she guessed his torment she said gently, 'She loved you. She told me so many times.'

He wanted to believe her and yet she had sown the seeds of doubt in him. She went on; 'Thank you for bringing me home. I hope Stella and Ruth won't make life difficult for you. I won't go back, I won't do anything until the child is born then we'll have a DNA test and you will see that I told the truth.'

'So, will you take the house?' He had to ask. When Max had died his own future had tilted precariously, filling him with insecurity. After the reading of the will it had steadied again, now with her news he felt as if the carpet of security had been whisked from under his feet again.

'I don't know what will happen, but I would never chuck you out, dear Philip. Mum would never forgive me and you've been so kind to me.'

They had arrived in her street now and he helped her out, telling her to take care, keep in touch with him. She leant forward and kissed his cheek, a gentle flutter of a kiss that smote his heart.

He drove back slowly, not wanting to face Ruth and Stella too soon. He could not bear it if Cinni was lying and yet it was the most extraordinary story.

# CHAPTER TWENTY-FOUR

THE flat smelt of stale dead things making Cinni almost retch. She must stop comparing each drab and dreary property with Sue's pretty, bright flat. She would make whatever she ended up with nice in her own way. She must see past the grubby walls and dusty curtains and imagine what it could be with a bit of flair and a good clean, but she could not. Over a month had slipped by and she had got nowhere.

It was autumn, the leaves changing colour, the sun becoming deeper as it prepared to leave them. She felt waves of panic, before she knew it Christmas would be here and then soon the baby would be born and she had nowhere to live. She would have to take one of these flats, either this one or one of the ones she'd seen last week. It seemed to be a toss up between having a larger living-room or two small bedrooms – all were depressing. She had some of her mother's furniture in storage and she would just have to decide on one of the flats and make it habitable.

Sue had not said anything more about Gerry's accusation about her making a pass at him but things were awkward between them. Sue was perfectly pleasant when she saw her but it was obvious that this was a veneer over her confused emotions. She had become very occupied with work and indeed with Gerry. Cinni had not seen him again but every so often Sue had asked Cinni if she would mind going out for the evening and once for a whole weekend. She had gone to other friends and kind though they were she felt as if she was an outsider unable to find the door back to their world. They did not exactly disapprove of her situation, after all, other friends had done the same, but they usually spoke of the fathers of their children, told of desertions, or falling out of love, or just being caught after some riotous party. Cinni barely mentioned the father of hers which made them think she was promiscuous, and perhaps should be watched in case she made a grab for their own men.

Cinni was disappointed that Sue had resumed the affair with Gerry but she did not question her about it and Sue did not tell her anything, just declaring she was still seeing him in that defiant way she had. For all Cinni knew he had left Helen and might even marry Sue after all, but so far there was no hint of that.

She had not heard from Ruth, but Philip had telephoned her twice to see how she was getting on, but he had not suggested another meeting. She had not felt so isolated since that time at boarding school when Sybella had managed to convince the whole form that no one should be her friend as her parents' life style was so shocking.

'I'll let you know,' she said without enthusiasm to the sparky young estate agent whose talents for describing the flats deserved an Oscar. She could not bear to look at the kitchen or bathroom, imagining them bleak and dirty beyond words.

'It's very good for the price,' the young woman enthused, 'and you'll make it so nice, it only needs a coat of paint and some bright furnishings.' Her smile held a hint of condescension as if Cinni should surely realize that if she wanted something better then she would have to spend more.

'I'll let you know,' she repeated, wanting to say that no amount of decoration would lift the miserable atmosphere of this place or the lonely isolated feeling but perhaps that was her fault and it leaked out of her and draped itself like cobwebs over every place she went.

The office of Magical Villas was in the chic bustle of the West End, just off Piccadilly, close to Bond Street. It was smart and clean and she felt much happier there, but she could not begin to afford even a cupboard in that area. Fiona, despite being so famous, had not made that much money. Not like today when models seemed to be able to demand the earth just for one quick photo shoot. She'd spent a lot of it on her cancer treatment and travelling with Philip, and Cinni didn't begrudge her one penny of it. What she'd been left would be just enough for a down payment on a grotty flat in the least smart area of Putney or Wandsworth. She'd have to watch her money like mad to keep up with the mortgage payments. If she moved further out she could do better but then she'd have the extra travel fares to think of.

The office was expensively decorated in accordance with the luxury villas they rented out. Cinni worked with three other women with whom she got on very well. They knew of her pregnancy but not how it had occurred.

After a couple of hours' work she volunteered to take the post to the post office. She couldn't settle, her worries kept crowding in on her; she'd noticed they were always worse after seeing a gloomy flat. She'd kept a notebook of all the ones she'd seen. She would decide this evening which one to take. She could not bear to go on trailing round any more.

She posted the letters and then walked slowly down Jermyn Street; she'd buy a comforting hot chocolate to take back to the office with her. The sun was out and it was quite warm for the time of year. And there, sitting with a young woman, young enough to be his daughter, younger even than she was, was her father.

'Daddy!' The word span into her mouth but then it died and she found she was laughing. How he'd hate her to call him Daddy, especially in front of a young girlfriend. He was Theo, the ever-youthful lover of life whose age had not left its mark. How ever would he react if she called him Granddaddy?

He had not seen her; he was draped elegantly over a chair on the pavement outside the café. He was dressed in a dark suit and blue shirt open at the neck. His hair, though greying, was to his shirt collar but beautifully cut. He did look young, not quite a boy though his face was unlined. She wondered if he'd had cosmetic surgery.

She went up to their table. The girl looked about twenty; she had short bubble-cut dark hair and a rather earnest expression as she hung on to his words. Cinni could not resist it.

'Daddy,' she said again and he looked up, startled. The girl threw her a look of horror. 'Daddy, how wonderful to see you. I haven't seen you for so long. I didn't know you were back.' She put her hand on his shoulder and bent to kiss him. He struggled to get up.

'Cinni, my dear, what a surprise.' He regained his composure, smiled at her, at the young woman. 'This is Paula,' he said, 'and ... er ... my daughter, Cinni.' She thought he might add, 'I had her when I was still at school.' But he did not.

'Hi,' Paula whispered.

'So, when did you get back from, well, I don't remember where – India or Hong Kong was it?' Cinni asked. She'd had the occasional card from him as he travelled about. He did not seem able to settle for long in England but that was probably because his older brother who had now inherited the title and the estate made life very difficult for him. Theo was by far the more attractive of the two but he was so hopeless with money and let loose would be in danger of bleeding the estate dry.

'Monte Carlo, actually. I'm going to move out there – for a while

A KIND OF LEGACY 163

anyway. Sit down, what fun to see you, you look . . .' he surveyed her. 'Well, tired, a bit low actually, life not treating you well?' He frowned at her and she felt the familiar sinking in the pit of her stomach. He hated ugly, scruffy women and she had not taken much care of herself these last few weeks.

She sat down. 'I'm not very well,' she said. 'I'll tell you about it some time.'

'Nothing serious?' He sounded frightened, half moved to get out of her range in case it was infectious. His selfishness annoyed her.

'Only pregnant,' she said and wished she hadn't told him so soon.

'Pregnant?' He looked even more alarmed. The girlfriend gasped.

'Yes, you are going to be a grandfather,' she said, getting perverse pleasure from the discomfort in his eyes. 'I wish Mum were here to see it, help me through it.'

'Yes, I do miss her,' he said slowly. 'I did love her, but . . . it was just too much . . . a child, the lack of money.' He smiled, contrite but a little boy smile that said he could hardly help it, he was too charming, too fey for the responsibilities of real life. This irritated her even more.

'I was that child, remember?' she said firmly. 'I needed a father and now my child needs a grandfather, but it will have no one else, only me.' The words spilt out of her before she could stop them. He looked annoyed now. He threw a reassuring glance at the girlfriend who looked visibly shocked.

'Come on, darling, I haven't seen you for ages and here we meet quite by chance and you go for me.' The honey charm that coated his words did nothing to relieve her temper.

'I do need you,' she went on. 'I thought you were abroad but now we have met up I can tell you what has happened. I've no one else who is family and your brother, my uncle, Simon, will hardly want to hear from me, will he?'

'He's a tight bastard,' Theo said. He took out a slim, black leather diary. 'Let's make a date.' He opened it and skimmed through it. Cinni could see that each page was taken over with lines of his flamboyant writing, the book looked full though there were still a couple of months to run until the end of the year.

She remembered Fiona saying, 'When you see him, hang on to him, for he'll disappear and the next time you hear from him it will be a postcard from some far off place in the world.'

Cinni smiled at Paula and then at the waiter who had appeared and they ordered some tea. Then she said, 'Now that I'm here with you, I want to talk to you, ask your advice. I might not have another chance.'

'Oh, but you will, we'll make a date now.' He waved his book at her.

'I want to talk now, it won't take long. I'm sure Paula won't mind?' She smiled again at her, wishing she would leave them alone for a few moments.

'We haven't time now,' Theo said and she watched him dispassionately as he made excuses to get out of it. Her pregnancy had shocked him and she could see he did not want to have to deal with it.

'I got pregnant completely by mistake,' she went on. 'The father's dead—'

'Dead?' He looked aghast. 'What do you mean, dead?'

'Dead as in dead, Daddy.' She was getting bored with his determination to avoid any responsibility. 'I'm on my own, but I still have you.' She put both her hands on his arm and leant towards him. 'I have you, Daddy, to confide in, to tell me what to do. I know you won't let me down.' Like Hell he won't, the thought snagged her.

He gave a laugh, half pleased at her flattery, half afraid. 'What am I to do? If he was alive I'd shoot him but it seems it's too late for that.' He frowned. 'But Cinni, didn't your mother,' he coughed, shot a glance at Paula then back at her, 'well, tell you how not to become pregnant?'

She very nearly told him how Max's age made her believe it wasn't possible but she stopped herself in time. She must keep completely quiet about that in case someone – well, Lucian if he was still interested – came to hear of it and smeared the news like graffiti all over the place.

'Yes, she did, but Daddy,' she emphasized his name, 'these things do happen.'

Paula who'd been looking increasingly uncomfortable said in her tiny voice that she wanted to get something from Fortnum's and would be back in a moment. She scurried away before Theo could stop her. This made him angry and he said, 'Now look what you've done. Couldn't it have waited until we met again?'

'No, because by then the baby may well be grown-up with babies of its own. It's extraordinary that I've run into you like this but now I'm here I'm so pleased to see you. I really am.' Tears came into her eyes and he saw them and patted her hand.

'I'm sorry, I'm no good at this sort of thing, never have been,' he said regretfully.

'You can try. I just need to talk to someone who cares. I'm having this child and I'm on my own. I don't want money, I just want someone to listen, be concerned for me. I want to keep in touch with you, wherever you are so we can talk sometimes and I know that I can tell you anything and you will support me.'

Philip's clumsy attempts at concern seared into her. She said accusingly, 'Philip Gardener tries to offer me support. He's completely out of his depth, but at least he tries!'

Theo looked rather ashamed, patted her hand again. 'Of course, yes, I could keep in touch with you. But you're pretty, lovely like your mother, surely some man will snap you up.'

'Would *you*?' she said, knowing he was hoping that some other man would take this responsibility from him. 'You know you'd run a mile if it happened to you.'

'I married your mother, I loved her very much and seeing you now brings her back to me.' He sighed. 'I couldn't take the confines of marriage, of a home life. I'm sorry, I know I let you both down, but I felt suffocated by it.'

She couldn't change him, she knew that and so had her mother. Fiona had loved him for his free spirit and she suspected, though she'd never asked her, that the two of them might have stayed together longer, both flying free but she had come along and tied them down, or her mother, anyway.

'Just be there at the end of the telephone for me now,' she said. 'Just so I can talk to you.'

'I will,' he said fervently. 'Give me your number and I'll tell you mine when I am settled. I'm leaving next week.'

'And taking Paula?' She couldn't resist asking.

He smiled. 'No, actually. She'll visit . . . but . . .' he eyed her ruefully. 'She's just a friend, nothing special. In fact,' he looked sad, 'I've never found anyone as special as Fiona.'

'I'm not surprised.'

'You are so very like her, it's quite uncanny.' He regarded her intently. 'So, who is this man who died?'

'No one you know but he was older than me. Had a heart attack, he never knew I was pregnant.'

'Married man?'

'No.'

'But you have a job, some money?'

'Yes. I've just to find a flat but it's proving difficult, they are all so gloomy. But I'll have to take one of them. I'm with a friend at the moment but I'm a bit in the way of her love life.'

He burst out suddenly, 'Well, take my flat. I'm going to be away at least a year if not more. It's standing empty – the family trust has paid for it on the understanding that I keep it in order and don't let it out in case one of them wants to use it. You can have it, you're part of the family, old Simon can't dispute that. I want someone there to keep an eye on things, you will be ideal.'

It sounded wonderful. 'But the baby?'

'There's plenty of room for a baby, it's got two bedrooms, though I use one as a study. Look, let's go there now.' He jumped up but then the waiter appeared with a tray holding a teapot and a plate of scones.

'After tea, maybe this evening.' She remembered the office, she'd better get back. 'Where is it?'

'In Chelsea, Crammar Court,' he said, sitting down again. 'Yes, what an ideal solution, move in there. But I can't do tonight.' He consulted his diary. 'How about tomorrow? We could lunch. Can you move in by next week?' He looked so pleased, relieved as if he had done his fatherly duty with very little effort for himself and solved the problem of worrying about his empty flat. She was not going to argue with that, for it was indeed an answer to all her prayers.

# CHAPTER TWENTY-FIVE

CINNI recognized some of the furniture in her father's flat. For a moment she was transported back to her childhood to the large nursery wing at Merriot where she had lived for a while when her grandparents were alive. She remembered the warm smell of drying clothes by the small log fire and that sideboard that held the Bunnikins china that her father and his brother used to use for meals when they were young.

Over the mantelpiece hung a seascape she remembered, frigates tossing on a glutinous sea. It had hung in her grandmother's sitting-room and she remembered her soft voice as she explained about the battle that was about to take place and how many of the boats would sink and have their sails torn to shreds by cannon fire. Oh, to go back to those secure days when she belonged to a family! Fiona's parents had a farm in Scotland but they seemed dazed by this beautiful child they had made together, a cuckoo in their nest and were not surprised when she had flown away. They had died when Cinni was very young. Theo – she didn't count his elder brother as she hadn't seen him since she was a small child – was the only member of her family left and he was feckless and ... but she stopped herself; he had saved her by lending her this flat.

She saw that he was watching her, perhaps even guessed her thoughts for he hastily glanced away, and said quickly, 'Well, here it is, not perhaps to your taste, full of cast offs from Merriot, but I'm not here very often.'

'It's wonderful, Daddy. So many memories of my childhood.' She gestured at the sideboard, the round table where she used to sit and draw. 'Thank you, I shall take great care of everything.' She wanted to ask what would happen if he suddenly returned, if whatever he was going to in Monte Carlo didn't work out, or if his brother and wife appeared to stay, but she didn't. Just to come here and settle was enough for the moment. Life with Sue was becoming increasingly difficult for apparently Gerry wanted to come and stay for more nights than he used to, but he did not want to see Cinni, which was hardly surprising after those lies he had told about her. Also she knew, because she had seen the unopened packet stuffed behind a bottle of cough mixture in the bathroom cupboard, that Sue was no longer taking the pill.

On the surface their friendship seemed fine, their conversations were about current affairs, both in the world and among their friends, they discussed the books they were reading, whose turn it was to buy the groceries, but they did not discuss Gerry, her pregnancy, or the monthly heartbreak when Sue discovered that yet again she had not conceived. Living together in such proximity Cinni sensed the change in Sue, the growing hope as each day passed followed by crushing disappointment. To move in here in a matter of days would be such a relief; even if her father came back, it could not be so bad as living with Sue under the influence of Gerry and the grief of failed pregnancy.

'So, I leave on Thursday, you can move in any time after that,' Theo said. 'Though I have to warn you I have a dragon of a daily. She's in love with me, I can do no wrong – she dislikes her own sex and probably will hate the baby.'

'She doesn't need to come while I am here,' Cinni said quickly. 'I'll keep everywhere clean and won't throw wild parties, I promise.'

'Oh, she has to come, she relies on the money and if I lose her I don't know what I'd do. I've had her years, she'll be a bit put out that you are here as she'll have to turn up. I'm sure when I'm away she barely comes but has a great deal to do just before I return.'

She tried again. 'Perhaps once a week and no more will be enough. When does she come? I'll be out at work until the baby comes.' With luck the cleaner would indeed hate the baby and never come back.

'She comes every weekday but I will tell her she can come less. She does my breakfast, all my clothes, everything really.'

'I won't need all that.' The idea of someone taking over so much of her life appalled her. She wondered what the woman thought of his young girlfriends; perhaps she had been one herself. 'What's her name?'

'Barbara, Mrs Simpson, as in the king's mistress.' He smiled.

'So what do I call her?'

'Mrs Simpson, until she tells you differently.' He said with surprise.

'I don't like the sound of her at all,' she said. 'Look, Daddy, can't you tell her, especially if she's not going to like me or the baby, just to come once a week, while I'm at work?'

'You must not fall out with her,' he scolded. 'Look, perhaps having the flat, it, well it might not be such a good idea after all. Have you really nowhere else?'

'It will be fine, Daddy, of course I'll have her,' she said quickly; she couldn't lose the flat now. 'I'll go out when she is here, don't worry, we'll be fine.'

'I cannot, *will* not lose her,' he said desperately like a child whose security blanket had been whipped away. 'And while we are on it, I don't want to be called Daddy. Call me Theo – after all you are grown-up now.'

'Whatever you say,' she said weakly, wishing she was alone and could lie down quietly.

'Let's have lunch,' he said. He went over to his desk and opened one of the drawers and took out a small box. 'There's a spare key in here.' He held it out to her. 'I'll show you the locks, tell you about the security.'

'And leave me your telephone number in case I need to get hold of you.' Despite everything, she did not want to lose contact with him.

'I'll ring you with that,' he said with a smile.

'But you have a mobile?'

'I have one, of course I have one, but I don't like it. I hate always being available, night or day.'

You would, she thought, juggling women would be much more difficult if they could ring you wherever you were. Of course you could turn it off but what if you forgot and it interrupted some crucial moment during a seduction? She changed the subject asking about the heating, how the cooker worked and such like.

'Oh, I've no idea,' he said carelessly. 'Barbara deals with all that. I'll tell her to tell you.'

Her heart sank again. What if Barbara didn't want to tell her? What if she controlled her by controlling the switches and timers, making her shiver or sweat according to her wishes? Oh, Mum, whatever would you have done, she thought desperately?

Theo was a good companion over lunch. To her relief it was just the two of them. She had wondered if the unfortunate Paula would turn up but she did not and he did not mention her. He told her amusing stories of his travels, work he had done – it seemed he did 'consulting' on properties abroad, designing them, buying them – and he showed some interest in her job in the South of France.

She told him about her work, exaggerating the awfulness of some of the clients and the mess they made, making him laugh and she was hit suddenly by a great bubble of happiness. She felt close to him, they seemed to share the same sense of humour, like the same places, same food. Perhaps now that she was grown-up and he was getting older they would see more of each other, he would enjoy being with her. But she was not going to voice this in case his fear of emotional commitment made him fly away again.

They were lunching at a restaurant in Chelsea Green. She had taken in the small room scattered with tables, the pictures on the walls, but once they had been seated she'd become captivated by Theo, engrossed in ordering and discussing the food and wine. But as she glanced up at the waiter to ask what tisanes they served she saw to her horror Lucian Fielding staring at her.

She looked away. She must go now, she could not talk to him. Yet she could not stop her gaze stealing up again. He was not alone; she could only see the back of his companion, a woman with glossy, blonde hair loosely tied back with a navy velvet tie. The tables were quite close together, though Theo had his back to them, but could they hear each other's conversation? How long had he been there? How long had he been watching her? One question was answered almost immediately when she saw the waiter bring them their starters. She and Theo had reached the coffee stage but he had ordered a crème brûlée. What excuse could she think of to leave suddenly? She'd told Theo that the day was free; she was not working this Saturday and had looked forward to spending the day with him and keeping away from Sue.

The crème brûlée arrived and he insisted that she try some, then as he finished it, he said. 'So, I suppose I must ask you about this baby, has its father no family at all to help you?'

She did not look at Lucian but she was convinced he had heard. 'Let's talk about that later,' she said quickly.

'I don't know when that will be, I'm going out tonight and am out of London tomorrow until Monday, then I'm off. Why can't we talk about it now? Who is the father? I think you can at least tell me that.'

'Let's go back to your flat for coffee, then I'll tell you.' She smiled as if she was only going to tell him something ordinary and safe.

'They do far better coffee here and I don't want to move. Come on, you can tell me. Is it someone I know? Or do you think I'll disapprove?' He smiled. 'Try me, I have no right to disapprove of your life, I have hardly lived the life of a saint, though . . .' he looked serious, a flash of sorrow in his eyes, 'if your mother had lived I think I would have gone back to her. Seeing you so like her, makes me realize how much I loved her.'

'She might not have taken you back,' she said sharply, remembering Fiona's tears and how Philip had cared for her.

'I think she would,' he said. 'But come on, tell me the name of this poor dead fellow, I won't tell anyone and there's no one here we know.' As if to humour her he turned round as if to check and saw Lucian.

'Ah Lucian Fielding, fancy seeing you here. How are you? Haven't seen you for ages. Do you know my daughter?'

# CHAPTER TWENTY-SIX

S HE would have got up to leave but the waiter arrived at that moment with her tisane and Theo's coffee. Lucian hovered round their table too, shaking hands with Theo and then turning to her.

'Cinni, good to see you.' His voice was clipped, his eyes skimmed over her face; she looked away, towards his companion, not wanting to see his dislike of her in his expression. He gestured towards the blonde woman who was watching them with interest. She had a large pouting mouth and slightly bulbous eyes reminding Cinni of a fish. 'This is Joanna Gibson,' he said.

'Hi.' Joanna smiled at them all.

Perhaps she was a mermaid, Cinni thought bitchily, then scolded herself. Why should she care if Lucian went out with a whole shoal of mermaids? She didn't want to have anything to do with him.

'So you know Cinni?' Theo glanced at her quizzically making her blush. She had a terrible feeling now that he did not believe her story about the father of her child being dead, and that Lucian was its father.

She said brusquely, 'Not really, he was out in France, staying with someone who'd rented a villa from us.'

Theo laughed. 'Oh, one of those dreadful people with hideous habits that would be better off slumming it in a pigsty?'

Lucian scowled at her, attempted a laugh. 'I hope not.' He regarded her with an expression of distrust as if he was convinced that she had told Theo lies about him. She said nothing.

'So, Lucian, I hear you are writing a book on Max Cavanagh,' Theo went on, making her start. How did he know that? Was it common knowledge? Would all sorts of people become interested and start scraping around for more information – notably shocking information – about him?

'Yes, I am. I'd hoped that Cinni would help me, after all her mother was one of his most famous muses.' He faced her now, regarding her with his topaz eyes. She looked down at her tisane, breathing in the minty scent, feigning an interest in it.

'Don't forget she was also my wife,' Theo said, puffing himself up like a small boy expecting attention.

'Of course I know that, but you didn't know Max well did you? Didn't you marry when he had moved on to another of his muses?'

'Yes, but I met him a few times,' Theo said. Cinni could see he was raking back through his memory to find memories he could bring out and offer to Lucian to embellish his book.

Lucian said, 'Well, if you think of anything that may be relevant please let me know.' He produced a card from his pocket and slipped it by Theo's saucer. Then he turned to Cinni. 'I do want to speak to you, Cinni. You knew him so well, from when you were a child. It would be so interesting to have a picture of him from a child's perspective and later as you grew up.'

Lucian could see that shameful last act in Max's life, she was sure of it. How it would lift his book and throw it out to a wider audience. She said quietly, 'I don't think his family want any more people to give infor-mation. I understand they have told you all you need to know about his private life. Surely his work is more important.'

'Nonsense,' Theo broke in with a laugh. 'People pretend they are dreadfully academic but there's nothing like a bit of gossip to get them going. I'm sure you saw a lot of things that would spice up Lucian's book.'

She longed to escape; they were ganging up on her though Theo could not know that she carried Max's child. Lucian saw her expression, laid his hand on her arm. 'We'll talk about it another time. Now I must get back to my lunch or it will get cold.' He went back to his table and sat down and said something to his mermaid, behaving as if he had not seen them at all.

But Theo would not let it go. He got up and sauntered over to Lucian's table. Cinni went to catch his arm to pull him back, but he reached the table, smiling at the mermaid who blushed and simpered up at him. 'I'm going away,' he said, 'but Cinni will be living in my flat for at least the next year. I'm sure she'll help you, won't you, darling?' He smiled back at her. 'After all, ours is a very interesting story. Max's wonderful picture of your mother was responsible for us meeting, for your existence, Cinni. It will bring a certain magic to the book, don't you agree, Lucian?'

Trust Theo to want to turn the whole book to his advantage. Cinni fumed, but bit her tongue. The other people lunching there were beginning to show an interest in them. She must not become conspicuous. Theo's eagerness to take centre stage embarrassed her, not just because he was determined that she would tell Lucian all he wanted to know – having first primed her what to say no doubt – but it troubled her that he craved so much attention. She got up and with a tight smile said, 'I must rush, thanks for lunch, Daddy. I'll see you before you go.'

'Don't be silly, you can't go yet. I thought,' he smiled back at the mermaid, 'that after lunch we could all go back to my flat then Lucian could ask you whatever he wanted.'

'No,' she said firmly, not even looking at Lucian to see what he thought of this idea. 'As I said, Max's family are not keen on any more information being given out on his private life. Not that I know anything anyway. I was a child, I probably noticed nothing. After all,' she looked at her father, 'it was Philip Gardener I saw more of. We lived with him, he was like my father.' She felt mean saying this, especially when she saw the hurt in Theo's eyes but she would never forget her mother's pain when he had abandoned them. Fiona had loved him and he had suddenly disappeared without a word. Cinni turned to leave. She had to find her coat that had been whisked away and that slowed up her departure.

Theo said, 'Just let me pay the bill then we'll go.' He moved back to their table, slipping his hand under her elbow and leading her back. Her remark had made him subdued adding to her guilt, which made her angry with herself. Did women like her always allow such men to treat them as they wanted? Theo had treated both her and her mother badly – never beating them or anything aggressive like that – but playing with them, loving them like cherished toys, before discarding them when they bored him. They, hurt and destroyed by his behaviour, could not help but still love him.

She thought of Sue and Gerry and how in the end he would destroy Sue's life. She would wait for him, led on by his honeysweet promises even though deep in her heart she knew they would not be kept. Why do we allow ourselves to live in such fantasy worlds, she asked herself, hoping and praying things will turn out as we want them to?

Theo paid the bill and they left, he waving extravagantly at Lucian and the mermaid, she just nodding vaguely in their direction. She thought she'd got away with it but Lucian was suddenly by her side.

'I'll get in touch,' he said gently, 'now I know where you are. There's not much I want from you and surely there's nothing you know that Ruth and Stella would disapprove of. Is there?'

He was too close to her – it made her feel claustrophobic and yet she longed to lean into him. She must be mad, she stood straighter, moved away, her face hard with the effort of keeping her secrets, but he'd guessed there was something, she was sure of it. She had protested too much and that had alerted the detective streak in him that there was something she wanted to keep to herself. She looked now into his face and saw the questions in his eyes, puzzlement as he wondered things and then discarded them.

'He didn't hurt you, did he?' he said quietly. 'If he did I . . . well, I understand your reticence,' he finished lamely looking upset and embarrassed.

She guessed at once he meant had Max sexually molested her when she was a child. She felt cold. A suspicion like that would blacken Max for ever, turn him from the jolly, endearing man into a monster.

'No,' she said vehemently. 'Of course he didn't.'

'I'm sorry.' He looked relieved. 'I didn't mean to imply he tried anything when you were a child, but he was well-known for seducing women and I just wondered if—' He stopped, looked awkward. 'Well, this is hardly the place to discuss it, but you seem so insistent not to answer any of my questions I just thought something unpleasant had happened that you would rather not remember.'

Her heart sank, she looked away. 'No.' She hoped her voice sounded normal. 'I just feel it would be better to concentrate on his working life, not turn the book into a gossipy thing but an academic one for people who enjoy his art.'

She left the restaurant then and joined Theo who was pacing about on the pavement outside. He said petulantly, 'I don't know why we couldn't have invited them back to the flat so that he could interview you. What have you got to hide anyway?'

'Nothing at all, I just don't see any point in it. Surely Max's work and, if he must, stories from his muses and girlfriends are more important than anything I could say.'

'You should leave that to him. After all, a good biography should show the whole person and only by collecting information from all walks of his life from many of the people who knew him in different ways and at different times can you paint a true picture.'

They were walking back to his flat now, the sun warm on their backs, picking out the colours in the shops and from the flowers that glowed in the hanging baskets and from the balconies. Cinni felt tired, drained by all the drama in her life. She'd thought it a miracle that she had found her father just when she needed him most and he had lent her his flat for at least a year but now it seemed there was a heavy price to pay.

'How well do you know Lucian?' she asked.

'Quite well. He came to Merriot when I was there on one of my rare visits,' his voice was sour, 'to write about some of the pictures there. He was doing a book on art in country houses. I went to the book launch; saw him at a few others. Nice chap.' They'd reached the block of flats and went inside. In the lift he said, 'What a coincidence that you met him in the South of France. Was he alone or with that girl, or another?'

'I think he was alone. He was staying in some villa and I met him in one of ours at a dinner party,' she said, not wanting to talk about him yet longing to ask if he had a steady girlfriend or even a wife.

They arrived at their floor and Theo unlocked the door and they went in. She flopped down on the sofa and closed her eyes, getting up her strength to go back to Sue and get on with her packing. In four days she'd be here. Alone until the baby came. She had booked into a hospital for the birth but she must start to plan for it. She put her hand on her stomach. Poor little thing, she'd barely thought of it as a growing thing, a person in its own right, but just a problem, a bomb waiting to go off and tear open the whole truth of its beginning. But with luck she could keep that hidden until after Lucian's book came out. How long would it take to write? When would it be published? If only Theo had not told him that she was living here and handed him the address. She could not look for somewhere else; the squalor of the places that she could afford seemed a hundredfold worse since she'd seen this flat. She felt too old to rough it as she had in her youth, and with a baby Why should it start its life that way when there was this, its grandfather's own flat on offer? It was the least Theo could do for her after abandoning them when they needed him.

Theo was sitting opposite her and though her eyes were closed she knew he was looking at her. 'So,' he said gently, 'this baby. I have a right to know who the father is. After all it is part of me too.'

'You didn't like being a father, thought it too ageing, too much responsibility, being a grandfather will be even worse,' she said.

'I know I was selfish and I'm sorry. I won't pretend that I'll change, become the perfect parent or grandfather but I would like to help, stay in your life.' He paused, perhaps wanting her to speak but she did not. 'A daughter,' he went on, 'is, after all, a very important person.'

She almost said, 'About time you realized that.' But she did not. He was trying to make amends in his own way. He was selfish and hated the ties of commitment and responsibilities, and was no doubt afraid of getting old, but he was her father and part of her did love him, had always loved him, though she had hated him too for what he did.

Still she did not speak and he went on, a little desperately, 'Will you ever forgive me for leaving you?'

'No,' she said, opening her eyes and looking at him. 'No, for there is nothing worse than thinking the father you thought loved you, did not after all.'

'But I did love you, always.' He looked hurt.

'But not enough to stay.'

'I did not leave you because I did not love you but because . . . oh, there was someone else, a young woman who offered freedom. We went to Greece, took a boat and spent the summer there. I couldn't have taken a child.'

'It doesn't matter,' she said, weary with it all. 'I can't change what happened, but stay with me now, let us try and build a good relationship. I need you.' A pang of pain hit her as she saw his restlessness. He wanted to appear magnanimous, the perfect father and grandfather in everyone's eyes but not at the expense of his life, his freedom. 'Anyway, thank you for letting me live here, that has really saved me,' she said briskly. It was pointless to harp over what she could not have but to be thankful for what she did.

'I'm so glad you're here, what a happy coincidence that we met like that.' He frowned. 'Now I understand why you are so reluctant to talk to him, it's Lucian's baby isn't it? You told me the father is dead because you don't want Lucian to be part of your life? Did you get caught out? Had a one night stand and are embarrassed to tell him?'

'No, it's not at all like that—'

'I don't mind if it is,' he interrupted her. 'He's a nice fellow. Does he know? You should tell him if he doesn't. Whatever the relationship between you, it is his child too; he doesn't want to lose another.'

Another? What did he mean? 'It is not his,' she repeated desperately. What could she say to get him off the track? He was determined to know whose it was, dead or alive. Should she tell him the truth or make up some story about an ex-boyfriend? She remembered how keen he was to help Lucian with his book, more from self-importance than altruism. Knowing Max was the father would be such a nugget of gold. Hastily she began to think up a story, a story she could tell everyone about a man, perhaps in France, whom she'd loved for a few weeks and later she'd heard that he had died.

'You must tell him,' Theo went on, seemingly oblivious to her denials. 'He had a sad time, a woman he loved got rid of their child just because she wanted some part in a film. He was very hurt by it, but this,' he smiled with delight, will be wonderful for him, for you too, for he is just the right sort of man to make you happy.'

# CHAPTER TWENTY-SEVEN

S UE still missed Cinni although she'd been gone almost two months now. She missed her in the evenings when she came back from work and the flat was dark and chilly and there was no one there but herself to cheer it up. It had been comforting having her there pottering around and even if they didn't talk together as much as they used to, she was there, alive and familiar, a companion to ward off the hollow feeling of loneliness.

She had wanted her gone for so many complex reasons. There was a great crack through their friendship like a dark line through a priceless piece of porcelain. She had believed Gerry when he had said that Cinni had thrown herself at him in France and this troubled her. She had not thought Cinni would do such a thing and even though she had protested, sworn she had not, the doubt had lodged in her like a stone in her shoe, rubbing her raw. Gerry had told her, often with tears in his eyes, about his difficult marriage yet Cinni had told her this was not true. In other circumstances they would both have become friends with Helen. Which one should she believe? Gerry had said they hadn't slept together for years yet there was another child barely ten years old. He'd explained this by saying it had happened when they were both drunk, but now as she thought of it in the lonely evenings she wondered how truthful he was. And how much was down to her so desperately wanting to believe him.

She was jealous too of Cinni's pregnancy. Since staying with her in France she'd been inexplicably gripped by a longing for a baby of her own. She could not wait for Gerry to leave his wife, she wanted one now and she hid away the pill, followed her time of ovulation like a slave and prayed he would come to her at her most fertile time. Nothing had happened and each month she mourned the child she longed for.

To make things worse she had not seen Gerry for three weeks. His job had changed and instead of working in the European market he now worked in the Asian one. This entailed longer trips away and though he still rang or emailed her she could not helping thinking his messages held a slight coldness as if he was only acting out the game of a dutiful lover.

In the daylight when she was busy at work she ridiculed herself for such thoughts, scolding herself for dwelling on them so much, giving them nourishment to grow and fester. But alone in the flat and in bed at night, unable to do more than cat nap, these thoughts grew like huge fungi, gradually squeezing out all common sense.

She had rung Cinni a few times and they had been to a film and out to supper but recently she too had been rather offhand, saying she was working too hard or was just too tired. The last time she'd rung she couldn't help slipping in the details of Gerry's new job and how much he travelled.

'Time to find someone else,' Cinni'd said. 'Don't waste your life waiting for a man you'll never get.'

This sentence clung to her like a burr, picking at her in the coldness of the night. Thoughts curdled in her head. Was Gerry visiting Cinni in her father's smart flat? At first the thought seemed preposterous but like a virulent weed it clung and grew. Little things she'd barely thought of sprang to life in her sleepless hours and took on importance. Cinni needed someone to look after her and her coming child. Max's family had disowned her, chucked her out. She remembered that evening after Philip had dropped her home. She'd been so hurt by it, curled up on her chair weeping, repeating, 'They can't think that. I'd never do such a thing.' Until she thought she'd go mad herself.

She knew that Cinni did not have enough money to buy herself a nice flat or much time and energy to change whatever she'd bought into something she liked. It was a stroke of luck that she'd run into her father and was now living in extreme comfort in his flat for the foreseeable future. But she was lonely, she knew that, not many men would be interested in a woman halfway through a pregnancy with a dead man's child. But why would Gerry be interested? He had begged Sue that they wait to have a child until they were settled, so she must be wrong, and yet at night her suspicions grew to alarming proportions.

Christmas was three weeks away and she had decided, as usual, to go to her parents. Gerry was always with his own family and it was a sad dead time for her. Everywhere there were images of families, laughing children, contented adults all together round sparkling trees, eating glistening turkeys, opening presents and there she was an ever older, single woman spending Christmas with her engaged sister and her elderly parents, and the photographs of her brother's children for them to marvel at.

When she got home one evening the light was winking on her answering machine. Praying it was Gerry she switched it on. 'It's Lucian Fielding. I hope you don't mind me ringing; we talked briefly in France this summer. I know you are a friend of Cinni's and I wondered if I could reach her through you.'

His voice seeped into the room and momentarily uplifted her, but she did not catch the number he gave out. She played it again and then again. He had wanted to interview Cinni for his book and she had refused; surely it was up to her to decide if she would talk to him or not? But then his voice sounded so persuasive and why shouldn't she give him Cinni's telephone number? That's all she had to do and it was up to him to get her to speak to him and for Cinni to deal with it.

'Thank you so much for getting back to me.' Just the timbre of his voice excited her. He went on, 'I do have her new number, address too but she refuses to speak to me. I just wondered if you could persuade her. I know it's a bit much of me to suggest it, but I don't seem to be able to convince her that I don't want to write anything spurious about Max just get her to give me some of her views on him when she was a child. I wondered if you could persuade her, even be there too as a witness, if that is what she would like.'

'I could try,' she said doubtfully, knowing the real reason why Cinni would not speak to him. But why should Cinni mention that Max was the father of her child? She could tell him about the times she spent with Max when she was a child and that was all. It would get Lucian off her back and that would be the end of it. After all she was not the only person Lucian would interview.

Perhaps guessing she was trying to think of a way to persuade Cinni Lucian said, 'Look, why don't you and I meet for a drink, then I will tell you what I want to ask her. I'll write down the questions and promise not to go beyond that. What do you think?'

It would be betraying Cinni to go and yet as he spoke, his words warmed the lonely embers of her heart. What harm would a drink be? It would be interesting to meet him anyway; she enjoyed his books.

They made a plan to meet at a bar in Knightsbridge. She worked in Kensington and that was not far away. The invitation excited her and for once she spent the evening uplifted, instead of slumping in front of the television with a glass of wine. She even got various overdue chores done as if he was going to come back and see her flat.

It would not be fair not to inform Cinni of their meeting. She rang her at her flat but the answerphone clicked in – a man's voice, presumably her father's, apologizing for not being available and suggesting they leave a message and also giving another number in Monte Carlo. She did not leave a message, not quite knowing what to say. Nor did she try Cinni's mobile and when she thought of ringing again it was past eleven and she did not want to wake her.

'How kind of you to come. I do hope you didn't mind me ringing you. I'm afraid I managed to persuade someone at your office to give me your number.' Lucian smiled at her, making her heart leap a little. With someone like him in her life she might find it easier to let Gerry go.

She had spent some of her day whizzing through some of his books, pretending at work that she was doing some research. Now she would be able to discuss them with him – the way he had portrayed various artists. She asked him if his book on Max would be written along the same lines.

'Yes, more or less. Now, this,' he produced a couple of pieces of paper from his briefcase, 'is all I want to ask Cinni.' He handed them to her. 'Nothing very frightening is there?'

She read through it, not noticing that he had ordered another bottle of wine. How old was Cinni when she first met Max? What were her impressions? How did her mother get on with him? All questions that seemed relatively innocent.

'Looks fine. I'll see what I can do.'

'She won't see me. I've left messages, tried to ring, even lurked round her block of flats but she refuses to see me. I know she's angry with me,' he looked ashamed, 'but it's nothing to do with this book. This is purely professional.'

'Why is she angry with you?' If she had not drunk so much wine she would not have asked.

'Oh, it's nothing, just something that happened this summer, but not relevant to this.' He clamped his mouth shut and she had a feeling that he would not be saying anything more on the subject, but his words seared into her.

'Something that happened this summer?' It concerned Gerry, she knew it did. Lucian knew Helen and Gerry and he knew Cinni, he had seen Cinni with Gerry, not just that time she had rescued them when the car had broken down, but other times too. After all, he had been out there a whole two weeks before she had come. So it was true and Cinni had lied to her.

All the old pain that had been banked up in her for years as she had waited for Gerry to leave his wife and marry her, burst out. Cinni kept telling her to dump him, find someone else, so it must be true that she wanted him for herself? She took another drink, aware suddenly that Lucian was regarding her with dismay. All her feelings must be showing like flashing lights upon her face. She took a deep breath, Cinni had been so hurt at Julian's betrayal, felt so alone that she had gone after Gerry. It was true he liked women and might have been easily seduced; after all, Cinni was beautiful, far better looking than she was. She hadn't wanted to believe it, warned herself that her lack of a decent night's sleep and perhaps too much wine for supper was clouding her judgement, but Lucian had confirmed it. It all fell into place now, Gerry's infrequent visits just after he had come back to her, swearing he could not live without her and Cinni being too busy or too tired to see her.

Lucian leant forward. 'Something is troubling you? Is it about Cinni, something that happened perhaps with Max that she's afraid of? I'll be discreet, you can tell her that. I'm not writing for the Sunday papers, or trying to discredit him. She need answer only the questions I have written here.'

She felt as if she was in another world, spaced out, the pain and the wine releasing her inhibitions, her loyalty. 'She will not see you,' she said, 'because she is afraid that you will find out that she is carrying Max's child.'

As she said it she saw his face change, she was was pierced with the anguish at what she'd done. She should not have said it; this was nothing to do with Cinni and Gerry. 'I mean,' she blurted, vainly trying to claw back her words. 'I don't mean that, I'm sorry, I'm tired, drunk too much. I didn't mean that at all, I meant someone else's child, only people might think . . .' she struggled on throwing in more and more ridiculous ideas to lead him away but she knew she was not convincing him.

'A dead man's child,' he said under his breath. 'That is what she must have meant.'

Sue was crying now, clutching at his arm. 'It isn't true,' she said, 'I made it up, don't believe it please. Oh, please don't believe it.'

# CHAPTER TWENTY-EIGHT

THE shops were overdressed for Christmas but Cinni hardly noticed. The London branch of Magical Villas was working at full tilt with people wanting reservations for villas in the Caribbean. It amazed her how many people made last minute decisions to spend Christmas and the New Year in more scorching climates. They were furious, insulted that none of the villas they wanted were free at that time; others, more prudent with their holiday planning had got there first. Cinni and her colleagues were worked off their feet trying to find other places and placate irate clients.

'Bloody same every year,' Gina complained. 'Seem to think just because they rented one from us before they have a right to any property they want at a moment's notice. How I'd love to tell them what I think of them but of course . . .' she put on a simpering voice, 'Magical Villas tries to act like a fairy godmother granting everyone's wishes.'

Cinni smiled, leant back to stretch her aching back. 'I know, we give them enough warning that Christmas is coming, sending out all those brochures but some of them seem to think we'll hold everything for them.' She steeled herself against the clients' anger, the men controlling, the women imperious, of the 'do you know who I am?' tribe, which made her hate them even more, but though she let them rant on, holding the receiver away from her ear – as indeed the others did, all laughing sometimes as these people spewed out their venom – it exhausted her. She was six months pregnant now, though still quite slim from the back and only a potbelly showed her condition. She could feel the baby moving; it was now quite an athlete or a dancer, especially when she lay down longing to sleep. She'd seen grainy pictures of it, a little bean with arms and legs. She could not discern the sex of it, nor did she want to know. It would make it more real somehow and yet it was part of her and she could not imagine being without it. The pictures fascinated her yet made her fearful too and reluctantly she began to realize that she must make plans to welcome it.

She'd gone for the scans alone, though some of her women friends had offered to go with her. She might as well get used to doing this on her own, she thought, besides she was so busy in the office she didn't have time to set up arrangements with other people. It was along to the hospital for the appointment then back to work.

She got on well with her work colleagues and she often asked them back to the flat or went out with them at weekends. They did not know her circumstances and accepted her as she was. She found them easier to be with than her old friends, especially Sue.

Sue had not contacted her for some time now and Cinni had not rung her. She suspected one of the reasons was that she had not conceived Gerry's child and could not bear to see her bulging with a pregnancy she had not asked for. Sue's last call had been late one night when, obviously the worse for drink, she had cried down the phone.

'I didn't mean it, I'm so sorry,' she kept saying, overcome with such sobbing she became incoherent. Cinni held on, making comforting noises not knowing what she was on about. She presumed she meant her believing Gerry's lies about her throwing herself at him, so she had reassured her it didn't matter and finally Sue had rung off. She was upset at Sue's state. If she had taken to the bottle because of her failure to secure a future with Gerry it was serious indeed. She did ring her back the following day but got no answer and the days sped away and somehow she never got round to ringing her again.

But one good thing was that Lucian had stopped trying to contact her. She'd been furious with her father over his belief that Lucian was the father of her child; fury that she later conceded was strangely edged in guilt that she could not help Lucian in his grief at his girlfriend aborting his child. 'It is definitely not his,' she told Theo. 'We barely spoke to each other let alone anything more intimate.'

'Well, that's a great pity,' Theo said. 'I like him, he's had a rotten time with this woman and you could have made him happy.'

'I doubt it. The child is not his so I'd be grateful if you did not go round suggesting that it is. We hardly know each other and that is how it will stay. I do not want to talk to him about Max; there are plenty of other people he can go to for snippets of his life.'

'If it is not his child whose is it then?' Theo had demanded. 'Surely I've a right to know who fathered my grandchild?' He almost choked over the word, angry perhaps that life had played such a trick on him and had forgotten that he was not the type to take on the responsibilities of being a father let alone a grandfather.

'I will tell you in my own time,' she said, afraid he would not keep the news to himself, boast about it and use it to his own advantage. Lucian would get to hear of it and would plan a massive offence to prise the details from her. Theo had been disappointed, reminding her of a spoilt child, sulking because the others would not play the game he wanted, but she had avoided telling him.

A week after that meeting in the restaurant, Lucian had left a message on the answerphone, later writing her a short note saying he wanted to see her for a few moments, any time, any place, but she had ignored them. Once when he had got her on the phone she'd just said 'no' and put down the receiver. Once she'd seen him hanging about outside the block of flats. 'Bloody stalker,' she muttered under her breath though she could not help but watch him a moment, eyes lingering on that dark head, the straight shoulders beneath the soft tweed jacket, before turning away and slipping out the back entrance. But for the last three weeks she had heard nothing; he must have given up. She hoped he was nearing his deadline and could waste no more time trying to interview her.

Philip had been the truest friend in all of this. He rang her every week and came to visit her sometimes. He did it because he had loved her mother, she told herself, but sometimes she caught him looking at her and saw something akin to love in his eyes. He'd been a better father to her in her youth than Theo had. Perhaps he saw her as the daughter he'd never had. Though Theo had saved her with this flat, she was grateful for that.

Another thought nudged her; so unkind she pushed it away. Once the baby was born and it was confirmed to be Max's it would inherit the house. If there were no other children she would have control over it until the child reached eighteen and could choose who could live there. But Philip was far too nice only to be kind to her because he wanted to keep a roof over his head. She suspected that he needed someone to look after. After her mother had died he had been left with such a void in his life. She remembered her mother saying, 'Philip is the sort of person who flourishes with caring for others. He knows I cannot do without him and so in some ways he is my keeper.'

She had laughed, said of course it was not like that, but now Cinni understood what she had meant. Fiona, helpless with her illness, depended upon him, had from the moment she had become homeless when Cinni was a child. Undemanding Philip had captured Fiona in her weakness and now Cinni too was in desperate need but somehow, and she scolded herself for this, she resented this. Had Fiona felt the same, yearning for a more exciting, passionate man yet knowing that one like that would not cope with the responsibilities a child and later an illness would demand from them?

Philip said, 'It's so nearly Christmas. Have you any plans?'

She was about to say no, she'd been too busy to think about it and time alone, just sleeping and preparing for the baby, mentally as well as practically, seemed a tempting plan, but feeling he might suggest spending it with her she said, 'I'm going to spend the time with friends.'

'I see . . . good.' She saw his disappointment.

'And you?'

'With Ruth and Stella and . . .' he grimaced, 'Aubrey. He may be a friend of Ruth's and we do need his rent but between you and me I don't like him. He hovers about as if spying on us. Stella thinks he's a kleptomaniac but then she's always been untidy and chaotic and loses things.'

'Sounds horrid. It's difficult sharing, even with someone you like.' She thought guiltily of Sue. She'd ring her later; suggest they go out for a Christmas supper or something.

When Philip had gone she was hit with despair. It crept up on her and pounced, digging its claws into her and pulling her down. Whatever was going to happen to her and the child? It moved within her, kicking against her as if to remind her it was there. How would she prove it was Max's? If Ruth refused to hand over anything with his DNA on she'd be sunk. She'd have to take legal advice and that would be a scandal in itself. It was not the house she wanted but recognition for the child. She wanted it to know who it was, what family it belonged to. Ruth could be dead before the child was old enough to understand but she wanted it to feel complete, part of a family even if that family no longer existed. Even though her mother and grandparents were dead and she had no contact, or little contact with the rest of them, she knew where she fitted in the scheme of things. She wanted the same for her child. She just had to find someone to help her achieve this with the least possible hurt.

Lucian came into her mind and she pushed him away. Why did she always think of him when faced with such a crisis? He was the last person she could confide in, the last person to help her. Think how he'd crow at her revelations, use it to promote his book.

The ringing of the telephone cut into her irritation. She picked it up.

'Hello, is that Cinni? It's Aunt Veronica here, we've never met but I'm married to your father's brother, Simon. I hear from your father that you've turned up again and are in his flat.'

'Y-yes, that's right.' Her heart fell further. Was she going to turn her out?

'I know this is short notice but we wondered if you were doing anything for Christmas and if not would like to come here to Merriot? We're a girl short and you, my dear, would be perfect.' She sugared over her unflattering reason for asking her.

'I . . . well. . . .' The request had so caught her out she was completely tongue-tied.

'Good, so glad, come for lunch on Christmas Eve and stay until the twenty-seventh. Will send the directions to you. Bye.' And she was gone leaving Cinni bewildered.

All the way back to Landsdowne Crescent Philip thought of Cinni. If only he had more money, to help her support the child. How would she manage with going to work, or if she became ill? Marriage – the most respectable solution – was out of the question, he was almost sixty and she wouldn't want him in that role, and he would find it difficult to settle, especially with a child. Yet he loved her, he understood that now, sitting in the tube staring at the advertisements across from him and the motley crew of fellow travellers. She was so much like her mother it was hardly surprising he loved her. But she was not her mother, he reminded himself firmly; if he loved her it must only be in the capacity of a father.

He had hoped to go straight up to his room to mull over his feelings but Stella caught sight of him coming in. 'That writer fellow is here again,' she announced with some glee. It was obvious that she had just come up from her room after sprucing herself up. Her newly applied scent tickled his nose and her lipstick glowed like a bright stain on her pale face.

'I suppose he has a lot of questions to ask,' he said feebly.

'He's a nice man, come and join us. We're having some wine, he brought it with him.'

He did not want to go and yet he followed her into the drawing-room. He was just in time to hear Ruth say, 'I want to make it quite clear that we want no more people interviewed. Some . . .' she coughed delicately, 'rather excitable people make up things that are absolutely not true, just for attention, I suppose. We do not want any unsavoury stories included,' she finished severely.

'Of course not,' Lucian said, then stood up to greet him. He shook his hand knowing Ruth meant Cinni as the rather excitable person. He was now certain that, bizarre though it was, Cinni was speaking the truth about her pregnancy. She was not one to tell such a lie, a lie that would be easy on the child's birth to prove one way or the other.

Stella made her entrance but as it was not noticed with Lucian listening to Ruth's remark, she made it again, wafting in as if she was the famous actress everyone was waiting for. 'I can tell you all you want to know,' she said mysteriously. 'I was married to Max for five years.'

'We all know that, thank you, Stella, but I don't think you can add anything of importance to Lucian's book. You have had your say,' Ruth responded sharply, fixing her with her piercing eyes as if willing her to disappear or be struck dumb.

Lucian smiled at Stella. 'You've been very helpful and I might get back to you later to clarify some dates.'

'Of course, any time,' Stella purred throwing Ruth a triumphant look.

'You have all been most helpful and I hope you will be pleased with the book. I want to make it a tribute to him, to his considerable talent,' Lucian went on. 'But there's just one more person I want to see, but she is . . .' he paused, 'rather difficult to pin down. Cinni Langley, Fiona's daughter.'

Ruth became agitated. 'Oh no, she is just the sort of person I was speaking about. She is far too excitable, with a very strange imagination. She would be a very unreliable witness.' She made it sound like a court case.

Lucian looked surprised. 'That was not the impression I got when I met her, although I admit she does seem very reluctant to speak to me.'

'I have forbidden her to,' Ruth said. 'I told her this was a serious, academic work, not one for the tabloids all smeared with filth and lies. Sex, that is all that interests the masses these days and just because Max had too many women in his life does not mean others can hope to benefit from it.'

Lucian was sitting very still watching her as if he was regarding the strange behaviour of some curious creature. Philip felt unnerved by this, afraid too that Ruth, in her desperation, would blurt out Cinni's announcement of her pregnancy. He must jump in or she would give Cinni away.

'Ruth's still very affected with his death,' he said quickly. 'Perhaps we could talk of something else. When your book is to be published for instance.'

'Next autumn I hope. Here have some wine.' He offered him a glass, poured some more for the others. Ruth was fighting to control herself, covering her mouth with a fluttering handkerchief as if it would block it but words kept coming out. 'There have been enough interviews, we don't want this sinking into the gutter.'

Stella sat down on the sofa beside Lucian, a little too close to him. 'Max was such a rogue where the ladies were concerned. I expect you've had all sorts of peculiar women crawling out of the woodwork all swearing he loved them.'

'No,' Lucian said. 'I haven't.'

Stella looked disappointed. 'You will,' she said. 'I'm sure you will, but he only cared for a very select few of us.'

A few minutes later when it was obvious that nothing more of interest was to be said, Lucian got up to leave, begging them all not to disturb themselves; he would see himself out. After a few moments Philip followed him, longing to get away from Ruth's anger – now conducted under her breath about Cinni's appalling behaviour with her wicked stories.

The passage along to the hall was dark and the light from the stained glass window over the front door fell in coloured splashes on the floor. He saw that Lucian was still there and paused for a moment to let him go, wondering for a brief moment if he was waiting for him to ask why Ruth was so upset. He was too drained for any more. But then he saw that he was not alone, Aubrey was there in the shadows near the umbrella stand. How he disliked the way he was always lurking around, like some thief in the night.

'About your book,' Philip heard Aubrey say. 'I wonder if you knew but a young woman, Cinni I think her name is, is going around saying she is pregnant with Max's child. Disgraceful don't you think?'

'How do you know this?' Lucian asked.

Philip leapt forward, arm outstretched as if he had a sword and would run it through him. 'How dare you tell such lies?' he shouted, making Aubrey shrink back against the wall, an uneasy smile twisting his mouth.

Lucian hastily made his escape and though Philip called after him to wait, he did not stop. Now he had got his prize he would not give it up.

# CHAPTER TWENTY-NINE

Cinni had not been to Merriot since she was twelve. Once, some years ago, she and Julian had passed it on the way to or from somewhere and she had made him stop and they had stared through the gates at the house half concealed behind the trees, until a red-faced man had come and shouted at them that they were trespassing and they had gone away, laughing.

Momentarily, she was poleaxed by a sudden rush of shyness and wished fervently that she had not come. Christmas holed up in the flat alone – or even with Barbara, as she was now allowed to call her, flipping her duster around – seemed so much more inviting. But she drove on up the drive and parked beside a muddy 4x4. Should she ring the bell or walk in? A middle-aged woman wearing an ancient wax jacket with a shapeless tweed hat crammed on to her head saved her. She was attacking some bushes by the side of the house.

'Cinni!' This must be her Aunt Veronica. 'Good to see you. Oh, my God, you're in pod – Theo never said. Is your husband with you?' She peered at the car, slightly annoyed as if the last thing she wanted was an extra man to spoil her numbers.

'No.' Cinni felt like a child caught out at some shaming misdemeanour. 'I'm not married, I came alone.'

'Oh, good,' her aunt said, relieved. 'No one seems to marry these days – no bad thing in some cases I'd have thought. Come in, you must be tired. The children can deal with your luggage.' She swept open the front door that was in dire need of a coat of paint and strode through the hall calling out, 'Cinni's arrived!'

Two Labradors came slowly up to greet her and then her Uncle Simon – a thicker, plainer and indeed older version of her father – appeared. He smiled then looked shocked as he noticed her bulging stomach.

'She's preggers – not married but that's the norm these days,' Aunt Veronica said briskly as if to stall his disapproval. But he was smiling, almost laughing.

'I bet Theo's delighted to be a grandfather, best joke I've heard for years.'

'Honestly, Simon, these brotherly squabbles,' she reprimanded him. 'Take no notice, dear. Come and meet the others then we'll have some tea.' She led her into the drawing-room.

The room seemed familiar, unchanged except that it had faded since she was last here as a child. The walls and curtains were blue silk, dried water stains spread like little islands in one corner. The furniture was beautiful, delicate and no doubt valuable, heavy gold-framed landscapes hung on the wall, one of a horse reminded her of a Stubbs. Two dog baskets lined with old blankets were near the fire.

A youth sprang up from his chair staring at her with fascination. Two girls with lanky blonde hair appeared through another door. Cinni had the feeling they had all been waiting to see what this cousin was like. Aunt Veronica swept her hand in an arc in their direction. 'Charlie, Sophie and Melissa,' she said. 'Your cousins.'

Uncle Simon coughed as if she was not a suitable person to be linked to his children – the daughter of his wayward brother and a model – that is how he saw her, Cinni thought with resentment. People like him and Sybella at school thought models were just smart tarts. Fiona could not have been less like that. She felt tears rise in her throat, wishing so much that Fiona was here, wishing she could be spirited back to her childhood when she was surrounded by love.

'Hi,' Charlie said in a friendly way, making her feel better.

One of the girls said, 'Funny we've never seen you before but Daddy's banned Uncle Theo; he says whenever he comes here something goes wrong on the estate.'

'That's not a very nice thing to say, Melissa,' Aunt Veronica said mildly. 'Her parents' behaviour is hardly Cinni's fault.' She smiled at Cinni. 'I told Simon it was ridiculous not knowing you and when I heard you were in Theo's flat I knew I could get hold of you. So,' she smiled triumphantly, 'here we all are, your family.'

Cinni smiled feeling strangely moved by this abrupt woman, then she wondered what she would think if she knew the parentage of her child.

'So, we'll have tea in the kitchen if you don't mind,' Aunt Veronica continued. 'Charlie will take your luggage upstairs, you're in the Green Room.'

'The haunted one,' Charlie joked in a quivery voice.

'I remember it,' Cinni said. She hoped it was haunted with her grand-mother's ghost, remembering how she used to come to kiss her each night on her way down to dinner, always dressed in something soft and smelling of flowers.

'Nothing much has changed here. Simon's kept it the same, no good doing everything up like a dog's dinner,' Aunt Veronica said. She was a few years younger than Simon Cinni saw now and the children were younger than she'd imagined. Veronica had obviously not been here when Cinni lived here as a child. She barely remembered Uncle Simon, he'd been away in the army or somewhere. When Theo had left her mother just after her grandfather died they had left Merriot too. Not wanted, as Fiona had told her, by Simon the new baronet. Her grand-mother had been poleaxed by her husband's sudden death, and soon after had a car accident from which she never recovered. Cinni had never seen her again.

Simon and Veronica had not come to Fiona's funeral but nor had Theo. 'I cannot bear to think of her dead,' he'd said having rung Cinni after seeing Fiona's death announcement in *The Times*. He had sent extravagant flowers with a note saying, 'My love always.'

They ate tea – crumpets and Christmas cake – round the table in the kitchen. They all quizzed her, even Uncle Simon, fascinated by this new member of their family. No one mentioned her pregnancy again or, to her relief, asked who the father was.

She had been told not to bring presents, only one thing to eat which would not need much cooking. 'We have a couple of staff but they won't be here much so that's what I always do, just ask for something to eat, ready prepared,' her aunt had instructed.

Cinni was relieved, buying presents for people she didn't know was a nightmare and who should she buy them for? Being told there would be twelve in the house and more wandering in – 'odd bods' as her aunt described them – she brought a large pâté in a round earthenware pot. It had a pattern of cranberries sealed under glaze on top making it look festive. She'd also brought a tin of savoury biscuits that could be nibbled at with drinks; both gifts were seized by her aunt with delight.

Halfway through tea another couple, friends of her aunt and uncle turned up. Cinni did not catch their names; one was an eager, red-haired man who reminded her of a terrier and his wife, small and blonde with a wide vacant face. There was a lumpy daughter, Annabel, who looked miserable, resigned as if she knew those better-looking children would taunt her and leave her out of their games. Cinni felt great sympathy for her and smiled at her encouragingly.

Just as she was about to go upstairs and unpack and have a few blissful minutes alone before dinner, there was the sound of another car arriving. Charlie opened the door and a young woman with sparkling eyes and a wide smile came in closely followed by a tall blond man, both laughingly complaining about the traffic and the lashing rain. They were obviously popular for the family crowded round welcoming them in. Cinni, hovering halfway up the stairs wondered whether to go down and be introduced or go on up to her room.

Another man came in behind them, shutting the front door behind him. It was Lucian. He saw her at once, standing there foolishly on the stairs higher than everyone in the kissing crowd below. He looked bewildered, almost shocked and she turned and went upstairs too horrified to say anything. She'd have to leave, she could not stay here for three days with him. But perhaps he had just dropped them, was going on somewhere else for Christmas and Merriot had been on his way. She lay down on the bed feeling faint. When they were all out of the way she could creep downstairs and get in her car and head back to London – send some explanation for her sudden departure, later.

But even as she planned this escape she knew she would not do it even if he were staying. Why should she? She was part of this family and in their own way they had welcomed her in. It was Lucian who should leave, not her. It would be a good two hours back to London in the dark and the rain. She might have a crash and be left bleeding and dying on the roadside. If he was staying here she would ignore him. This should be easy with so many other people around; she would make it quite clear he was not to mention his dratted book.

She went down to dinner in fighting spirit. The drawing-room was full of everyone drinking and, she was pleased to see, eating the biscuits she had brought. Uncle Simon greeted her and gave her a glass of champagne, asking if she knew everyone, leading her over to the new arrivals and to Lucian, who looked away, pretending without much conviction to study one of the dusty landscapes on the wall.

The two people who had arrived with him were called Henry and Alice, but their names were blurred in with Lucian's. All smiled and nodded to each other, only Lucian remained aloof – his Darcy look firmly on his face. He did not talk to her nor she to him but he was put next to her at dinner. She was filled with a sick dread yet her heart was fluttering most alarmingly. How foolish one's body was, could it not connect that he was the enemy, the last person she wanted to see.

He said when they had settled, 'I shall not mention my book at all.'

'I would not listen if you did.'

'I didn't know you were still in touch with this family,' he said.

'Well, I am.' She felt he had intimated that she was not good enough to be sitting here with them all in this icy dining-room, but perhaps she was just being paranoid.

The man who looked like a terrier and she'd since learnt was called Colin sat on her other side. He pounced on her with polite conversation, but when he heard that she did not hunt, fish or shoot he became disconsolate and did not speak to her again so she was thrown back on to Lucian although she would have far preferred to sit in silence.

Aunt Veronica, seeing the icy manner between them, said loudly, 'You'll never guess at this extraordinary coincidence but the book Lucian is working on at the moment is about Max Cavanagh who painted Cinni's mother Fiona – Theo's former wife, you know. So, Cinni, I'm sure you and Lucian will have lots in common. After all, you knew Max quite well, didn't you?'

Cinni blushed as everyone's eyes swivelled towards her, regarding her with interest. If only she could escape, get back to the flat and peace and obscurity in London. She would go tomorrow in daylight even though it was Christmas Day.

Lucian's voice was strong and commanding. 'While I'm here I'm on holiday for a few days and I have a strict rule never to work on holiday.'

'Oh, how odd. All the other writers I know are forever scribbling on the napkins or in grubby notebooks. I always think they are writing nasty things about me.' Her aunt shrieked with laughter.

Lucian said gallantly, 'There's nothing nasty to write about you, Veronica.'

Colin's wife sitting on Lucian's other side immediately began to question him on his profession so Cinni was not able to thank him for not turning Veronica's remark into a free for all about her connection with Max. She only hoped he would keep to it.

# CHAPTER THIRTY

MERRIOT was heaving with people, not only with those staying in the house but with groups of visiting young who were always on the move somewhere like a swarm of locusts, all jostling and laughing and ragging each other in their public school voices.

Aunt Veronica took it all in her stride, occasionally shouting good naturedly, 'Oh children, do be quiet, settle to something, Monopoly perhaps, or go out in the fresh air.' Cinni thought there was enough fresh air gushing in through the gaps in the windows and under the doors to save them going out to find any more.

Uncle Simon took the men out after Christmas lunch – Cinni supposed round the estate – but at least it took Lucian away, not that he had spoken to her since last night's dinner apart from wishing her a happy Christmas. She had watched him surreptitiously, a hard, closed look on her face as if she had built a prickly hedge around herself, and he had kept away. He was popular, she saw that, his Darcy look quite gone as he joined in the animated conversations that rose and fell among them. Once or twice when she had unconsciously let down her guard and expressed some opinion or told some story she had seen him watching her and his gaze lit a fire in her that she held like a hot water bottle, but she made sure he would not know of the ridiculous effect he had on her and use it to prise her secrets from her. But as the day went on and the evening too, he did not seek her out or try to catch her alone. She put down her feelings of disappointment to tiredness; she was not used to so many people and so much noise.

Wonderful large meals were produced with no apparent fuss at all. Sophie and Melissa and some of their friends helped and Cinni, glad of the familiar comfort of the kitchen where she remembered making pastry and icing tiny cakes as a child, was happy to help too. Unlike other women Cinni knew, Aunt Veronica could not care less who cooked the meal. She shoved things into the Aga and often sent one of them to check on it, or take out the baked potatoes and, as Colin's wife kept bleating she knew a 'frightfully good way with the leftovers', thanked her profusely and told her to get on with it.

Christmas Day passed and on Boxing Day there was a meet in front of the house. The breath of the horses and hunters wafted like dry ice in the sharp air. Cinni had not seen Lucian at breakfast and then there he was mounted on a satin black hunter. She might have gasped – she hoped she had not – and turned it quickly into a cough, but he caught her eye, lifted his crop to her, a maddening smile playing on his lips. She scowled, how she hated him, hated the way he kept turning up like a stalker. Did he find out where she was and then somehow inveigle an invitation? She turned away but not before she saw him laughing.

Most of the house party was out hunting. She was left with the unfortunate Annabel and Alice who said she had hurt her back in a fall earlier in the season. Alice was grumpy and bad-tempered to be missing the day and Annabel was grumpy and bad-tempered because nobody liked her as she didn't fit in anywhere, so Cinni decided she'd escape them both, find a comfortable corner and settle down to read. After a while Alice came and found her curled up in the little sitting-room.

'I'm sorry I'm such a cow; I just hate missing a day out. The hunting round here is marvellous too but it would have been mean of me not to let Henry come here just because I can't hunt.'

'Will you be able to hunt again?'

'Hope so, if I'm good and let this heal.' She sighed. 'I'm just so impatient. I'm dreading when they all come back boasting of a lovely day. But there it is.'

'I didn't know Lucian hunted,' Cinni was annoyed to hear herself saying.

Alice frowned. 'Yes,' she said as if it was the most obvious thing in the world. 'He's ridden since he was a child.'

How Cinni longed to question her further but she didn't want Alice to imagine that she was at all interested in him. But Alice went on. 'It's extraordinary that you know the artist he is writing about. I must say he's being very constrained about it not firing questions at you all the time. How well did you know Max?'

Her question was friendly without guile but Cinni felt herself seizing up. 'My mother knew him very well; she was one of his muses. I met him through her.'

Alice clapped her hands. 'Yes, and your mother was Fiona right? She married Theo, Simon's wicked younger brother.' She laughed. 'Sorry, that's a bit crass of me, but it's quite a story round here. We, well my parents, all adored Theo but Simon ... well, I suppose I shouldn't be telling you this,' she giggled, 'but he refused to have him here as he said he'd bankrupt the estate. It is said however that Theo didn't want to come here anyway, wanted to live abroad. Is that true?'

'I don't know really; he wasn't much good at being a father, taking responsibility. He was so young, though now,' she felt she must defend him, 'he's been marvellous, letting me live in his flat.'

'That's what Veronica said. She's been longing to meet you for years, only Simon ... well,' she laughed awkwardly, 'these huge estates are hell to run, never enough money after death duties and I suppose he was afraid your father might get in the way of his ideas to make money, or spend it all on a riotous life or something.'

'I don't know anything about it,' Cinni said, not wanting to say how different the two brothers were. Simon had probably been born middle-aged: 'constipated with convention' was how her mother used to describe him. His father had died suddenly and catapulted him into his role and there was his brother, the charming, feckless man-child refusing to take life seriously, to grow up at all.

Alice went on, 'Veronica often asks Henry and me over. He's a cousin of hers and when she heard that Lucian was staying with us she insisted that he come too. She knew his mother and—' She blushed. 'Oh nothing. I do talk too much, Henry's always telling me off. Sorry, I'm disturbing your book. There's not much peace here is there? And soon they'll all be back and it will be chaos again.' She got up. 'I'll leave you to it.'

Cinni did not want her to go, she wanted to hear more about Lucian. She said, 'I don't know Lucian, is he a good writer?'

'Oh, I thought you *did* know him. He said he met you in the South of France. I thought ... well,' she laughed awkwardly, 'that's me jumping to conclusions again.'

'What do you mean?' Thoughts chased themselves through her mind. She hated it when people half told you things and caused bizarre conclusions to spawn like mushrooms in your mind. Had he said that she was a tart who threw herself at married men like Gerry? Perhaps he had warned Alice to keep Henry well away from her?

'Oh, nothing at all. He just said he'd met you. Now he needs to clarify things about you and Max. How fascinating to be the daughter of such a beautiful woman. You look quite like her actually. Did you ever pose for him?'

'No. I was too young.'

'Of course, but now, now you are older. He must have been tempted to paint you, as you must have reminded him of Fiona. Though perhaps you never saw him again after you grew up. When did you last see him?' To Cinni's imagination Alice's carefree voice now held an edge of steel. The interrogator first nibbling gently round the subject before digging her teeth into the heart of the story. Had Lucian put her up to this, suggested that she use this quiet morning for a girly chat, winkle out the information from her? Resentment seethed through her. That was surely it. Thinking she had snatched Helen's husband just for a bout of fun he despised her, could not even be bothered to talk to her. But she was jumping to conclusions again, if only he had not appeared here, he unsettled her so.

'Can't remember.' Cinni stared determinedly at her book.

'Oh well.' Alice moved towards the door, then added in a friendly way, 'You must get quite tired being pregnant. When is your baby due?'

'March,' she said in what she hoped was a dismissive voice.

'Will the father be joining you here? Veronica loves having people around her, the boyfriends and girlfriends of people she knows, even their parents and grandparents. She loves to know about everyone, quite a gift – or I suppose it could be seen as an intrusion – what do you think?'

'I don't know,' Cinni smiled, refusing to be drawn further. Alice looked as if she were gearing herself up to ask her more questions, so Cinni said, 'Hope you don't mind but I've got to finish this book for my book group and I haven't much time.'

' 'Course, sorry.' Alice left her reluctantly.

Later when they had all returned and were in the drawing-room eating huge slabs of Christmas cake for tea, Cinni saw that Lucian and Alice were sitting a little apart from the rest of them, their heads together deep in conversation. Was it her imagination or did their eyes keep flickering in her direction? Anxiety prickled through her; she hoped she hadn't said anything to give herself away.

Aunt Veronica sat next to her and said, 'I'm so glad you're staying here tonight. With all these people I don't feel I've spoken to you at all. There will just be the three of us for dinner. Everyone else is leaving and the children are going to some party.'

Cinni smiled, but inside she felt uneasy. Here with the crowd, the children noisy and boisterous, she could be left alone, but with them all gone, she would be the centre of attention. Her aunt and uncle would no doubt question her on the years they had not seen her and perhaps even criticize her father. But she was too tired to drive back now, she would have to stay.

After a prolonged tea everyone began to leave. Cinni gathered that Uncle Simon was dropping the children off at their party later on. The hall was filled with suitcases and people began their goodbyes, the dogs in constant danger of being stepped on. Cinni, somehow caught up in the wash of the departing guests, hovered in the hall with her uncle and aunt. She did not see Lucian approach her in the shadows until he was next to her and he startled her, though she had secretly been searching for him in the merry crowd. Before she could protest he took her arm and led her a little away from the others.

'We've had no time to talk at all over these two days, but I want to say I shan't be wanting to ask you anything for my book on Max. I have all the information I need.'

'What?' She squinted at him, had she heard right or was this some new ploy to get her to speak to him?

He smiled. 'I don't need to know any more. Philip told me quite a lot; after all he made quite a few visits with your mother and you. There really is no reason for me to bother you again.'

They were standing in a kind of alcove, the only light coming from the interior of a cupboard with glass doors showing off a collection of china. Cinni noticed a dusty piece of holly among the cups that must have been put there some Christmases ago. He was standing close to her but was not touching her. For a mad moment she was seized with a compulsion to lay her hand on his face, she even lifted her arm a fraction then hastily whipped it down by her side. 'You mean, you have all you need? You don't want to ask me anything?'

'Yes. I'll stop chasing you. I'm sorry if I was a bore but . . .' he laughed, 'like hunting, once you catch the scent madness takes over. But I promise you, from now on I shall leave you in peace.'

She was surprised at the force of disappointment that hit her. She should be rejoicing, she had won and yet perhaps she had not, perhaps he knew everything and at this very moment the words describing Max's last act on this earth were lying fresh and jubilant upon his page.

Alice called to him and he put his hand on Cinni's arm. 'Must go, good luck.' His eyes skimmed over her stomach. He took a step away from her towards the front door, then he turned back. 'Take care of yourself, Cinni. If you ever need any help, ring me.' With a quick, stiff smile he had gone, calling to Alice and Henry, embracing Aunt Veronica. She watched him go out into that cold night, the brightness of the carriage lamps on the outside walls lighting him up for a second before he was gone. She felt empty, sad, betrayed and yet she told herself she should be glad he was gone and she need never see him again.

# CHAPTER THIRTY-ONE

'WE'VE so many lovely leftovers, your delicious pâté, Lucian's wild salmon and of course turkey, ham and Stilton, we don't have a thing to cook,' Aunt Veronica said with satisfaction, sitting down opposite Cinni in the little sitting-room that was the cosiest yet most dilapidated room in the house.

The house was strangely quiet after the fever of the last days. Simon had taken the children to the party and now there were just the two of them with the dogs snoozing by the fire.

Cinni was feeling sleepy, lulled by the flickering fire and could have happily dropped off but Aunt Veronica was in fighting form. She beamed at her as if she had invented her. 'I'm so glad to meet you at last. I do like your father but he is a dreadful liability so we can't have him here, but there's no reason why you shouldn't come whenever you want to.'

'That's very kind,' Cinni murmured then felt she should perhaps support her father and not come here unless he was allowed to as well. Before she could think of a tactful way to say this, Aunt Veronica settled herself in the deep nest of the sofa as if preparing for a long gossip.

'So, tell me about the baby. When is it due?'

Cinni's heart sank, she'd been expecting this and wondered again if Lucian had put her up to it. He seemed to be friends of everyone but her. 'March,' she said.

'Will you marry the father? Will he support you?'

'No, he's . . . well, he's dead,' she said, and then wished she hadn't. She really must make up a plausible story about this child's father and keep to it.

'Dead? That's very unfortunate. How did that happen?' Aunt Veronica looked suitably shocked.

Cinni was tempted to tell her everything. She liked her, didn't mind her plain speaking and she was her relative – even if only by marriage – and yet she thought of how Veronica would tell Uncle Simon and how he would disapprove and no doubt refuse to let her come here again. And Lucian, how well did he know Veronica? Would she tell him? She well might. Cinni could hear her saying at some dinner party in that cut glass voice of hers, 'You'll never guess, Lucian, but Cinni is having Max's baby, no less.'

'Yes,' she said. 'I don't really want to talk about it. It's so upsetting.'

'Of course it is. Well, my dear,' Veronica leant forward and patted her hand, 'you must make the best of it. Has he family?'

'Not really.' Cinni was not going to say that he was old and only had a sister; it would be too easy to guess his identity then. 'But I'll be fine.'

'You can always visit here, any time you want.' Aunt Veronica smiled. 'I love little ones, mine are so big and out of control now and I hope it will be a long time before any of them have children, though you can never tell these days. I've masses of stuff in the attic; Nanny put it all away so it will be spotless, carry cots, Moses basket, clothes and so forth. We'll go through them tomorrow. I must say,' she laughed, 'it does amuse me to think of Theo as a grandfather. How will he feel having his smart, bachelor pad turned into a nursery?'

'I don't think he's thought that through. He is going to be away after all.'

Aunt Veronica chuckled delightedly. 'Life always catches us out, doesn't it? You must invite me up when the baby is born, I'd love to see the transformation.'

'But you can come any time. I understand it is a family flat.'

'Strictly it is, but Simon would never dream of going there. He thinks it is a den of vice,' she giggled. 'He's not much good at fun, dear man, and your father can't get enough of it. Now't as queer as folk.' She went on to ask her about doctors and which hospital she was to go to, and would she like to have it here at Merriot?

Cinni explained about her work and how she was booked into the local hospital but she found herself wishing that Aunt Veronica with her common sense and sturdy presence would be there to help her through it.

Uncle Simon appeared and during dinner asked her about her father, almost in fear as if at any moment he might appear and demand something. Then he said to his wife, 'That book Lucian is writing. It won't have any thing unsavoury in it about our family will it?'

Cinni choked on her tangerine. If Lucian had his way it would.

'Whatever do you mean, dear?' Aunt Veronica demanded.

'Well.' He glanced at Cinni looking pink and awkward, throwing his wife a pitiful look as if she should know exactly what he meant without having to spell it out. 'Do you think he will embellish it with some sort of sordid story about how Cinni's parents met, had her, married.'

Cinni guessed at once that he was too polite to say that Theo got her mother pregnant with her so was forced to marry her. She knew it was not like that, but Simon seemed to think it was.

'I don't see why she should. What sort of questions has he asked you, Cinni? I know he wanted to interview you, get your views of Max. Did he ask about your parents?' asked Veronica.

'Intrusive questions, muck-raking, you know?' Simon glared at her as if he were ashamed of his brother for smirching the family honour so.

Cinni wished the ancient floor beneath her would open and suck her down into oblivion. Her parents' behaviour, though more shocking in those days, was nothing compared to hers. She could imagine what a lurid picture some tabloids could make from it; they'd delight in bringing in this family, a baronet's niece killing a famous artist by seducing him then having his child and upsetting his will.

'Of course he didn't.' Aunt Veronica saw her face and mistook it for offence at Simon's words. 'Lucian is honest, decent, not like some of those unscrupulous writers who make up stuff just to sell their book. You may be shocked at Theo's behaviour, Simon, and I know he's irresponsible and up to goodness knows what, but that has nothing to do with Max. After all, he left Fiona and Cinni years ago, he's not in the equation.'

Cinni had managed to pull herself together. Should she confess all now and ask them what to do? Perhaps they had some influence over Lucian. She said, 'How well do you know Lucian?'

'I've known him since he was a child. His mother and his father too were childhood friends of mine. I don't see much of him but he is friends with Alice and Henry so it was lovely to have him for Christmas. Cheer him up, after . . . well, a sad business.'

She longed to ask what the sad business was, wondering if it was the same her father had hinted at – his girlfriend aborting his baby. She went on, 'Do you think he would want to sensationalize his book or will it be a more academic work?'

'He only ever writes the truth as he sees it,' Aunt Veronica replied. 'I've got all the books he's written; you can read them in bed if you like.

He'd never make anything up or exaggerate it out of all proportion, but he would write his story as it happened. That's why his books are so interesting. He has the gift of showing you the person and how their character and life style affects their work.'

He wouldn't have to sensationalize her story. The truth was all he needed. 'If you asked him not to include something would he do that?' she said.

Uncle Simon's head jerked up like a retriever catching a scent. 'What sort of thing?' he demanded, his eyes boring into her.

Aunt Veronica took over. 'Oh I'm sure Cinni meant nothing, did you dear?' She barely paused for breath, giving her no time to answer, not that she could anyway. 'Stop bombarding her like that. The precious family name will be safe, you know that. This is a book about Max not this family.' She smiled, soothing over his feathers but leaving Cinni feeling wretched and ashamed.

Christmas had been a bore as it always was, Olivia, Sue's younger sister had left already to be with her fiancé. Her parents had the same people over on Boxing Day as they always did and they greeted her with suppressed sympathy. Yet another year had gone by and she had not managed to find a man, let alone get married. Photographs of grandchildren were produced like rabbits out of a hat and passed round with furtive glances as if to check that their grandchild was better looking than other people's.

Sue had vaguely told her parents about Gerry. Her father never discussed it, except for to ask, 'When's he going to do the decent thing?' Her mother especially was embarrassed about the relationship. While she chatted during her turn to do the church flowers or help on various committees Sue knew she had made up some story about her elder daughter being unable to marry this unhappily married man. She suspected that her mother hinted at some honourable reason why she could not marry him and this year it suddenly grated on her and the sympathetic looks and descriptions of their children's weddings and new grandchildren – not to mention Olivia's engagement – cut her to the quick.

When Hilary Barton began to boast about her rather plain daughter's wedding, throwing her rather smug looks as she discussed the price of dresses and flowers, she heard herself saying, 'I am engaged; we'll get married soon.' This remark brought the whole group to silence, suddenly broken by excited chatter. Sue stood smiling foolishly, watching the news speed out of control like a forest fire around the room until it reached her parents who hugged her, delighted.

'Darling, you never said, how lovely,' her mother said hugging her, relieved at last to be able to join in the boasting at getting all her children settled. Only her brother, Jeff, caught her eye and guessed the truth.

'Why did you do it?' he asked as they passed each other in the kitchen getting more food and drink to hand round.

'I'll explain later,' she said miserably, not realizing how such news would be seized. She was behaving so strangely at the moment, telling Lucian Cinni's secret about the baby and now this. She was going mad, worn down by the stress of life with Gerry or rather these days without him. She had hardly seen him these past weeks though his last telephone call had been warm, laced with promises to make his absence up to her.

A lurid picture of him enjoying Christmas with his family and the saintly Helen rose up to attack her. At other Christmases when she'd thought of him, she'd imagined him trying to have fun for his children's sake with such a bitch of a wife, wishing he were with her in her loving arms. None of it was true, he wanted them both, she realized now, alone in the kitchen hearing the excited chatter in the next room, and only she could stop it. Only she could refuse to see him and make a concerted effort to go out and move on.

Sudden tears seized her, her heart wrenching at the thought of life without him. She had told that room of people, some who had known her since she was a child, that she was engaged and they had rejoiced for her; worse still, her parents had been so thrilled as if they'd feared she was some sort of odd ball who would never find a man to settle down with. She had lied and betrayed one of her dearest friends, though Cinni, she reminded herself, had thrown herself at Gerry. But had she? Her mind suddenly became very clear. She had been blinded by Gerry, wanted to believe him when he said he was in an unhappy marriage and would soon leave his wife and marry her. He never would, she knew that now, there would always be some excuse and she would never be married or have a child. Why ever would Cinni who disapproved of him and said she liked his wife make a pass at him? She might well want a man to look after her in her predicament but she'd hardly go for a man with a family still to raise and another woman in his life as well.

Gerry had ruined her life and she had let him because she did not want to lose him. Caught up in the mesh of his lies she had allowed herself to believe his story about Cinni. He – and to be honest she was as much to blame – was responsible for breaking one of her strongest friendships. Not that Cinni would ever want to be her friend again when she heard how she had told Lucian about her baby. She could sink no lower. It was now up to her to find a way to make amends.

# CHAPTER THIRTY-TWO

HER waters broke all over her smart chair in the office. For one terrible moment Cinni thought she had wet herself, then she realized what it was. Terror gripped her. The baby could not be coming now, it was almost a month early. She cried out and Gina, halfway through a telephone call, dropped the phone and came to her.

'Your waters have gone,' she said unnecessarily.

Jill gasped, jumping up and coming to her, arms outstretched, as if to catch the baby as it shot into the world.

Cinni sat there, damp, stunned. She was not ready either mentally or practically for this baby – she only had a few things in the flat that Aunt Veronica had insisted she take from Merriot. She was still working, really because she couldn't bear not to and be alone in the flat waiting, though she would hardly be alone with Barbara, the cleaner, who contrary to her father's prediction, enjoyed the drama of having her there in her predicament.

'He never mentioned he was a father, let alone a grandfather,' she kept repeating with relish, before launching into the most horrific descriptions of her three labours, each of which could have killed her. 'The doctor said I am a living miracle,' was another of her favourite phrases. But she was kind and fussed over her the few times they were in the flat together. Beth, who managed the office had been understanding and said she could work shorter hours, and although she had not strictly worked for them long enough, take some paid maternity leave. None of this she had really taken in, thinking she had plenty of time to cope with it but time had run out and the baby was on its way. Panic now seized her, it was coming too soon, it might not even survive. She grabbed Gina's hand and held it. She must not think like this, but birth and death were both too momentous to cope with at the same time.

It was nearly the end of the day and Gina took charge. She'd had two children and knew what to do. 'Don't worry, you'll be fine,' she reassured Cinni, rescuing her hand from Cinni's fevered grip. 'I'll ring the hospital, which one are you booked into?'

Jill calmed down and cleared up the mess clucking with sympathy and reassurance as she did. As they both comforted and helped her, Cinni relaxed a little, feeling that a mysterious bond had grown between them, filling her with a sense of security to be with other women who felt instinctively for her and the birth ahead.

Gina drove Cinni home, packed an overnight case for her as she washed and changed. Seeing her put in some of the baby clothes, tiny garments, lovingly washed and ironed and wrapped in tissue paper by some nanny long ago, it hit her suddenly that in a few hours the baby – the person whose existence might cause such ructions – would be here.

'It's so early, will it be all right?' She voiced again the fear that loomed in her. How relieved Ruth would be if this child did not live.

'Of course, a month is nothing and the hospital will cope.' Gina went on to tell her stories of various friends' babies who had been far more premature and were now as bright and normal as anyone else.

The doctor, who seemed almost too young to make such a decision, told her to rest as, if it did not come on its own, they would induce labour the following day but the baby had its own plans and arrived after a short, hard labour at three in the morning.

'A boy.' Cinni was handed the small, squirming object. She could not believe that this had come out of her. As she took him in her arms staring with surprise and wonder at this tiny being, she was seized with an overwhelming love. He did not look like Max; his features were finer, more like Theo. She called him Roland, she didn't know why. The name came to her as she held him.

She rang Gina, who had promised to come back for the birth but now felt rather disappointed that she'd missed it. The only other person she rang was Aunt Veronica who insisted that when she left hospital she must come to Merriot to recuperate. She agreed with relief, not knowing what on earth to do with this baby on her own.

They stayed in hospital a week. Roland was small but tough. The girls from the office came to visit but as she had not told anyone else about his arrival no one else came. She should tell Theo that he was a grandfather but as the days went by she did nothing about it. She felt curiously isolated here caught up with the rhythm of motherhood and the hospital routine, there never seemed to be any time to do anything else. It was hard seeing the fathers marvel at their new child, two happy parents cradling their child, filling her with loneliness. But Max would have come if he had been alive. She imagined him, proud and loud with delight, taking over the ward with his presence. But maybe he would not have come, refused all contact, she would never know now.

At the end of the week Aunt Veronica arrived in some battered ancient car and took over, scurrying her and the baby away to Merriot as if to escape the dangers of the city as quickly as possible.

She felt very close to her late mother during the following days, feeling her there beside her, laughing in that way she had, tossing her head, her hair rippling down her back. Or regarding her grandson with that inscrutable look, keeping the secret of his parentage. Fiona had come here too with Cinni just after her birth in the local hospital. How strange that life had repeated itself.

'Stay here as long as you want,' Aunt Veronica said. 'Simon's often away shooting and the children have gone back to university.' She laughed. 'I must tell you he took enormous pleasure ringing your father and calling him Grandpa.'

'What did he say?' It amused her too.

'Not much, asked if you were all right, sent his love. He's sending you some flowers.'

It took a fortnight for her to recover and come to grips with motherhood and she did not have time to think much about Max in this strange limbo of caring for a new life. Roland was Roland, his own person and she did not want to think beyond that.

One morning when she going through seed catalogues with Aunt Veronica to choose plants for the garden, the phone rang. Aunt Veronica answered it and handed it to her, a quizzical expression on her face. It was Philip.

'I heard through your office that the baby has come. Are you both all right?' She sensed that he was disappointed that she had not rung him with the news herself.

'Yes we are, thanks.' The sound of his voice was like a cold wake-up call. This was the outside world intruding on her cosy nest. Roland was changing, his fine features filling out and sometimes she fleetingly saw a slight look of Max.

Aunt Veronica was pretending to be concentrating on her task, ringing round the code numbers of the seeds she wanted in the catalogue, writing them down on the order sheet, but Cinni could tell that she, like her father, suddenly did not believe her story of Roland's father being dead and now suspected that Philip was the father. She could say nothing to give herself away.

'He looks like my father, he's so sweet,' she said.

'He's early. Didn't you say he was due in March?' She sensed Philip's accusation. Perhaps she was pretending he was early when in fact he'd been born on time or even late and so could not be Max's. Ruth must have worked all this out.

'He was a month early, you can ask the doctor,' she said firmly. 'When I come back to London in a few days you can come and see him.'

After he'd rung off, Aunt Veronica looked at her expectantly. When Cinni said nothing she said, 'Was that Roland's father? I mean I never really took to that story of him being dead, though of course it might be more convenient for you to say that.'

'No, that was Philip who took my mother in when Theo left her.' Her voice must have sounded harsh.

'It must have been tough for her.' Veronica said. 'I didn't know Simon then but I know he was dreadfully shocked when his father died so early. Jasper was barely sixty. Died of a heart attack while out shooting on a very cold day. Quite a common way to go apparently. Bit like the poor Queen, Simon didn't expect to inherit so soon.' She sighed, patted her hand. 'Your father, though delightful, is hopeless, spends money like water and the estate just couldn't take any more of his extravagant onslaughts.'

'I know that.' It was too late to go into it all and after all Veronica had nothing to do with it and was at least trying to help her now.

'Brothers! They can be so resentful of each other, one thinking the other has more than him – probably something happened in the nursery years ago.' She smiled. 'But to give him his due your father does keep away, lives this strange wandering life that wouldn't suit Simon at all. But it's such a bonus to have you and that dear baby.'

'It's wonderful to be here, I don't know how I would have coped alone in the flat – but the flat's lovely too so in the end my family has been marvellous.' Determinedly she pushed away images of her mother, abandoned and frightened; that was in the past, she must only think of the good things now.

Aunt Veronica, ever helpful, had produced a young, rather large girl, unfortunately named Petal, who simply adored babies and had looked after numerous brothers and sisters.

'Her mother's a slut, no other word for it, but Petal is above that and needs a break. Why don't you take her to London with you as a nanny? I know she is trustworthy and devoted to Roland and it will give you a break. We'll pay for her for six months as a present, then see!'

She'd protested said she had to think about this. Though Petal had been wonderful in helping her out here under the watchful eye of Veronica, how would she behave with the lure of London nightlife? But Petal had declared she was nervous of big cities in the dark and as long as she could have a television she'd be fine. Cinni had agreed to give it a try, and thought that perhaps Barbara might take to her and keep out of her hair while entertaining Petal with her stories.

The afternoon before they left for London she was reading in the cosy sitting-room. It was a raw, cold day and though she had been meaning to ask Petal to watch Roland so she could go for a walk, she had not done so yet. Aunt Veronica had gone on one of her 'do gooding missions'. Roland was lying asleep beside her on the huge, squashy sofa. She half dreaded returning back to the world but another part of her longed for it. It was cold and damp in the country and so dark – the day had hardly started before it was teatime and black with nightfall. There were no bright shops to sparkle like jewels in the night. It had been a magical time getting to know her baby, but now it was time to brave the real world.

She heard the doorbell ring, jangling on down the corridors. Elsie the daily was there and she would deal with it. A few moments later Elsie appeared. 'For you, miss.' Her eyes were agog, her simple face shining as if she was handing over a present. It was Lucian.

The shock was so great she could say nothing for a moment. He regarded her gravely. 'Hello, Cinni,' he said.

Elsie left slowly, blocking the door for a moment so he had to wait to come in. She whisked up the baby in her arms, holding him close to her but she moved so abruptly that he woke and cried.

'Are you well?' he said, coming in and standing by the mantelpiece, rubbing his hands against the cold, staring into the glowing embers.

'Yes, thank you.' She rocked the child back and forth, whispering to it, keeping his face against her shoulder. Had he known she was alone and had come to catch her unawares? Did he suspect that Max was Roland's father and had come to check the likeness?

'Veronica tells me you've been here a fortnight.'

'That's right.' Why had Veronica told him? Had they met by chance, or had she sought him out? Did she, and the thought made her blush, think like Theo that Lucian was the father? No one seemed or perhaps wanted to believe that Roland's father was really dead.

He said, 'So, you had a boy? He looks a sturdy little fellow.'

'He's fine.' She could not look at him, she wanted to get up and leave but Roland was quiet now and she did not want to disturb him again. She wanted Lucian to go and yet the feel of him in the room made her heart race. What a fool she was letting such ridiculous emotions affect her. She'd been starved of male company too long and her hormones were all over the place, that was all it was.

'Can I see his face?' he took a step forward, smiling.

'No.' She clutched Roland to her, got up to go. 'I don't know why you are here. Aunt Veronica will be back soon.'

'I came to see you.' His eyes held hers, defiant, determined.

'Now, you've seen me. You said you didn't want to ask me anything for the book. Have you finished it?'

'No, but it's true I won't ask you any questions. I came to see you because. . . .' He paused, glanced away as if he had changed his mind, then with a look of determination went on. 'I care for you a great deal, I . . . I want to be with you. You needn't say anything now,' he rushed on, his Darcy face on now and she realized that it covered a sort of shyness, a fear of rejection, but she was too stunned at his words to react to it. 'But I'd like to see you, slowly at first if you want. I'm sorry I jumped to the wrong conclusions over you and Gerry, but Helen was so upset and told me it was you and I had seen you together in that field, but it was unforgivable of me to do that.'

She frowned, she could not believe this. It was a dream surely and then reality kicked in. It was just another way for him to get his smut for his book. He had waited until the child was born and had come hoping to find a mini Max and be able to write it all up in his book.

'No,' she said, finding the words sticking in her mouth, 'it will not be possible.'

'Why? I think we get on well. I know I was wrong believing you'd behaved badly with Gerry and I've apologized and will do so again, most sincerely. Helen has been a great friend for many years and a loyal wife to Gerry and I hated to see her hurt, besides Gerry confirmed it. You must see it was difficult not to believe it.'

'So, why do you now?'

'Sue rang me, told me the truth.'

'Sue?' There was the faint ring of alarm bells but before she could challenge this he went on.

'I'm truly sorry. Can't we put it behind us and at least try to be friends? And also,' he smiled. 'I never believed Colette when she insinuated that you were gay.'

His smile warmed her and yet she must not let herself be lured into his trap. She said more sharply than she meant to. 'I have a child; he is the most important person in my life. I have no time for anyone else.'

'Of course you feel like that now, I understand that, but soon you'll want to have more from life, go out, do things.' His face became serious; he talked almost as if she were not there. 'I didn't want to care for you but every time we met there was something about you that drew me to you. I find this difficult to say.' He paused. 'I'm not used to declaring myself like this. But it nagged at me and I thought I had better say it and then I would know where I stand.'

He stood before her proud and defiant and yet she saw the softness there, the uncertain pain in his eyes and she knew this had cost him a lot. Yet even as she softened towards him she thought of the ruthlessness of an author wanting maximum publicity. What a coup for him it would be. Max's last act on this earth, to father a child.

'I'm sorry, no,' she said, half covering Roland's face with his shawl as she got up and, trying not to touch Lucian as he was so close to her, walked past him to the door.

His voice was gentle. 'Cinni, I know that Max is the father of your baby.'

# CHAPTER THIRTY-THREE

Aunt Veronica, bustling in with dogs and bulging shopping baskets, disturbed the scene. They heard the front door slam and her firm footsteps coming down the passage. She was calling out to herald her arrival. 'What a wind, sharp as a knife. Hope that baby is wrapped up and not in a draught.' She stopped at the door of the sitting-room on her way to the kitchen and seeing Lucian carried on as if his presence was no surprise to her. 'Ah, Lucian, lovely to see you, all well?'

In a moment she realized things were not all well. Cinni was crouched down on the sofa holding the baby in the curve of her body as if she expected him to be snatched from her at any minute. Lucian was hovering in front of her.

He said, 'I'm just going Veronica, good to see you.' He touched her arm as he passed her and with a sharp, tight smile left the room. Veronica navigated herself through her baskets and the dogs and sat down beside Cinni. 'Want to talk about it?'

Cinni pulled herself back from her shock. He had said that he knew Max was Roland's father. How did he know? Then she remembered he had said something about Sue. She had apparently told him that it was her not Cinni having an affair with Gerry, but she must have also told him about Max. Or perhaps she had told him about Max and then, feeling guilty, had told him the truth about Gerry.

The pain of Sue's betrayal took over from her shock, filling her with fear. When had she told him? It must have been before Christmas and that was why he had said he no longer needed to interview her for his book. Then there was Sue's tearful, incoherent call when she was obviously drunk. She'd been apologizing for something and she'd thought it was her believing Gerry's claim that she had made a pass at him. She tried to curb her fury; perhaps Lucian had seduced it out of Sue – he certainly could lay on the charm. And his declaration now, what was that for? For a moment she had believed his words, felt the warmth seep into her heart, feelings she had denied had ignited within her. She'd almost been caught. He knew this, it was what he was aiming for and no doubt by pretending he cared for her he would have prised out the sordid details of Roland's conception.

Aunt Veronica, who had been sitting in an edgy self-imposed silence, now could bear it no longer. 'My dear, you need not talk about it but sometimes it is better to air things. I'm very broadminded you know and discreet. Having a baby outside marriage is the norm today whatever we oldies may think. I quite understand – well, I sort of understand, after all, it must have been quite a shock – that you said Roland's father was dead, if his father refused to acknowledge the child, or was unpleasant, or . . .' she looked awkward, 'you were raped or something, not that I think Lucian would do such a thing, but if he is the father then I'm sure he will look after you both even if you don't marry each other.'

'Lucian is not the father,' Cinni protested.

'If you say so, dear.' Aunt Veronica smiled as if she knew better. 'But he's something to do with it, I'm certain of that. Does he think Roland is his, even if he is not?' Her expression suggested that even though she disapproved of promiscuity, if Cinni had slept with a whole string of men she would remain unjudgemental. 'I perhaps should not be telling you this, but he's been through a traumatic time with a woman he loved and thought loved him. He might have found if difficult to find himself in the same predicament again and be afraid to care for the baby in case you got rid of it too.'

Cinni hardly took this in. She'd have to tell Aunt Veronica the whole story now, she might as well. When Lucian's book on Max was published the world would know all about it. Some tabloid would be bound to snatch it up and shout it to the world. Roland shifted on her shoulder, snuffling down into her neck. She stroked his head, suffused with love. He was all that mattered; somehow they would make their life together. She said, 'Max Cavanagh is his father.'

'Max? But he's dead,' Aunt Veronica burst out.

'I know, the effort killed him.' Quietly Cinni told her everything.

'Well, I'm amazed. I have heard of old men fathering children, it's only our body clocks that run down, but this is extraordinary. Shows what a strong force life is; no doubt this little chap was meant to be born.' She looked at Roland reverently as though he were the Messiah. 'But Max has a family doesn't he, what do they think?'

'He has a sister.' She thought of Ruth and how she would deny this. They would have to go through the palaver of a DNA test, go to a solicitor to prove his parentage.

'But where does Lucian fit in all of this?'

'His book, don't you see? Think what this will do for his sales. Max's last act, fathering a child before he died.'

Aunt Veronica frowned. 'No, Lucian would never do that. He's far too honourable. How does he know anyway? Did you tell him?'

'No, I think a friend of mine did. Oh, it's a long story and I think she did it under duress or when drunk or something. But now he knows, I must warn Max's sister.' She moved to get up to telephone but Aunt Veronica put out a restraining hand.

'Don't rush into anything. He's hardly started his book; nothing will be out until at least next year. You must not upset yourself; you are still in a delicate state after giving birth. Leave it with me. Now, won't you stay here a little longer. I don't like to think of you coping with this alone in the flat?'

'I don't know what I would have done without you.' Cinni embraced her awkwardly with the child on her shoulder. 'But it's time I went. I must protect us, don't you see; find out what I can do to suppress the story. I don't know who else knows now.' Had Sue told Gerry, who'd told Helen and goodness knows who else?

That evening she telephoned Sue. She could have waited until she returned to London but the fizzing anxiety of unravelling the truth made her impatient. The phone was snatched up almost immediately; no doubt Sue hoped it was Gerry.

'Sue, it's me, Cinni. I've had the baby, he came early. I've also seen Lucian and he says he knows Max is the father. Did you tell him?'

There was a gasp, almost a sob. 'I didn't mean to. I told you, it just slipped out. I feel so awful about it, about everything I thought about you. I quite understand if you never want to see me again.'

She could hear the panic in her voice and felt an instant buzz of sympathy. She said, 'So, did he seduce you, make you drunk?'

'No, none of that. I'm just so unhappy, I've broken up with Gerry, well I hadn't then but Lucian asked if we could meet to go over some questions he wanted to ask for his book, and he was so nice and kind. I didn't mean to tell him, Cinni, I feel so awful about it.' She went on describing what had happened at some length, telling her that later, appalled at what she'd done she'd rung him again and told him the whole story about her and Gerry and how Cinni had taken the rap to save Gerry's marriage. Cinni recognized that Sue was at the end of her tether. She tried to soothe her; it was done now and it was no good beating her up about it. With promises to come to see her when she had settled in London, she rang off.

With reluctance Aunt Veronica drove them back to London. She and Petal set to arranging things for the baby and when finally everything was done and Veronica had left, Cinni rang Philip at his office.

'So, someone – I'm pretty sure it was a girlfriend of mine – told Lucian the truth about Max's death.' Even as she was speaking to him she was hit with another terrible thought that perhaps it was Philip who had let something slip.

Philip said, 'I don't know about that but you know this new lodger we have, Aubrey? Well he told Lucian. I don't know how he found out, lurking about listening to Ruth I suppose. Anyway I know he told him.'

Anxiety seized her again – how many people knew? Would it be out before the book was even written?

'So, what's he going to do about it?' She could see the headlines already, screaming their story for all to see.

'Ruth was furious with him. She's afraid he'll sell the story to some downmarket tabloid, but I think she's got something on him and she's sort of blackmailing him. If he tells anyone she'll see his misdemeanour comes out. I think she's frightened him enough, but you never know.'

'But she doesn't believe that Roland is Max's anyway?'

'I think she might now. She doesn't want to believe it of course and they – well,' he laughed hoarsely, 'all of us are worried that you might take over the house.'

'Of course I'm not going to,' she exclaimed. 'Even if Max did leave the house to his children – and for all we know there are others – it can't be until you are all gone.'

'His children have precedence over us,' Philip said. 'Perhaps he did it as a joke, not knowing that he had any children. That is just the sort of thing he would enjoy doing – having control even after death.'

'You have my word that I will not take over the house for Roland until you are all gone,' she said. 'But what shall we do about Lucian's book?'

There was a pause then he said, 'I'll get Ruth to talk to him. That's all I can do. But . . . well I'd like to see you and the baby. I think they all would, though they won't admit to it.'

'Come round, any time. I'm not back at work yet. I've got a young woman helping me; she's a godsend, means I can get things done.'

Philip said, 'Look, come round here. I'll square it with Ruth. Does . . . does the baby look like Max?'

'Not really, more like Theo if anyone. I see a slight resemblance to Max sometimes but that may be my imagination.'

They made a plan for her to go round to the house that weekend. Ruth's invitation came through Philip. Tea on Sunday and to bring 'the nanny'. This made Cinni smile, knowing that Ruth's idea of a nanny was locked in some far off time of crisp uniforms and nursery routines run with the precision of a military exercise. She explained this to Petal who took whatever life doled out with calm stoicism and said, 'I'll put on me best shirt then.' And she went to iron it.

Roland had more luggage for his short visit than Cinni and Petal together. Stella opened the door, her eyes at once going to the baby as if he were a reincarnation of Max and would rise up and bluster at her. She seemed quite disappointed as Roland slept on in his baby carrier. Philip was close behind her and he too stared at the sleeping child as if he were a grenade with the pin out primed to destroy their lives. They made their way to the drawing-room where Ruth sat imperious in her chair with all the calm dignity of a monarch about to be deposed.

'So, Cinni,' she greeted her, 'let me see my supposed nephew.'

Petal, whose own siblings had been fathered by whoever had been around at the time and had never heard of Max, and cared even less, put him down before her.

Cinni fought to control her rising anxiety. Ruth stared at Roland, his tiny face bunched up in sleep. Stella and Philip stood either side of her, also looking down on him, tense, waiting for her reaction.

'He's just a baby,' she said at last. 'He could be anyone's.' She turned accusingly to Cinni.

'He is Max's,' Cinni said firmly. 'I'll do a test, go to a solicitor to prove it, but he is your nephew.'

'I'm too old to have a nephew,' Ruth said at last, defeated yet still fighting on. 'And Max was certainly too old to go fathering children. What was he thinking of, the old fool?'

'I don't suppose he planned it,' Stella said. 'It does sound most unlikely but I can see a look of him in the brow. What colour are his eyes?'

'Still that sort of grey-blue,' Cinni said.

'Max had green eyes,' Stella went on, as if that put up a case against it.

Philip said, 'Have a test if that would make you feel better, Ruth, but I think you know in your heart that Cinni is telling the truth and the baby is his.'

'He doesn't look like Max,' Ruth retorted.

'He doesn't look much like anyone, perhaps a little like Theo, Cinni's father,' Philip went on.

The doorbell went again and Stella, all pink and girly, went to answer it, returning with Lucian. Roland woke and howled so Petal, at Ruth's insistence, took him into another room to feed him. Cinni, feeling nothing could get any worse, sank down on the nearest chair. Philip went to get the tea.

'I thought it best to get this all out in the open,' Ruth said defiantly, glaring at Lucian and Cinni.

Lucian, smiling politely at everyone, avoided Cinni's eyes.

'He's a dear baby,' Stella said, as if Roland was the one on trial and she must give him a character reference.

Philip lumbered in with a huge tray of misshapen scones, a very dark fruitcake and a teapot. This he proceeded to unload on the sideboard among a delicate line-up of china cups and plates. Ignoring him, Ruth went on, addressing Lucian.

'Cinni swears that my brother has fathered her child. I find it hard to believe that even he would be so stupid, but you are writing this book about him and I shall refuse my consent if you write one word, or give one hint about this. Is that clear?' Her voice could have cut down a battalion.

Lucian forced himself to smile, let his eyes linger a moment on Cinni. 'I can write whatever I like but I have no intention whatsoever of mentioning it,' he said. 'My book is about Max's work, as well as his life as I feel it had a bearing on his work, but this last act has no significance at all for his work. Had he lived it might have been different.' He smiled as if amused. 'Who knows how fatherhood would have influenced his work? It's a great pity we will never find out.'

As he spoke Cinni felt a great weight lift from her, yet still she wondered if she could really trust him and this was not just another ruse. Ruth went on giving orders, adding that if 'Aubrey breathed one word' some sordid incident with a past well-known MP would be on the desk of the editor of the *News of the World* within hours. Philip and Stella handed out the tea but Cinni felt she would never eat again.

After a while she realized that Ruth had accepted, was even a little excited at having a nephew, though she decided – indeed, ordered them all – to keep quiet about it. She would keep an eye on him and would introduce him in a few years when public interest had waned. Cinni promised she would not turn them out of the house. Theo had telephoned to tell her he had a new life, and no doubt a new woman and would not be back for the foreseeable future, and after all she now had Aunt Veronica on her side and an open invitation to Merriot.

As they got up to leave Lucian came up to her. He said quietly, 'Is there any hope of you having dinner with me? Tonight or tomorrow?'

Her heart leapt and yet she curbed the warmth that infused her; she was still vulnerable, she must keep her head.

'Please.' His eyes sought hers and she saw the tenderness there, the anxious fear of rejection, the pain he had once suffered. We are all carrying some suffering, she thought; it is not fair to judge too harshly. But is it me he wants or my story?

'As long as it is not too late,' she said at last. 'The baby keeps me up half the night.'

'I'll pick you up at 7.30.' He turned from her, making his goodbyes and leaving the house.

She didn't know what to wear and then scolded herself for caring. She'd just had a baby for goodness' sake, nothing would look good. He picked her up in his car and she felt as nervous as a teenager on a first date. You are overreacting, she warned herself, you must keep vigilant.

They drove down the King's Road. He said, 'All my favourite restaurants are closed on Sunday night so I hope you don't mind that I've organized dinner at my flat.'

She did not want to be alone with him and yet sitting here beside him, she did not feel threatened. She could tell him she'd changed her mind and wanted to de dropped home but she did not. He drove on down past World's End, into the New King's road and over Putney Bridge and parked by an oval shaped block of flats made of glass glistening in the dark beside the river, a necklace of blue lights edged the windows. She made some remark about how modern it was and he said he had recently moved in. Explained that he hadn't got everything straight yet.

They were both silent, like strangers, as they went up in the lift. He only put the light on in the hall then let her walk in to the main room suspended above the glistening water pulsating below them, the dark sky above, speckled with stars. It was another world, isolated magic, like being in a ship alone at sea, safe and yet unnerving too.

She stood there looking out for a long time. How small and insignificant they and their problems were against the universe? A wind ruffled
the water, sending a couple of moored boats bobbing precariously on the
surface, spurring on the clouds to cover the moon. It would be majestic
here in a storm.

Behind her she heard him gently moving about, opening wine, setting
dishes, she felt disarmed, close to him suspended here alone in the night.
She said, 'I can trust you, can't I, over this story? I could not bear my
child to be hurt over it; it's hardly his fault. Blame me if you must, but
not him.'

There was silence for a moment, he stopped doing his tasks. He said,
'Will you ever trust me? Because if you don't or can't, I'll take you home
now. I can't go through this sort of thing again.'

The anguish in his voice made her turn. She could see him outlined
against the light in the hall, a bottle of wine in his hand, a glass in the
other.

'I was very much in love with this woman, I thought she loved me,
wanted to marry me, have my children. She got pregnant by mistake and
aborted the child without telling me.' The words were laboured, each one
rung out with pain.

'I'm so sorry.' She could feel his anguish from where she stood and
took a small step towards him, but she did not move further.

He put down the bottle and the glass and came closer to her. 'I cannot
stop thinking about that child, my child, who was not given a chance of
life. People might think that men don't feel anything until the child is
born especially if they were not planning to have one. But she gave me
no choice, had it ripped out and thrown away, my child.'

She went to him then, she could not stop herself, and put her arms
round him and held him. He held her too and they stood there together
in that magical darkness comforted at last.

He said, 'I admired you for keeping the child, after all you were in a
desperate situation, and many a woman would understandably have had
a termination. Let me be with you and Roland, I love you, do you not
know that?' He smiled, stroked her cheek gently with the back of his
fingers. 'I didn't want to love you, or love anyone ever again, but it's
happened and I don't want to let it go.'

Deep down she still wondered about his book. Would his passion for
writing all the facts take over from the passion that simmered now

between them? She loved him too; she'd known it a long time though she had denied it.

'Let's take things slowly,' she said, the force of her feelings for him overwhelming her a little. 'If Roland is anything like Max he will rule our lives.'